THE L

are key to focusi -
ers scattered acr those
gifted with such p to master their
talents lest they go wild. Those especially skilled are chosen to serve in the Towers, to work the matrices for the benefit of all.

To all who have fallen under Darkover's spell, the Towers and those who dwell and work within them are one of the most fascinating aspects of this amazing world. And now, in these new stories chosen by Marion herself, and including a tale of her own about Dyan Ardais, readers can explore the many facets of Tower life—the powers, the perils, and the pathways walked by those who wield the forces of *laran*.

A Reader's Guide to DARKOVER

THE FOUNDING:

A "lost ship" of Terran origin, in the pre-empire colonizing days, lands on a planet with a dim red star, later to be called Darkover.

DARKOVER LANDFALL

THE AGES OF CHAOS:

1,000 years after the original landfall settlement, society has returned to the feudal level. The Darkovans, their Terran technology renounced or forgotten, have turned instead to freewheeling, out-of-control matrix technology, psi powers and terrible psi weapons. The populace lives under the domination of the Towers and a tyrannical breeding program to staff the Towers with unnaturally powerful, inbred gifts of *laran.*

STORMQUEEN!
HAWKMISTRESS!

THE HUNDRED KINGDOMS:

An age of war and strife retaining many of the decimating and disastrous effects of the Ages of Chaos. The lands which are later to become the Seven Domains are divided by continuous border conflicts into a multitude of small, belligerent kingdoms, named for convenience "The Hundred Kingdoms." The close of this era is heralded by the adoption of the Compact, instituted by Varzil the Good. A landmark and turning point in the history of Darkover, the Compact bans all distance weapons, making it a matter of honor that one who seeks to kill must himself face equal risk of death.

TWO TO CONQUER
THE HEIRS OF HAMMERFELL

THE RENUNCIATES:

During the Ages of Chaos and the time of the Hundred Kingdoms, there were two orders of women who set themselves apart from the patriarchal nature of Darkovan feudal society: the priestesses of Avarra, and the warriors of the Sisterhood of the Sword. Eventually these two independent groups merged to form the powerful and legally chartered Order of Renunciates or Free Amazons, a guild of women bound only by oath as a sisterhood of mutual responsibility. Their primary allegiance is to each other rather than to family, clan, caste or any man save a temporary employer. Alone among Darkovan women, they are exempt from the usual legal restrictions and protections. Their reason for existence is to provide the women of Darkover an alternative to their socially restrictive lives.

THE SHATTERED CHAIN
THENDARA HOUSE
CITY OF SORCERY

AGAINST THE TERRANS —THE FIRST AGE (Recontact):

After the Hastur Wars, the Hundred Kingdoms are consolidated into the Seven Domains, and ruled by a hereditary aristocracy of seven families, called the Comyn, allegedly descended from the legendary Hastur, Lord of Light. It is during this era that the Terran Empire, really a form of confederacy, rediscovers Darkover, which they know as the fourth planet of the Cottman star system. The fact that Darkover is a lost colony of the Empire is not easily or readily acknowledged by Darkovans and their Comyn overloads.

REDISCOVERY *(with Mercedes Lackey)*
THE SPELL SWORD
THE FORBIDDEN TOWER
*STAR OF DANGER
*WINDS OF DARKOVER

AGAINST THE TERRANS
—THE SECOND AGE (After the Comyn):

With the initial shock of recontact beginning to wear off, and the Terran spaceport a permanent establishment on the outskirts of the city of Thendara, the younger and less traditional elements of Darkovan society begin the first real exchange of knowledge with the Terrans—learning Terran science and technology and teaching Darkovan matrix technology in turn. Eventually Regis Hastur, the young Comyn lord most active in these exchanges, becomes Regent in a provisional government allied to the Terrans. Darkover is once again reunited with its founding Empire.

*THE BLOODY SUN
THE HERITAGE OF HASTUR
*THE PLANET SAVERS
*SHARRA'S EXILE
*THE WORLD WRECKERS
*RETURN TO DARKOVER

THE DARKOVER ANTHOLOGIES:

These volumes of stories edited by Marion Zimmer Bradley, strive to "fill in the blanks" of Darkovan history, and elaborate on the eras, tales and characters which have captured readers' imaginations.

THE KEEPER'S PRICE
SWORD OF CHAOS
FREE AMAZONS OF DARKOVER
THE OTHER SIDE OF THE MIRROR
RED SUN OF DARKOVER
FOUR MOONS OF DARKOVER
DOMAINS OF DARKOVER
RENUNCIATES OF DARKOVER
LERONI OF DARKOVER
TOWERS OF DARKOVER
*MARION ZIMMER BRADLEY'S DARKOVER
*SNOWS OF DARKOVER

(*forthcoming in DAW Books editions in 1994)

Marion Zimmer Bradley

Towers Of Darkover

DAW BOOKS, INC.
DONALD A. WOLLHEIM, FOUNDER
375 Hudson Street, New York, NY 10014
ELIZABETH R. WOLLHEIM
SHEILA E. GILBERT
PUBLISHERS

Cover art and border design by Richard Hescox.

DAW Book Collectors No. 919.

First Printing, July 1993

1 2 3 4 5 6 7 8 9

DAW TRADEMARK REGISTERED
U.S. PAT. OFF AND FOREIGN COUNTRIES
—MARCA REGISTRADA,
HECO EN U.S.A.

PRINTED IN THE U.S.A.

Contents

Editorial

When I sat down to work on TOWERS OF DARKOVER, I looked back and found that I've been editing anthologies for ten years. My anthology career began while Don Wollheim, the lamentably late Editor in Chief and founder of DAW Books, allowed me to do THE KEEPER'S PRICE. The SWORD AND SORCERESS volumes began when he was working with an individual who, though a really crackerjack editor, had an abrasive personality. Don was heard to say that he wished he could find an equally competent editor who was a little easier to work with. I said I'd always wanted to edit an anthology, so he let me try it. And in spite of the conventional wisdom which says short stories don't sell, all of my volumes are still in print, and I'm still paying royalties on them.

I think it's about time to take a long retrospective look at ten years of Darkover anthologies. As I write this, LERONI OF DARKOVER has just come out, and it is piled with the other volumes here on my desk. What have I been doing right? Well, I credit my success as an editor to an undiminished enthusiasm for the slush pile. Many editors burn out, but I still greet each new load of manuscripts with enthusiasm, even though I know at least half of the stories will be all but unreadable. There are exceptions; I can't read dot matrix or hand-written manuscripts, so I return them with advice about the nuts and bolts of professional writing. Rule 1, of course is: Make it legible!

In 1983 or 84, when I was teaching a creative writing course at a local high school, I told the kids this. A raised hand interrupted me and a very bright fifteen-year-old boy asked distressedly, "You wouldn't reject a really good story just because it wasn't typed, would you?" Perhaps to his disillusionment, I answered promptly that I certainly would. The first and most important lesson a would-be professional should learn is that proper submission is *very* important; so I send them a little advice about making their manuscripts look professional, You'd be surprised at how many young writers resent this sort of fundamental help; but if they really aspired to being professionals, they'd be as grateful as I was.

Jerry Bixby sent me the best rejection slip I ever got. It started out, "For gosh sakes, Marion, quit trying to impress me with how well you can write, and tell me a story." Then he went on, "If you can't think up a plot I'll give you one you can use for the rest of your career: 'Joe has his fanny in a bear trap, and he has all kinds of adventures while trying to get it out.' " No doubt he said "fanny" because he knew I was both young and female. (Jerry himself was the author of one of the best early STAR TREK episodes, and wrote "Share Alike," one of the best sf stories I ever read.) I often repeat Jerry's suggestion to young writers: skill at writing, per se, can't be learned; but anybody can learn to *plot.* I did, without much talent for it; and my writing got better with practice.

I remember many of my other early rejection slips, because, believe me, most editors are such overworked and busy people that every word they write over and above "We regret that your story does not meet our needs at this time" is worth its weight in gold. I've been rejecting manuscripts for years, and I know. I don't waste my time. If I bother to write something on a manuscript, you can take it from me: I think you can do better and I'm willing to gamble a little of my time on it.

I could paper a room in my house, and not the smallest, with rejection slips from both before and after that crucial first sale. You can't afford to get cocksure; I still get some rejections, and I've never met a writer yet who was immune to them.

I remember Fred Pohl writing me one that read "Marion Zimmer (I wasn't even Bradley then) writes well; she just writes too much." Another editor whose name I may never have known, typed "Irrelevant, incompetent and immaterial" on one of my early mysteries. And another—the late Tony Boucher—wrote "I neither understand nor believe in the science behind your 'Gravity Shifts.' " I did rewrite that one; the thing that helped me most was an article in WRITER'S DIGEST that told me "The editor will never miss all the good stuff you leave out." I could rephrase that: your story isn't cast in stone, at least not before it's printed. Remember, the editor is right, even when he's wrong."

One of those starry-eyed young writers with more idealism than professional know-how once tried to tell me she would not feel honest if she changed anything—even a single word—in a story, just to make it more salable. That would have been "shamelessly pandering to commercialism." This may be all right for highly artistic writers—or those with independent incomes; but if you want to make a living in this ruthlessly competitive business, at least at first, the attitude you should adopt is that *the editor is always right; he knows the business and you don't.* When you have a major reputation, you can push back quite successfully. Most editors I have worked with will accommodate a writer if he feels strongly about something, but wait till the editor knows your commercial value to his magazine. Then you can do what you need to—or whatever your artistic conscience directs. While you're still an unknown, however, it's wise to listen to the editor's voice of experience.

Early in my career, I was accosted by one of those feminist types who knew I had put myself through college and supported my family by the commercial writing of romances for schlock paperback houses. She took it upon herself to enlighten me about what she called "artistic integrity." She accused me of being a literary prostitute and stated flat out that I should not write for money, but for higher artistic ideals. I told her that was all very well, but I had kids who were in the habit of eating; and the landlord, grocer, and local power company did not wait upon my artistic dreams. A literary prostitute, I told her, does not endanger anyone's health or morals—and at least *my* son never had to steal milk out of other people's refrigerators (a low blow, because I had found her own son doing just that).

Well, if your artistic integrity is worth all that much, maybe someday they'll discover your work in that Great Slush Pile In the Sky and call you a great artist, long after you're not around to care. Me, I'd rather gaze upon this very real heap of successful anthologies full of stories by hard-working, receptive young writers, and consider the last ten years as time well spent.

—Marion Zimmer Bradley

Love of the Banshee

by Lynn Armstrong-Jones

Lynne Armstrong-Jones is a writer who sends me several stories for every anthology. The only trouble with that is the inelasticity of typeface; one of the policies I have had to make in these anthologies is to print only one story by any given writer per volume. Lynne sent me four stories this time, and I think this is the best of them. I could be wrong—but in editing, the editor is right even when she's not. (Gosh, I like playing God. . . .)

Lynne lives in Canada and has a son who was an infant when I first began reading her stories; he is six now. Her stories have appeared in four Darkover anthologies, three SWORD & SORCERESS anthologies, and in four issues of my Fantasy Magazine. *She has sold poetry to WEIRD TALES and various small press publications. Her novels, she tells me, are still in various slushpiles; well, that comes with being a writer. By the time this volume is printed, she will have had her second child. The doctors say it will be a girl—isn't science wonderful? When not producing either babies or stories, Lynne works in adult education. She is very grateful to all the people she's met at conventions, for their encouragement and their kind words. That's the nice thing about sf and fantasy; other writers are not hated rivals, but fellow workers and friends.*

I must say, when I wrote about banshees in some of my early work—long before Darkover was in print—I never expected anybody, on or off Darkover, to love them. But some people evidently do. . . .

She remembered.

And it was not easy to be thinking of something *else,* not when she was face-to-face with a rather irate banshee.

She remembered. All the time she stared into that grotesque face, she was remembering. . . .

Remembering why she was here. Recalling only too clearly the disgust with her life; her too-small cottage, her exasperating three children, her husband's continual absences while he chased some sort of dream, and yet another child now growing restlessly in her too-large belly.

And the need to somehow try to escape from her disappointing life. To come into the woods to feel the fresh air. . . .

And now, to be stuck inhaling the banshee stench.

Her heart was pounding. She had only a small dagger with her; how was she to defend herself against this great and horrid bird?

The child within kicked again, this time a good, solid one. Although her one empty hand moved to her belly, Mirella was silently cursing this new life. It was the last thing she needed.

What she needed was *laran!* If only she'd been blessed! Why, then she'd be able to do almost anything to stop this creature's threat. Better yet, if she'd had *laran,* she'd have married a *dom,* been *Domna* Mirella with her own great house—or even been developing her skill with the Tower-trained.

Instead she was just another poor woman struggling to feed her family while her husband chased a dream of becoming a paxman to *Dom* Cedric. Instead she was facing a banshee, and wondering how in Zandru's hells she might escape with her life!

For a moment she watched a fantasy flash through her mind. She saw herself use *laran* to will the unwanted child from her belly, sending it to the banshee to satisfy the horrid bird's hunger.

The banshee screeched again, and Mirella's heart seemed to leap into her throat once more. Mirella thought that, if she just kept very still, the bird might relax and leave. But, although the banshee had grown quiet for a bit, an end to the dilemma was certainly *not* in sight.

For the horrid creature remained, perched on a large branch easily within lunging distance, while the woman, wondered if there was any use in her clutching the dagger—which was beginning to seem more and more small and useless.

Blessed Avarra, thought Mirella, *I MUST do something!* Very slowly, carefully, never taking her eyes from the awful, sightless creature, she began to back away.

But, blind though it was, the banshee's hearing was keen, and it leaned forward quickly, another horrible screech filling the air. Mirella jerked as though struck, but she did not stop. Again she withdrew, quietly, slowly, trying to ignore the horrid cries of the awful creature.

It was working! There was more distance between them! Perhaps she *would* get out of this yet! Still not taking her eyes from that bird, she moved back, back, until she'd reached the cut-through to the main path. But she was tired, her heart still pounding. She wanted to take the short cut.

So she cursed the child within once more as she made her way up the twisty path to the ridge. As pregnant as she was, it wasn't easy to make her way; she certainly didn't need the distraction of this new inconvenience's kicks.

"Oh, look at me," she moaned to herself. "I should've been a great *domna* in a grand hall, not something breeding like a beast! If it wasn't for those children, I wouldn't even have come out here!"

She pulled herself atop the ridge, eyeing with distaste her broken fingernails and the rip in her skirt. She stood erect, hands now massaging the ache in her back.

Her home might be small, but it was suddenly looking better and better.

So she trudged down the small, twisty, shorter path which led along the cliff edge, then away and into the brush. She shoved some low-hanging branches aside, following the path back toward the edge—

And was quickly ducking, the terrible cry of the banshee once more sending icy chills up her spine. She could feel a rush of air, the thing lunging much too closely past her as she knelt down, her hands covering her head.

"Blessed Avarra! Why won't you let me *pass?*"

But there was no reply other than the strange and horrible cry as the creature moved away. Hesitantly,

Mirella took her hands from over her head, her throat very dry as she gazed after the banshee.

What could she do? She could continue along this shorter route, risking further contact with the awful creature, or return to the main path. But, although that way would take her away from this area, it was also much, much longer.

"Curse you," she whispered hoarsely. "What makes you think that this whole wood is *yours?*" But this route really *was* the only choice. Surely, if she could just make it a little further, she'd be past the territory of the awful bird!

"Just a little further," she promised herself. "Just a bit further now."

She rose awkwardly to her feet, her gray eyes searching for something—*any*thing—that might protect her. She used her dagger to help her get the loose branch from a tree. Silently she cut and pulled the smaller twigs from it, then used her dagger to sharpen the end to something like a point.

"All right, bird," she muttered, "any time you're ready."

Clutching the stick for support, she stepped back toward the cliff edge, eyes scanning the area for any sign of the *thing*. At first, all she saw was the crimson glow of the sun, now closer to the horizon. But again *it* came, almost as though it had a personal grievance with this one woman. Downward it swooped, Mirella jabbing upward desperately, once more cursing the fates for not having giving her *laran* instead of useless, noisy children.

The banshee moved off once more, leaving Mirella a chance again to catch her rasping breath, and wonder if it was over.

But another screech had Mirella hurrying past,

following the narrow path as carefully as she could without losing time. Here the ridge curved in a different direction, and she wondered if the banshee would follow her this way, too. She slowed to a walk, her heart pounding and her chest heaving.

A sudden pain had her gasping, doubling over. Her hands clutched at her belly, horror shooting through her yet again. The babe! If it came now, it would be too early! Much too soon! Surely it would die—

From somewhere inside, a voice—which seemed her own and yet not—was asking if that would be so awful. Certainly she hadn't wanted another child, anyway. . . .

Another twinge, from deep within her body. She cried out, then drew in a long breath— The stench! The banshee must be near.

But the stench seemed somehow different now. Of course! The wind. She'd changed direction . . . and that would mean she should be safe. After all, if she could smell it, then *it* couldn't smell *her!*

She sniffed the air again, one hand still on her belly. The breeze continued to carry the smell in her direction. Mirella moved ahead, gritting her teeth against another twinge. She stepped carefully around a boulder—

And gasped. Not from pain, but in response to the strange sight before her. Pulling her skirts from dragging on the ground, she stepped toward the edge of the cliff and looked down.

There, in a huge tree not that far away, was an enormous nest. Mirella sank to her knees, unable to tear her eyes from the sight.

"So that's why," she murmured softly. *That's*

why you were so anxious to keep me away; you're protecting a little one of your own!

A wry smile suddenly pulled at her lips, for if the banshees were ugly, then there was no word at all to describe the naked chick! Angrily, she realized that cursed chick was the cause of all this difficulty! Teeth clenched, she lifted a rock, prepared to send it in the chick's direction, happily anticipating the sight of a smashed skull.

Yet she hesitated; there was something about the naked, helpless thing. . . . And suddenly an enormous shadow blocked the sun's glow.

The woman cringed, then relaxed, as the banshee settled beside the chick. Mirella's hand rubbed at her swollen stomach as the mother banshee gently—oh, so gently—deposited a strip of something into the chick's eager, wide-open beak. And Mirella watched in fascination as the huge banshee rubbed her great head against the chick's little one. That head. That great head with the strength to take a human life so easily . . . could be so incredibly gentle, even loving. . . .

Another twinge, but this one not so painful.

Mirella watched the caresses of the two banshees, her hand once more seeking contact with her own moving babe.

She closed her eyes, savoring the intensity of the movements inside of her belly. She took a long, relaxing breath.

"No, my little one," she murmured. "You'll not come now, not too soon. . . ."

Mirella continued to breathe slowly, very deeply, sending soothing messages to her impatient belly. Her mind was filling with images. The images of the love between the birds became her own remembrances.

A babe held close against her breast, the touch of soft, perfect infant skin, the joy of a tiny hand in hers.

Mirella tried to clear the lump from her throat, but it didn't want to go. Instead she allowed release of a few tears. She glanced at the banshees just once more, then wiped her hand across her eyes, and rose.

"Thank you," she murmured in the birds' direction.

The rest of her homeward journey was quite uneventful—although almost anything would have seemed uneventful after what she'd just faced.

She walked inside her cottage, shivering and tired. First she stepped to her son's small bed, and, thirstily, drank in the sight of his sleeping face. She turned to find her elder daughter staring, her young face a question.

Mirella smiled at the sight of her child, the girl's radiant auburn hair as soft as rabbit-horn fur. Mirella moved to her, anxious to once more feel that hair, touch that face.

She kissed little Kinetta's cheek, her fingers caressing the soft skin. She thought of the love of the banshee. . . .

And of her own.

The Wind Man

by Dorothy J. Heydt

It's getting to the point where I hate to say what kind of stories I don't *want, because somebody—all too frequently Dorothy Heydt—seems to delight in sending me a forbidden story so good I just* have *to buy it. And then I have to explain all over again that I will violate my own guidelines, but only if I simply can't resist the temptation to share the story with my readers. And every time I do this, I know I will get a flood of stories—all infinitely resistible—trying to bring Jaelle or Dorilys back to life, or I'll get more recycled Free Amazon stories which are just rehashes of Subject A. Ah, but if the stories are as good as this one is, I'll have to keep printing them. . . .*

"The Wind Man" relates to the fairy tale of the Traveling Companion (I know, I know—I usually don't buy recycled fairy tales, either. You win again, Dorothy!)

Dorothy Heydt lives in Albany, California, a few miles from us. She has two children, one of whom has a story in this anthology. David Heydt is one of a legion of second generation writers who enjoys telling me that his grandmother introduced him to Darkover many years ago. And they wonder why I feel . . . well, I suppose "ancient" leaps readily to mind.

But I can forgive even that, as long as the incoming stories continue to be of such high quality.

" 'Didn't we just leave this party?' " Donald murmured, as the little snowflakes drifted into his face and powdered his beard.

His classical reference was lost on Marguerida, but she agreed that things were being awkwardly cyclical of late. The Terran spaceman and the Keeper-in-training had met like this, months back, on an inaccessible mountain between two wrecked aircraft. Here they were again, high in the Hellers' meager summertime, with a plane that no amount of plastic surgery could reclaim. Donald had been piloting this time, not Marguerida, but a gust of wind had caught them aslant, and here they were.

"Fortunately, there does seem to be a way down," Donald said.

Marguerida was not so sure. That streak of white below them was probably a road, cut into the mountain's side and now filmed over with the light snow. The problem was in getting down to it, twenty fathoms or so down the steep rock. "Donald, I do not think I can climb down that."

"You won't have to." His voice came muffled from the inside of the plane; he was filling backpacks. This time, at least, they had adequate provisions: lightweight Terran shelter bubble, thin insulating blankets, and freeze-dried food, enough for weeks. Marguerida would have been happier with thick Darkovan wool and canvas, but they could not have carried it all on their backs.

"You won't have to climb it," Donald repeated as he emerged from the plane. "I'll lower you on a rope, and myself, too. We've got plenty of rope. Here, *domna,* put this around your waist. That's the vaccine." He handed her a small waist-pack colored virulent orange, and helped her to fasten it at the small of her back. She settled the little cluster of vials against her belly, slight and precious as an unborn babe. Without the vaccine to deliver, they could have camped in near-comfort in the wrecked plane till Thendara Base could spare a flyer to pick them up—but without the vaccine to deliver, they wouldn't have been out there at all.

The morning sun had just cleared the eastern peaks and was creeping down the slopes, and the fierce morning wind had died almost to a murmur. When Donald had lowered Marguerida to the road, and their laden backpacks after her, he doubled the rope around his body and made his own way down the mountain's face. While he did this, Marguerida explored the road a hundred paces in each direction. When he reached the bottom, she was waiting for him with a grave face. "There's something you must see."

She took him to a little gully that ran down out of the rocks above. Coarse rock and gravel provided drainage where the roadbed crossed it, and in the little hollow upstream of the road lay a heap of weather-bleached bones. They had been scattered by water or scavengers, washed together again by water; most of the skeleton seemed to be still there. Donald retrieved the lower jaw and fitted it gently to the skull. The nameless man had fallen to his death long ago: the crown of his head had cracked and splintered away.

"A dozen paces along," Marguerida said, "there's a flat place where we can lay the bones and build a cairn."

"We? You and me?"

"We're here: the task is for us. So may some kind friend do as much for us when our time comes. Come *on,* Donald." She gathered an armload of the long leg bones and set off along the road.

Donald sighed, but he had sworn obedience. He picked up the skull and followed. "I *was* hoping to have reached the village by sundown," he muttered. "No offense, Yorick, old chap."

They laid out the bones in some approximation of a human shape, and Marguerida laid a Terran chocolate bar among the heaped finger bones. They laid stones over the place till the pile rose to shoulder height and was plainly a cairn made by men for their fellow man, not a chance-fallen heap of stones. And Donald took from a pocket of his trews a small Terran blaster, set it to its lowest notch, and carved a cross in the rock wall behind the cairn.

"There's no religious significance," he explained as he turned back to find Marguerida staring at him. "It's a conventional mark, a way of saying 'Here lies . . . whoever.' "

"I don't give a straw for your religious significance," Marguerida said. "That is an energy weapon, forbidden by the Compact."

"I know it is," Donald said, and made it disappear. "I won't use it unless it's absolutely necessary. But in a year when most of Darkover's values have fallen about its ears, when there are brigands and masterless men prowling between here and the Kadarin, I want an ace in the hole."

"An ace— Never mind, I don't want to know. Very well." She picked up her pack. (It was bulky but light: he must have taken the heavy stuff himself and given her the freeze-dried food and the latrine paper.) "Which way do we go from here?"

"Let's see." From a jacket pocket he pulled a folded sheet of thin plastic, and shook it out flat. It was printed with aerial photographs, tessellated together to make a rough map of the mountains.

"That way is south—this way is north—and we were flying that way." His finger traced along a winding mountain pass. "We're somewhere along here—see? there's the road. If we follow it north and northeast, we'll reach MacKenna's Halt in—" he marked off rough distances with his thumb, "—eight or nine hours, if nothing gets in our way. Shall we go?"

Marguerida was still looking at the map. The machines that had taken the photographs had also done radar scans. Marguerida was unclear about just what radar meant, but the analogy about shouting down the valley and waiting for the echoes made sense. So the photos were overlaid with red contour lines, whose use was also still fairly unclear to her, but that place where six or seven lines ran together must represent the steep cliff above their heads. "What's this?"

"What's what?" He looked where she was pointing. "That thing? A building, I'd say, or a cluster of buildings." He looked up. "Nothing to be seen from here. It could be centuries old and ruined. Shall we go?" he repeated.

"We'd better have some water for the march. We

can carry the bucket till it melts.'' Marguerida dug the collapsible bucket from her pack and looked around for snow.

In spite of the old saw ''as cheap as snow in the Hellers,'' there was not much to be found. It was summer, after all, and the wind had blown away every flake it could reach. She found a drift between two rocks, crusty from freezing each night and thawing by day, but it was red with mountain algae and would make them sick. Unless Donald could contrive to boil it.

''There's some clean ice over here,'' a voice said, and Marguerida almost dropped the bucket. There was a young girl standing on an outcrop of rock, a girl of maybe twelve or fourteen years, wearing a shabby jacket and trews and boots that had been good several years ago. Her hood was thrown back to expose short-cropped red hair that glinted in the morning sun. Something inside Marguerida's head woke up and started ringing like a tiny bell.

''Thank you, I could use some,'' she said aloud, and followed the girl into a shadowed crevice where long icicles hung like a row of crystal teeth. They picked up stones and hammered at the ice till the bucket was full of shining fragments. They carried it between them back to the road.

There are people with red hair but no laran *at all,* Marguerida told herself. *Terra has islandsful of them. She could have never heard the call that went out to gather at Comyn Castle—or hearing it, assumed it didn't mean her—or else she didn't* choose *to come.* Marguerida had had to shed a few layers of anti-Terran prejudice herself.

So she said only, ''I am Marguerida Elhalyn, once Keeper of Albà Tower, and this is my paxman Donald. We came from Thendara, and we hope to make MacKenna's Halt by evening. Do you know the place?"

"Down the road, yes, about a day's journey. I know it. My name is Shaya. I was traveling, too, but I lost my companions and," she smiled ruefully, "my bearings, too. I am *supposed* to go to Armida, but I'm not sure where it is any more."

"West of here," Donald said. "If you come with us to MacKenna, we can set you on your road from there."

"I was hoping you'd say that," the girl said, and grinned. "What takes you to MacKenna? It's a tiny little place, no more than an inn and a few houses."

"There's plague abroad," Marguerida said. "It hit the valleys last year, and we thought it had gone, but now it's come back and running through the mountains. We've got medicine for it, and we need to get it to MacKenna's folk, not only for their own safety but for those who pass through."

"Plague!" The girl's green eyes were shadowed. "I've been out of touch for longer than I thought. Has it reached Armida?"

"Last year, I believe," Donald said. "I'm sorry, I don't know what kind of losses they had. Communications have not been good lately."

"Well," Shaya said. "I won't find out any sooner by fretting about it. If you'll take me with you, I'll do my best to be useful. Do you have anything to eat, or should I keep my eye out for rabbit-horns?"

"We have plenty of food," Marguerida said. "Donald, do you have the breakfast bars? or do I? No, here they are." She shared out three and shouldered her pack. Shaya took the water bucket in her free hand and tore the wrapper from her breakfast bar with her teeth. "Chocolate!" she exclaimed gleefully. "I haven't seen chocolate in I can't remember *how* long." Chewing briskly, she set off down the road.

They walked at a steady pace, through patches of blistering sunlight and frosty shadow, along a tolerably smooth roadbed. Only once did they have to stop and clear fallen rocks and rubble.

The girl Shaya led the way, unaware perhaps of how her companions watched her. Her name meant "grace," Donald recalled, but was a common nickname for girl-children before they grew up. Donald had had an Aunt Grace at home, a tall old lady with iron-gray hair and an eye that could spot a little boy's unwashed neck through two shirts and a windbreaker. So he was ready to treat this confident mountain woman with respect.

And after all, Marguerida thought, *she may not have reached the age of puberty and threshold sickness yet—though she's certainly tall enough. The important thing is not to press her or frighten her; by the time we've dealt with things at MacKenna I may know her well enough to know how to persuade her. If there is any* laran *in her, they'll find it at the Castle.*

The air was dry, and they took pieces of ice from the bucket to melt slowly in their mouths. The wind sang softly in their ears, a thin mountain summer song, full of sneers and sarcasm but not much serious threat. *Just wait till I grow up,* it said, *just you wait till I'm a big wind, I'll huff and I'll puff and I'll blow your house down.*

"Hold," said Shaya suddenly, and stopped. The path ahead of her was growing narrower as it ran on toward a hairpin turn a bowshot away. It might have been a trick of perspective, as if the gods before the gods, the ones who had made the mountains, had wanted to make the road look longer than it was.

"I'm afraid we may have had a rockfall since I was here last," Shaya said. The cool, measured voice made her sound older than her years. "If you'll get out your rope, Donald, I'll investigate." She tied one end of the rope around her waist, and Donald belayed it around a spur of rock.

Shaya picked her way along the narrowing track, testing each step before putting her weight on it. By the time she reached the turn, she was walking on a ledge no more than a span wide and keeping her balance by gripping the rock wall with her hands.

"Donald, stop her," Marguerida said softly. "You can't let a child take such risks." And Shaya looked no more than a child out at the end of the rope, but maybe it was the perspective. She shifted her grip and slipped round the turn. In a moment she was out of sight.

Donald and Marguerida looked at each other. "I can't pull her back now," he said. "She'd fall."

"May I have a little more slack, please?" Shaya called. Donald paid out a few more meters and snubbed the line against the rock. Slowly they saw the slack taken up. Then it loosened again, and in another minute or two Shaya reappeared, inching her way back.

"There's not much of the road left," she said, "but there is a foothold all the way round. Then it widens out again. I think we can get across, but I'll have to do something different with the rope. Here, double it—and give me the two ends—" and in a moment she was out around the turn again.

Donald put the single loop of rope around his rock, and Shaya from her end drew it snug, running breast high around the turn and out of sight. "Will you go next or shall I?" Marguerida asked.

Donald hesitated for a moment, as if trying to decide whether it would be less dangerous for Marguerida to go second or third. Not coming up with any answer, he shrugged. "Alphabetical order?" he said, and slipped in between the rock and the rope. His feet turned sideways, his body close against the wall. Like a bas-relief or an espaliered tree, he made his way around the rock and out of sight.

Then it was Marguerida's turn. She pressed forward along the wall, one foot shuffling ahead of the other, the rope tight under her armpits. As she came round the turn the wind hit her in the face, dry and bitterly cold. It chuckled in her ears, *gotcha gotcha gotcha.* She set her teeth and kept moving. The rock was crumbling under her right foot. She angled her left ahead, her knee braced against the rock and her back against the rope, till she found solid footing again. The wind whined in her ears like whole generations of swamp gnats. It blew dust into her eyes and mouth. She closed them and shuffled on. *Gotcha gotcha gotcha. Gonna freeze your fingers off, drop you down the shaft and flatten you like a pancake—*

And a hand was gripping hers so hard the bones ached, Donald pulling her onto the road and out of the wind. He half led, half dragged her to shelter, an inward curve of the road with a gravel shoulder that gave them all room to sit. "The vaccine," she mumbled, and felt Donald unzip her waist pouch and finger through the vials.

"They're all right," he said.

"Aldones!" Marguerida said when she had her breath back. "What a malicious wind! Why didn't you warn me?"

"Sorry," Shaya said, coiling up the rope. "Around here they don't call the wind anything, lest it come."

"Oh," Marguerida said. "You mean, this is the Wind Man's country?"

"So they say."

Donald looked from one to the other. "Who?"

"Is it safe to tell him?"

"Tell me what?"

Marguerida touched Donald's wrist, then Shaya's. "We all need a rest," she said, "and something to eat. Something hot would be good, if you think you can boil water at this altitude, Donald. And we'll tell you. Because if we don't," she said to Shaya, "he'll *think* about it, and that will be just as bad."

Donald opened a package and added water to the chips and flakes that would turn into soup. When it was heating in its pressurized bubble over the pale glow of the little Terran campstove, Shaya began, "Once upon a time there was a wicked wizard."

"A *laranzu* from the Ages of Chaos," Marguerida translated.

"He was the brother of a king," Shaya went on, "and served him in the wars, making *clingfire* and poison dust, breathing fire and destruction wherever he went. He had a starstone that shone like the bitter heart of a glacier. He was proud of its power, and of its size," Shaya said dryly. "His royal brother was feared, and he was feared, from the

Dry Towns to the sea. And then came Varzil the Good, and the king swore to the Compact.''

Marguerida gave Donald a sharp look, and he turned away to shake the bubble of soup, where little bubbles were starting to rise.

''And when the wizard realized that his dominion was done and his skills forbidden, and that no one would fear him any more, he became angry; and he said, 'If I must lay down my power, none will ever pick it up again,' and he slew the king his brother and laid waste the country for a day's march all around, so that even now nothing but scabweed will grow there.''

''Mostly because of erosion,'' Marguerida added. ''The dust he used—no, I don't know what the 'half life' was!—but it burned out long ago.''

''Soup's done,'' Donald said. He took the bubble from the stove and carefully let the pressure equalize. When the bubble had deflated, the soup was cool enough to drink, and he poured it into cups.

''Then the wizard's own people rose against him, the *laranzu'in* in their Towers, and he cast many of them down; but even so they overcame him and drove him into the mountains.''

''He overturned Alba Tower, so they say,'' Marguerida said. ''That's how I come to know the tale.''

''They drove him into the mountains,'' Shaya repeated, ''and no one ever saw him again. But they hear him in the howling of the wind. It's said the wind blew his skin away flake by flake, and carved his bones into lace, till nothing was left but his starstone.

''And that's what you hear in the wind, that evil murmuring, that poisonous laugh: the Wind Man.''

''Interesting,'' Donald said, collecting the empty

cups and rinsing them out with a little water. "Have you ever heard him yourself?"

Both women stared at him. "Just now," Marguerida said. "Rounding that outcrop," Shaya said. "You didn't hear anything?" Marguerida demanded:

"Only the wind," Donald said. "A nasty sound, I'll grant you—it sounded like a leak in the hull—but quite inanimate. Of course, I haven't any *laran.*"

"Neither have I," Shaya said firmly; and if neither Donald nor Marguerida believed this, they said nothing about it. "We had better get moving again."

It was not long after noon by Donald's watch. They walked in silence for a couple of hours, slowly climbing through thin air and drifting strands of mist to a smooth saddle where the road ran like a ribbon over the shoulder of the high-crowned peak. Donald struggled for air and wished in vain for just a little *laran,* the kind that might have let him foresee this adventure and bring along some supplemental oxygen. Marguerida sucked in deep lungfuls of the diamond air, and seemed to find it adequate. Shaya strode along steadily, like one born to the place. Once she stopped long enough to refill the water bucket with clean snow. They passed over the saddle and descended for another hour, a steep descent that made their toes ache and their ears pop.

The grasses grew thick beside the road, and small indigo-colored flowers began to appear, and even insects and a few birds, taking hasty advantage of the short Darkovan summer. The landscape began to remind Donald of the Alps instead of the Himalayas, and the tops of the highest trees rose ever closer to their feet.

After another brief rest they descended into a gorge whose depth Donald's map could only guess at, because of the trees. The leafy branches closed in over the travelers' heads, slim paper-barked poles like birches and the pungent resin trees. Donald shifted his pack on his shoulders and breathed in the richer air with gratitude. Marguerida was still silent, but Shaya had begun to sing, rhyming couplets in a minor key and in a dialect Donald couldn't quite follow: something about a lonely shepherd.

They found the bottom of the gorge in the shadow of the trees: three meters across and a hundred meters deep, and the bridge gone. Shaya flung the weighted end of Donald's rope over a branch and they swung across, one by one. After taking that exhilarating leap they were all merry, even Marguerida who had been quiet and abstracted since mid-morning. The air was just cool enough to be pleasant, the sun warm enough to comfort their bones as they climbed out of the wooded gorge.

They had risen out of the trees, out of the bushes and flowers, out of the whine of the insects into the whine of the wind. The road was curving back and forth again in narrow switchbacks. Shaya broke off in the middle of her song, and stopped and listened.

"What is it?"

"I thought I heard something." She listened again. "I guess not." She stepped around a lichen-crusted spur of rock. They heard a gasp of suddenly taken breath, and a muffled grunt.

Donald put Marguerida firmly behind him and peered round the curve. Two unpleasant-looking mountain men were holding Shaya against the rock wall, a woolen rag stuffed into her mouth.

The third man had a sword in his hand, flecked with rust around the hilts but very bright along the edges. He took a step toward Donald, his shiny sword point tracing little figures-of-eight in the air before him, grinning with a mouth full of dirty, broken teeth. Donald sighed, and looked at the man with distaste, drew out his blaster, and fired. The brigand fell flaming into the abyss.

His companions retreated hastily, dragging Shaya with them. They vanished between two rocks, where the hooves of small chervines had worn a path into the shadows. There were sounds of scuffling, and a howl of pain. Shaya was putting up a good fight.

Donald was about to go after them when Marguerida caught his arm and pulled him back. "Wait," she said. "And watch out. . . ."

"Ugly bitch," said one of the unseen men. "Take that cord and tie her hands."

There was a moment of silence. Then the sounds began. They were not the kind of sounds that normally come from the throats of grown men. A pair of banshees, put to torment in the fire, might have sounded like this. Marguerida stepped back against the wall, drawing Donald with her. She was paler than usual and looked ill. Donald, attending to her, missed the moment when the brigands came stumbling out of the shadows, their faces torn and bloody from their own nails. He never saw them step blindly off the road and into empty air. What Marguerida saw, she forbore to tell him.

She took a breath and let it out again, and called out, "Shaya, do you need us?"

"I'm all right," came the answer. "Be with you

in a moment.'' She came down the path, unwinding a cord from her wrists. She flung it into the gulf. ''Dirty *bresu'in* made me drop the bucket,'' she said. ''Good, there's some left.'' She lifted the bucket and drank, then passed it to Marguerida and Donald.

Shaya looked at the sun, westering toward the peaks across a sea of air. ''If we're to reach MacKenna by dark, we shall have to pick up our feet,'' she said. She took the bucket back and led the way down the road.

''What did she do to them?'' Donald whispered.

''One learns a lot of strange things in the mountains,'' Marguerida said. ''Perhaps she showed them something they didn't want to see.''

They were climbing again; the road bore eastward. The falling sun was warm on their backs and tinted the rocks around them to the color of blood. And the wind began to pick up again.

It sang in Donald's ears. *Pressure dropping, hull leak, meteorite, bad gasket, losing air.* He drew deep breaths and looked sternly at the world around him, whole cubic kilometers of air, a natural storage tank. He had been trained to let his mind rule over his emotions, and for the most part he succeeded.

Little rabbits on the road, it said. *Little rabbits on the run. Run away, I'll let you run, and then I'll bring you back, and I'll—*

They were almost to the top of the ridge, and the wind's ugly whisper was at their backs. Marguerida ran nervous fingers over her waist pack. The vials were still there. It would be hard for the worst malice of a Wind Man to blow open the Terran zippers, and once they got over the ridge the wind ought to let up.

They stood at the summit for a moment to judge how much daylight was left, and how long a road. "I don't know if you can see that little spot down there," Shaya said. "I don't know if I can either, but it's there. We should get there in an hour, maybe an hour and a half, and," she held up two fingers to the horizon and squinted at the sun, "we've half an hour before the sun falls behind the mountains. There'll be enough twilight to get us there."

They stepped forth onto the descending road, and the wind came round and hit them like a bludgeon. They staggered forward, and Shaya fell to hands and knees. Marguerida clutched at her hand and pulled her to her feet, and stretched her other hand backward for Donald to catch. Hand in hand they stumbled down the road, keeping close to the rock wall on their right lest a sudden gust twist them off the road.

Welcome to my house, it muttered. *It has a floor and no roof, and one wall, but you don't know where it is. Is it there? No, that's only me, and you're falling away, falling, falling.*

It had begun to snow again, and the white flakes billowed around them till they could barely see each other, much less the road.

Down and around, the wind howled, *down and around. You're walking right into my lap. Right into my mouth. I'll chew you up and spit you out.*

Down and around. The wall was still at Marguerida's shoulder, but she could hardly feel it. She knew her hands were still tightly gripping Donald's and Shaya's, but she couldn't feel them at all. Yet it didn't feel like the numbness of cold. The shining white of the snow was shading, not into the rose of sunset, but into a luminous bluish-gray that seemed to radiate from all around and from very far away. Marguerida had walked out into the overworld without seeking it or knowing.

The wind had died away from her ears, but not the voice that muttered hate and greed, death and cruelty in a breathless stream like a poisoned river. Her Keeper's training let Marguerida follow the wicked voice upstream without listening to the obscenities it said.

There was a sharper light ahead, harsh and painful to the sense, and a human shape stood in it—two shapes?—no, only one. No, beside the human shape that drifted past, feet dragging like one who walks in fetters or against a gale, there was something else. It had been a man once, or manlike, but something had taken the image and a pair of shears and cut it into lace. Its flesh was tatters that fluttered in a wind of their own making; its bones were perforated like the casts of sponges. Through the holes in its skull the light shone like bitter stars.

Marguerida looked at it with disdain. It could not touch her. Here in the overworld she wore not her ugly Terran jumpsuit but the red robe and veil of the Keeper's office, the garb that was hers by right. Centuries-old rituals and lessons, the dedication of her teachers who had trained her and were dead: these armored her. The shreds that had been hands reached toward her and drew back as if burnt by her fire.

But the other figure, the one that was still human—Marguerida saw her as if with the eyes of a god that looks out of the high places and sees all time and human history together. Past, present, and future wrapped up together like a nut in the palm of the hand. Young girl, maiden grown, woman heavy with child, battered body with its last breath on its lips, all at once. She held out her hand. "Come, Shaya. We're getting out of here." As their hands met, they fell back as through a sieve and were back in their bodies with the wind howling about them, thick with snow, brilliant with a poisonous blue.

Marguerida drew in both her arms, tugging gently at the hands she could not see, till they met. She set Donald's hand in Shaya's and fumbled her way up his arm, like a lifeline, till she found his ear. "Donald. Give me your blaster."

He said something, she couldn't hear what, and with his free hand dug out the blaster. She felt it cold against her cheek, took it carefully in both hands and found its muzzle and its trigger. Donald's hand moved over hers and did something—opened the mysterious safety catch, she supposed, that Terran stories were always going on about. She moved a few steps forward, till Donald and Shaya were both safely behind her, and fired into the wind where the blue light was strongest.

All the colors of the spectrum erupted around her, spiraling outward like deadly rainbows. Everything was dancing in it, images of men and horses, chervines and trees and tall towers bright under the moons, all fading, fading. The wind was slackening, the great wheels of color slowing down. Marguerida held the little blaster steady, trying not to wonder how much power it had in it, how many breaths of firing time before it was exhausted. She understood drained batteries; she'd often felt like that herself.

But the power held. The blue light died just as the blaster began to chirp and flash its "CELL LOW" panel. The wind fell away so suddenly it was like going deaf. The sun was just vanishing behind the mountains, but the sky was still light. They were standing on uneven gravel in the bottom of the crevasse; a few meters ahead of them, the rock walls were still glowing orange-red. Whatever had lain between them was atoms now.

They made their way back to the road. Donald found a single bone fragment among the gravel, and carefully ground it to powder under his heel.

"All those centuries," Shaya said.

"Just bad luck he fell into the crevasse," Donald said, "where the walls would protect his starstone from the elements."

"Bad luck, or bad purpose," Marguerida said. "Can't you see him, at the end of his life, creeping into that shelter so that the evil will he'd poured into his stone would outlive his body? Here's your ace-in-the-hole, Donald. I'm afraid I've drained it."

"And I've dropped the water bucket somewhere," Shaya said. "But look, that light down there is MacKenna. We can probably make it before dark."

They nearly did. Two little moons gave a pale illusion of light for the last mile of their march. Then the lamps shone through the inn's horn windowpanes, and the smell of nut-porridge leaked round the edges of the door.

"I won't be coming in, if you don't mind," Shaya said. "I know my road home now, and I'm ready to take it."

"Don't be silly; you can't go on in the dark," Donald protested.

"She isn't," Marguerida said. "The gods go with you, Shaya, and thank you."

"Thank *you,*" Shaya said. "But—yes, I think my debt is paid. Good night."

And she was gone into the darkness, only a swirl of snowflakes where she had been. Donald opened his mouth to protest again, but Marguerida took his arm and led him inside the inn.

The people were gathered around the fire, telling stories, as they did every night of their lives. Hard to judge in the dim light, but only a few showed the bright eyes of fever. They had come in time.

"—So he took the child behind him on his horse and rode with her to Armida. But as he rode up to the great house, she slipped from the crupper and was gone. He searched in the darkness, but he never found her. So he went up to the house—"

Donald put his hand to his mouth. He had heard this kind of tale before, they told variants on every planet, but this time—

"And when he told the tale, the people wept and said—"

"She died long ago," Marguerida said in his ear. "She's been trying to get home ever since; but the unhallowed dead wander and can't find rest. We gave her burial, and she paid back the favor, and now she can go home. Not, of course, to Armida, but to her real home. Now that it's safe." She drew him closer to the fire, and smiled at the astonishment in his eyes. "Didn't you realize, when you touched her, that she wasn't *there?*"

"In the middle of a howling blizzard? Was I supposed to take her pulse?"

But the people in the inn had seen them now, and beckoned them in to places at the fire. Marguerida put on a smile and sat down next to the old man with the copper armring. If she could talk the MacKenna into being vaccinated, the rest of the village would follow him without argument. The wind outside moaned softly, like an old scold grumbling herself to sleep.

Shelter

by Nina Boal

Nina Boal has been a Friend of Darkover since back when we were printing Darkover stories in a fanzine.

''Shelter'' is a story which must have happened many times in the history of Darkover. It's an intensely involving story, one that draws you in at the first paragraph and then holds you tightly till it's finished.

This is the kind of story I am always looking for and am occasionally lucky enough to find. . . .

Corrina leaned toward the guest room's tiny window. It was late afternoon, and a solid white sheet filled the window almost to its borders. Resignedly she shook her head; a red-gold braid wriggled over her shoulders. The storms showed no signs whatsoever of clearing. There was no way she could continue her journey.

Somehow—*somehow*—she would have to find a way to spend another night here at the Copper Cauldron Inn. Slender, pale fingers felt their way through the leather coin pouch, finally turning it inside out.

It was empty. She had spent her few remaining *sekals* for last night's stay.

She stared at the wood paneling on the floor. Some nights during her journey, she had paid her way at inns and guest houses. But she'd also been able to earn a few nights' boarding sweeping floors, washing plates, doing other odd chores. In that way, she had stretched out the money she'd received from the sale of the stolen *oudrakhi* she'd been riding. Now she had reached the absolute end of her money. She would have to work again for her keep.

Corrina swallowed hard. There was something about the way *Mestro* Piedro had regarded her when she had checked in. Muscular fingers had dwelled longer than needed, almost fondling her hands as she'd laid the coins in the innkeeper's palm. Corrina had hurriedly jerked her hand away. Pulling her cloak well around herself, she had scurried to her room.

But maybe she'd somehow drawn the innkeeper's attention. Perhaps she'd walked in a certain way, curving slim hips or curling her face into the folds of her hood so that her silken hair would display itself.

Silken red hair. That had been the curse of her existence. She had heard stories from others, had inquired, had put two and two together. Had she been born into one of the great families of the ruling Comyn, the "spells" she suffered would have been considered a blessing, a gift. A teacher in one of the high Towers would have honed her *laran* to a fine edge.

But instead, her mother scratched a bare living from the gritty soils of a Serrais border village near Carthon. Her mother's sandy-haired husband—"*not your father,*" he'd said, pointing to her flame hair—had tolerated her until her thirteenth year. That was when her strange "spells" had taken her over, causing her to stare at visions, making her scream out in her sleep.

She shrugged her shoulders, shutting her mind on her memories. The world went as it would and not as she would have it. There was nothing she could do about her lot except search out the best way. She would have to ask *Mestro* Piedro for work.

The thick fingers trailed along Corrina's slim shoulder as she stood at the kitchen's door. "I don't need a cook or dishwasher tonight," the stout innkeeper laughed. "My wife and daughter take care of that."

Corrina twisted away from the wandering hand. "I . . . I could wait tables, sir," she stammered out.

The bearded, dark-haired face stared at the ceiling rafters. "Yes, you could, couldn't you?" A guffaw escaped. "My best customers are coming tonight, a contingent of Lord Serrano's Castle Guard. You could serve them at table." The hand stretched out, threading underneath the headscarf Corrina wore. "You could also serve these fine customers in *other* ways. You're young and pretty enough, and you need the money. I could pay you quite well."

The fingers tightened around her chin. A white light exploded inside her head. The invading fingers suddenly retreated. A knife flashed in the kitchen flames, moving as if following its own command. Corrina sliced the blade through tan skin, leaving a thin line of blood. *Mestro* Piedro's screech filled the kitchen's empty spaces. Corrina clutched the blade in her whitened fist. "Don't you come near me," she whispered, staring straight into the innkeeper's gray eyes.

"Get out now, bitch!" *Mestro* Piedro growled. "You should be grateful that I offered you gainful employment. Now you can go out into the storm and see how *that* will give you shelter."

Corrina struggled to control her shaking. "Don't come near me." She repeated her warning. Still holding the bare blade, she rushed to her room to pack her few possessions.

The night winds howled and whistled. Wet snow brushed and stung her face as Corrina placed one booted foot in front of the other. The land was very different from the cool, arid plains of her Serrais home. Thick forests of towering firs surrounded the scattered farms and inns of the foothills which bordered the high Hellers peaks near Alderan.

She cursed her temper. She'd gotten herself in real trouble this time, disputing with the innkeeper. She had survived these past few tendays, a young woman forced to travel alone. But she'd never last through this storm.

Does it matter? A voice of sheer desperation echoed in her mind. She could never return to her home village. She was a "six-fathered" bastard as far as her family was concerned; her "spells" had made her useless in the fields. But her youth and red-gold hair had made her a desirable commodity for a starving family to peddle to the highest bidder. She'd been sold to Dry Towns slavers passing through the village.

She wrapped her hand around the handle of the

sheathed knife, buried within her woolen cloak. Memories rose, unbidden. Somehow, she had found her strength the night one of the slave sellers decided to "try her out." In her struggles, she'd reached for and found the knife, plunging it deep within the heaving chest. The others had been held helpless, perhaps by the powers she knew were connected with her red hair. Taking the dead man's *oudrakhi,* she'd ridden off alone into the desert night.

The swirling wind sang to her. This wasn't the desert. Winter lashed this place, as if avenging a great, unnamed wrong. Her woefully untrained powers wouldn't help her here. *Shelter,* the wind hummed. *Let me embrace you, keep you warm.* She sank to her knees. *No harm will come to you,* the wind's melody murmured. *No more pain, no more terror.*

She stretched her body out in its bed of snow. "*Lay your head on my lap,*" the strains of her mother's lullaby cooed to her, as if she were once more a child. A snowdrift's frosty pillow cradled her head. "*Sleep, little one. Sleep in peace.*"

Shivers coursed through her. Numbness threaded itself through curled, aching fingers. Then a head-splitting cry. . . . She was in one of Zandru's nine hells, she was sure. The scream was one of torment, the torment she deserved for . . . *for what?* The anguished question.

The scream, again. Her snow-wet fist balled, then rubbed across her eyes. Her head throbbed with pain, with indescribable terror. Someone *else's* terror.

A wail, disintegrating into ragged sobs, ripped

through her. She crawled to her knees, forced her eyes to open.

She was still somehow alive. The storm shrieked, curling around her shaking body. The sobs flailed through her mind, cries not her own. A child's sobs were emanating from behind snow-laden branches.

She clambered to her feet, pushing against the wind—one step, then another. The child's cries were now soft waves, washing in her mind.

There. Inside a particular thicket in the forest. She crouched beneath one of the firs; she enveloped the small, quavering form with her woolen cloak.

A muffled crunch of steps pattered toward her. A bass, male voice was penetrating the depths of flakes. *Piedro?* A stab of panic pierced through her. She curved her body around the child; her fist wrapped around the hilt of her blade.

A hand grasped her shoulder. The voice spoke again, its roughness brushing across her—laced with a kindness she knew never existed in the Copper Cauldron's lecherous keeper. She dropped her hand from her knife's hilt as her ears sought out the stranger's words; they seemed to flow to her from a far passageway. "You've found my child. Come, let me warm you in my house." Her own exhaustion suddenly seized her. She could only sink into the steady pair of arms which lifted her up and carried her.

A shrill clatter—Corrina's legs were thrashing against heavy quilts spread over her.

Her eyes opened wide. Red streams of sunlight poked through a window. She lay in a bed which was pressed against the wall of a one-room cabin. Her breath's puffs disappeared into the frigid air. A huge pot of water simmered over embers, within a stone fireplace.

She folded the thick blankets well around her as the images of the past night raced through her memory. She'd withstood the advances of an innkeeper, she'd found a child in a storm, a strange man had found her. . . .

The ringing clatter shot through her again. A child of about seven or eight years was kneeling on the hearth, spinning a piece of kindling. Jet-black hair tumbled over a brown wool tunic, draped around thin shoulders. Eyes as pale as the coarse strands were dark stared intently at the wooden shard; each rap of the whirling object brought an eager, wordless yelp.

The cabin's lone door thumped open. A huge man lumbered inside, slamming the door shut behind him. Corrina gave a start as the man piled a load of firewood onto a stack directly across from the door. The child continued twirling the kindling piece, seemingly unharmed by the storm, oblivious to the existence of either the man or his guest.

The man poured water from a small pot into a clay mug, then reached for a jar of herbs. "So you're up," he said, holding the steaming cup toward Corrina.

Corrina grasped the mug's handle. The leaf-scent floated into her nostrils as she tasted the bitter sweetness of tea. The man pulled a wooden chair to the bed, lowering his bulk into the seat's expanse. Blue eyes twinkled underneath shaggy chestnut-brown hair.

Still, it was a strange man. Instinctively, Corrina huddled herself into the protection of thick bedcovers. The clatter continued echoing through her ears.

The dark-haired child persisted in spinning the kindling woodpiece.

"I'm Carlo MacFiona," the man introduced himself. "This is my foster son, Felix," he pointed toward the figure crouching pensively on the hearth. "Don't worry about my intentions," Carlo smiled. "When I have desires, which has not been often these days, I am a lover of men."

Corrina gazed squarely at her host. She had heard tales of *ombredin.* They were all slender and "feminine" in countenance, or so she'd been told. Carlo was stout; a dense red mustache grew profusely across his upper lip. Corrina shook her head—another untrue tale. *As false as my parents' protestations of love and devotion,* Corrina told herself.

She let her body relax, taking another sip of the refreshing tea. She was grateful she had found this host, who was so unlike her last one.

A loud crash—and the clattering stopped. Felix was ambling toward Corrina's bed. Fine-boned fingers began stroking Corrina's forearms, then reached for her face. Corrina turned her head, laughing. The slender fingers tickled. She gazed into Felix's eyes—and a chill spread across her.

The eyes were completely blank. Corrina had once known eyes like these on the face of a village child, a girl. The girl's eyes had been green rather than Felix's pale gray—but had carried the same vacant stare. A "changeling child," the village elders had told the girl's frantic mother while the girl had sprawled on the ground, spinning a leather hair clasp.

Soft fingers brushed across Corrina's nose. Something crackled inside her mind as if two forces met. It was connected to her mind powers, Corrina surmised, even though the child's hair was dark rather than red. A twinge flickered, the force inside released. Felix grunted. He lifted his hand toward his eyes, rapidly flicking his fingers in the air. He piled his body on all four limbs and loped back to his fireside spot. Loud squeals of ecstacy filled the air, blending in with repeated clacking. Felix once more was twirling his piece of wood.

Carlo poured himself a mug of tea. "My foster son has been that way," he shrugged his shoulders, "for as long as I've taken care of him."

Corrina leaned up on the bed. Her eyes took in the self-involved boy. Line-forces still pattered in her mind. She would have to find out about them, ask her host. *At a later time,* she told herself. Lifting an instinctive barrier, Corrina studied the furnishings and implements of the small cabin, primitive by the standards Corrina knew in her village, yet clean and neatly arranged. She noted the thick pelts of furs hanging along the length of one of the walls. "It must be hard," she said, "for you to care for your boy and support yourself as well."

"We do adequately," Carlo answered. "I once was a mercenary soldier until Felix came to live with me. Now I hunt and trap for a living, here in these woods."

Suddenly, Felix darted toward the door, tugging at the bolt. Quick as a cat, Carlo leapt from his place and ran toward the child. "No, no, Felix, *chiyu,*" Carlo admonished. "You don't go outside without me. It's dangerous. Besides, we have a guest. Perhaps later." He wrapped his broad arms around Felix, who screeched in consternation. Gently, Carlo guided the squalling child back to his accustomed place.

Felix gave out an inconsolable, ear-splitting shriek. Corrina's head pounded. Just as quickly, the pressure let up—and Felix settled himself down on the hearth. Finding his favorite toy, the piece of wood, he commenced his spinning and twirling as if the previous incident had never happened.

Carlo's eyes opened, an amazed sky-blue. "I can feel it inside my own mind as well," he said. "Something is connecting between your mind and my foster son's." He pointed at Corrina's red hair.

"I am . . ." Corrina braced herself. "I am six-fathered, born after the festival when Comyn lords mingle with the common people." Corrina's cheeks grew hot. *How can I explain to him that my parents actually sold me to the highest bidder?* "My mother and stepfather were tillers of their fields. They . . . they cast me aside when my 'spells' became too much for them." She lifted her chin. "I've made my own way since then."

Carlo relaxed visibly. "You're like me, a cast-off *nedestro.*" He pointed at the red hues in his own hair. "But I was taught something of matrix science before being sent away." He smiled warmly. "We can discuss this a little later, over breakfast. Let me take Felix out to gather more wood, so you can dress in privacy." The blue eyes dropped. "I'm sorry I have no proper guest room for you. This one-room hovel is the best I've been able to do."

Corrina could see the flushed cheeks as Carlo turned away. "Come, Felix," Carlo commanded. "We're going out." At the word "out," an almost animated expression crossed briefly over the boy's face. He leapt to his feet and loped over to his foster father's side.

* * *

Carlo carefully spooned porridge into Felix's waiting mouth as Corrina sipped her own. The rich salt-sweet taste bathed Corrina's tongue; Carlo was definitely a skilled cook.

"My mother was a kitchen maid at Mariposa Castle," Carlo explained. "My father is Lord Rannirl Lanart, closely related to the high Altons of Armida, though he has chosen not to acknowledge me."

He reached a hand beneath his undertunic, pulling out a small leather pouch attached to a thong around his neck. "When I was fourteen, the castle *laranzu* had me taken to Corandolis Tower for *laran* testing. I was keyed into this matrix, found to have a *small* measure of the Alton Gift of forced rapport. But the Tower's Keeper determined that my gifts were not strong enough for Comyn purposes, though I was not a danger to them. So I was sent back to my mother's kitchen. When I came of age, I left Mariposa to make my own living."

Carlo lifted a cup of *jaco* to Felix's lips. The boy eagerly drank it. "Two years ago, I found this boy wandering alone in the woods, without any clothes. I took him in; my gifts, though not strong, revealed his name to me, 'Felix.' No one has ever acknowledged his existence. I am the only one he knows as his parent."

Corrina found herself watching foster father and foster son, observing their interactions with each other. She noted the tenderness which Carlo used, the matter-of-fact way he accepted Felix, with all his limitations. *No,* she corrected herself. Carlo didn't see Felix as "limited"; he saw merely the child's unique differences.

She found herself longing to be a part of the

peaceful life displayed before her. In her own life, with her disruptive "spells," she'd always felt a freak. Could she dare to think that she could find a place here, with these other outsiders?

A flying shape whizzed by Corrina's ear; it would have slammed into her head had she not ducked. A crash against the wall, up above the wooden wash tub—and shards of what once was a ceramic tea mug fell in pieces to the floor beneath the tub.

Felix was rocking violently in his chair. A low moan rose to a screech, ripping a ragged hole in Corrina's mind. Carlo once more leapt catlike from his chair, running over to soothe the boy. Felix curled himself against Carlo's chest, his screeches muffled in the folds of the man's wool tunic.

The bass voice began humming a soft melody as Carlo moved his body to the rhythm of Felix's rocking. His hands stroked Felix's hair. The hammering in Corrina's mind began to recede.

Corrina rushed to fetch the broom she found standing by the hearth. She swept the pieces of ceramic into a pile, then pushed them into a dust pan.

Carlo's earlier explanation shot into her, "*Something is connecting between your mind and my foster son's.*" She swallowed hard. A despair, new yet bitterly familiar, welled up inside her. Her damnable "spells" were disturbing the the tranquillity of this house. She had no choice but to leave, and continue her journey.

She strode to the bed where she had slept, then began bundling up her clothes and meager possessions. She fought the tears which threatened to burst out. "I must go, right away," she muttered. "For your sake."

Felix broke away from Carlo. He ran to Corrina

and wound his arms tightly around her. He moaned quietly as he pressed his face against her blouse.

Carlo was close behind. "Please, *mestra,*" he pleaded. "Stay with us; don't leave. You saved my son's life."

Corrina, her arms held firmly by her side, could only stare at the shaking figure wrapped around her. "Yes," Carlo continued. "Something is happening in both of your minds." His smile opened. "This is for the good, I am sure; Felix has never displayed this sort of feeling to a stranger." He pointed to his matrix bag. "We will work this out together. I sense that there are some secrets which may unfold."

His fingers barely touched Felix's dark head. "Come, *chiyu,* our guest isn't going anywhere, so don't worry." Felix released his arms, then turned his pale gaze at Carlo. "Come, let's finish our breakfast." Felix clambered onto his chair while Corrina found hers again, her doubts still darting through her. Carlo began spooning porridge into Felix's mouth once more. Felix eagerly lapped it up, his pale eyes placid. Once more, it was as if nothing at all had happened.

Dreams drifted through Corrina's head that night. Pleasant pictures floated before her—golden flowers bathed in crimson lights, bowing to the caresses of crisp mountain breezes.

A scream cleaved her head in two, pulsing again and again. The flower field became a vast white mass of ice flecks, knifing through tender bare skin. Tears formed frozen rivulets on her cheeks. She lifted leaden feet, one after the other, plunging them into drifts which towered far over her head.

The cry trembled through her. An aching, weaving sob crawled into her ears, lanced through her skull.

She sat bolt upright on her bed. An owl whistled outside, muffled by the thick layer of snow. A shrill coo followed, it's mate's mirrored reply. A creak resounded from the hearth, bathed in the shimmer of Kyrrdis. Two shadowy forms rocked, a synchronous dance through the pale-green moonlight. Carlo was sprawled on the floor, sheltering Felix's shivering form.

A scream pierced *inside* her; Felix's mouth had shut tight. A crackling invaded her consciousness. A thin white thread of force began burrowing into her mind, spinning from an outside, unseen place. A hammering resounded in her head. Shields sprang up to stave off the intrusion.

An explosion. . . . Pieces floated, swimming along waves of a purplish mist. She was drowning in its swirls.

A blue-white light blazed, a beacon amidst the muddied swirls. A voice spoke to her mind. *It's me—Carlo. The blue light is my matrix crystal. We are in the overworld. I'm going to try and pull us out.* A rope formed, twisting through the mist. Corrina's own hand, a wraithlike image of itself, reached in desperation for the lifeline.

The white force-thread wound around her arms, then divided into strands, writhing toward the blue stone. The strands pulled together, forming fine-boned fingers. They parted the purple mist, as if drawing a curtain. A jet-haired figure revealed itself. *Felix,* Corrina recognized Carlo's foster son. Pale gray eyes stared from a paler face.

Secrets unfolding, Corrina remembered Carlo's

words from the morning. The blue matrix held steady. Without speaking, Carlo communicated to her: Hold still; do not fight it.

. . . A nursery. A flame-haired man, dressed in the finery of his rank, leaned over the canopied bed where his wife lay. The midwife lifted up a squalling infant, the son of Lord Gareth Serrano. ''Something is wrong, *vai dom,* the midwife said. ''He is male, yet not quite. He'll never sire sons of his own.''

''Then the breeding project is a failure,'' Lord Serrano murmured. Bitterness creased his forehead. ''All the work, the research the *laranzu'in* put into it has been for naught.'' A screech from the infant drew his attention. ''Get it away from me,'' he commanded, turning away. . . .''

A blank space formed within the mist's curtain. Corrina gazed, questions arising in her. *Male, yet not quite?* She'd heard vague tales of *emmascas,* pale-haired and barren, born occasionally into Comyn families. Felix had dark hair. How could he be one of those? Why should it matter anyway?

And the pictures had shown Felix as an unknowing infant. How could he have perceived the images from outside? How could he have known his father's motives? Carlo's mind brushed against her own, his own puzzlement joining her own.

Corrina felt her rage seething inside her. How dare Felix's father throw his son aside in such a casual way? *Your own parents cast you off,* she had to remind herself. Her rage flowed, blending in with white lines that emanated from bright gray eyes. Forms began filling the space, another scene from what seemed to be outside the boy's range of consciousness. . . .

Lord Gareth and Lady Drusilla, his wife, stood next to Mikhail of Tramontana. The Tower's Keeper spread his crimson-draped arms; his hand held a gleaming matrix.

"Your child has gifts never seen before in one so young," the Keeper said. "They will aid in the wars. Felix can form force-lines which rival the Alton Gift in entering unwilling minds. His mind is able to leave his body and look down upon himself, storing images. But he'll be useless in siring sons," the Keeper knitted his brows.

Lord Gareth smiled with satisfaction. "One gift to use in battle, as a battering ram against minds," the Comyn lord said. "The other for spying from far ranges. Perfect. So we'll follow the planned procedure for extracting the gifts from him."

"They'll be stored in this lattice," Mikhail indicated the wide screen. "Until you produce a more normal son to name as Heir. The mind of the one not-quite-male will be left as empty as his loins. He'll be no further use to you. No further threat."

A dark-haired boy, about six, was escorted into the mirrored matrix chamber. "Father," he asked, his eyes alert and unafraid. "What new lessons will I learn about my Gifts?"

"You'll soon see, Felix my child," Lord Gareth said dryly. "You'll soon see."

The visual images fled. A yellow, billowing smoke curled inside the portals of gray mist. Corrina found herself floating in the overworld, pitching and yawing on the furious sea of smoke.

A blue matrix shimmered amidst the clouds. Carlo's voice spoke. *Now we're inside Felix's mind. Hold on tight; keep your eyes on my stone.*

. . . A prying, a burrowing. Mind-shields struggled to stay whole. Thick fingers, like gaping maws, reached in to pluck out fancied jewels of power. Something clutched at Corrina. She was hurtled through a curving tunnel of time—the prize of Dry Town merchants, she twisted her body against grasping fingers. Her hand found the knife's handle. . . .

A light burst. A scream she knew all too well split her mind in two. . . . *Running, gasping for air. Slipping out from perspiring hands. Dashing down a castle's secret corridor, then out a hidden door. Snowflakes knifed through tender skin. A blanket of sheltering snow. Run into the trees, away from invading, slicing pain. Run. Far away. . . .*

The swirling mists of the overworld, the familiar blue light of Carlo's matrix reappeared. Corrina breathed deeply. Another light shining, a tight ball protecting a cherished treasure. . . .

Corrina found herself crouched on the fireplace's stone hearth. Carlo was sprawled next to her; Felix lay next to him. Crimson beams, the dawn's first lights, poked through the window.

She rubbed her eyes in amazement. "Is . . . is it over?" Carlo could only nod in fatigued assent. Felix pressed himself into his foster father's eager embrace.

Corrina's stomach churned. Felix wasn't quite

"normal" enough for the Comyn lords. So they had planned to . . . Corrina couldn't find the right description; it had been something unimaginable and unspeakable. Felix's parents had cared more for *laran* weapons than for their child.

The last image, the tight ball of light, flickered briefly before her. "Lord Serrano didn't succeed, did he?" she queried. "Felix still has his powers wrapped inside him."

Carlo ruffled Felix's hair. "Still contained, right here." A smile of gratitude spread across his face. "Where they'll never be used for the wars." Felix peered up from the hollow of Carlo's arms. Tears streaked his cheeks.

Carlo gave a slight shrug. "Lord Serrano never sent search parties for any son, as far as I know. I remember hearing news last year that a peace treaty was signed. The *laran* weapons aren't needed anymore—so neither is Felix."

The boy's gray eyes glittered. They flitted around the cabin, taking in the fur pelts, the dining table, the kitchen implements, the large wash tub. The eyes were alert, no longer the blank eyes of a changeling child.

Felix lifted his hands, stroking Corrina's nose, her long red hair. He looked directly at her, then grinned widely. Rays of rapport reached out tentatively into Corrina's mind.

The boy was forming his lips into a round circle. He pointed at the middle of the room. He puffed out a breath, then a sound. "H-h-h!"

The pale eyes brightened. The wide grin became even wider. Carlo's face glowed with the unbounded pride Corina felt inside her. Felix took another breath. He opened his lips. ‘‘H-h-h . . .’’ His fingers held Carlo’s and Corrina’s hands. He spoke distinctly, just one word.

‘‘Home!’’

Carmen's Flight

by Margaret L. Carter and
Leslie R. Carter

Margaret Carter's stories have appeared in four previous Darkover anthologies and in SWORD AND SORCERESS V. She has an impressive list of publications, both scholarly and fictional, in the field of vampires and vampire literature. She is currently employed as a proofreader for a small biweekly newspaper, and lectures occasionally on her academic specialities.

This story was plotted by her husband, Leslie, who is the commanding officer of the U.S.S. Reid, *a frigate based in San Diego. His other literary credits include a textbook,* Principles of Naval Weapons Systems; *perhaps if he were not committed to his naval career he would write a lot more fiction. . . .*

''Carmen's Flight'' is their first collaboration, and I think you'll enjoy it.

Surely the discolored sky and the bloated, red sun weren't enough to account for the crawling sensation under her skin. Carmen Delorien had spent shore leave on far stranger worlds during her career in the Space Service. Cottman IV ought to seem downright homey. The people, after all, were human; rumor had it they were descendants of an ancient lost Terran colony. Not that Carmen had seen much of the native culture so far. This tavern in the Trade City resembled spaceport bars on a score of planets. In her Security specialty, Carmen had learned to trust her instincts. But this time there seemed no justification for the sense of wrongness she'd felt ever since disembarking from the ship.

She took a long swig of the sweet, fruity wine, called *shallan,* in an attempt to drown the feeling. *Just another liberty port,* she told herself. *Sometimes I wonder why I bother. Why not stay on board, if all I'm going to do is swill cheap booze with other Terran personnel?*

''How goes it, Delorien?'' A loud baritone broke into her ruminations. Carmen jumped, sloshing her drink on the marred wooden tabletop. The skinny, mustached blond who'd just taken the seat beside her said, ''Twitchy, aren't we? Not enjoying the night life of scenic Darkover?''

''Slade, how about a 'hello' or something next time, before you yell in my ear?'' She considered Gary Slade, another member of Security Division, one of her better friends aboard *Arcturus,* though all her friendships were little more than casual. Although she didn't feel like company at the moment, she briefly explained her foul mood, repeating aloud her thoughts about sticking to the Terran Zone.

''Well, that's easy to fix,'' Gary said. ''According to the briefing we got, Darkovans aren't crazy about us, but recently they've loosened up enough that they do let Terrans travel outside the Zone. Why don't you hire a guide and see some of the country?

Maybe you're just tired of being cooped up on the ship.''

Carmen expressed her skepticism with a wordless grunt.

''It always takes a day or two to adjust to a new planet, anyway.''

''It's more than that,'' she said. ''I've never felt this way before.'' The moment she'd left the ship, the illusion of eyes on her back had started plaguing her. She'd actually whirled around to confront the imaginary follower a couple of times. Nothing, no local footpad with designs on her pay or her person. Yet the feeling wouldn't go away, and the itch inside her skull—as she thought of it—kept getting stronger. The idea of a tour of the countryside, or at least a stroll outside the Trade City, appealed to her. At the same time, however, she shied away from it. She knew she would attract attention out there, not only for her uniform. Though her black hair wouldn't necessarily set her apart from the natives, its close-cropped style would. Respectable Darkovan women didn't cut off their hair.

A dark, burly man in Space Service uniform slipped into the chair on her other side. This time she was alert and didn't start with surprise. ''Anton Polaski, off the *Iberia,*'' he introduced himself. ''Buy you a drink?''

''I already have one.'' Unattached loner that she was, she normally had no qualms about picking up a night's companion in a setting like this. But tonight the brief distraction didn't seem worth the trouble.

Taking the hint from her brusque reply, Polaski wandered off in search of a likelier prospect.

''I don't feel like sitting around,'' Carmen said

to Gary. "Think I'll take a walk and then head back to the ship."

Gary shook his head in mock dismay. "Not the Delorien I know. Maybe you're coming down with something—better report to the medics."

Ignoring him, she abandoned the dregs of her drink and headed for the street. The chill air cut through her synthetic clothes, making her envy the leather jackets and fur cloaks she'd seen the natives wearing. *And this is supposed to be spring!*

Without much thought for her direction, she found herself meandering toward the spaceport gate. She flashed her ID and nodded to the guard, then stepped through. The black sky overhead made the night air seem colder. Carmen drew her inadequate cape tighter around her shoulders and strode briskly across the plaza. She ignored the row of shops that catered to Terran sightseers. The inexplicable restlessness drove her into the narrow, cobblestoned lanes.

She spent an hour wandering between rows of low, stone houses, many adorned with windows of colored glass. Spicy odors tickled her nose. She paused at a stall in the old market to buy a couple of fried cakes. She regretted eating them; the snack didn't help her unsettled stomach. The curious stares of the locals affected her like veiled threats. *Maybe that's why I feel so jumpy, because I'm the center of attention out here.* Carmen knew better, though; she'd felt the same way in the bar. It took conscious effort to keep her hand away from her holstered blaster. *Watch it, don't want to cause an incident.* For some reason, these people were touchy about firearms.

When she caught herself heading toward the

fringe of the city instead of back toward the Terran Zone, she forced herself to stop and think. Curfew couldn't be far off. She imagined getting lost, with the humiliation of asking directions from some amused Darkovan. Or getting waylaid by those hypothetical footpads.

Snap out of it, Delorien. Get a move on if you don't want to find yourself in deep you-know-what. Yet when she turned in the direction of the spaceport gates, the crawling sensation under her scalp got worse. She felt there was something she'd forgotten, something she ought to be doing out here. Shaking her head, Carmen mentally snorted at the ridiculous idea. *Maybe I do need to see the medic.*

The next morning, Carmen woke up with Gary Slade's suggestion that she tour Thendara and the nearby countryside buzzing in her head. Today it didn't seem like a bad idea. Except that she felt an urge to explore farther than a few kilometers around the capital. Why not? She had liberty today; she wasn't on the duty roster until 0700 the following morning. That schedule left plenty of time for a private expedition. Flyers were available for rent, and she had enough credits saved up. In space she had little opportunity to spend her pay.

She rushed through a shower and started packing. The surge of activity eased some of the pressure at the back of her mind. Halfway through, she realized what she was doing. She paused to stare at the gear laid out on the deck. What did she want all this stuff for? Five changes of clothes, a first-aid kit, toiletries— *You'd think I was going on a week-long camping trip, not an easy day flight.* And she'd also made a mental note to requisition a week's worth of rations.

Well, what was so odd about taking precautions? She had to be prepared in case of an emergency landing. This was a rugged world; in some locales, settled communities were small and scattered.

After dressing in a thermal cold-weather outfit, she picked up her blaster. *Shouldn't take this. Outside Thendara, it's contraband.* But she couldn't stand leaving it behind. She tucked the weapon into her pack.

After breakfast, she signed out for the day. She'd told Gary where she was going but evaded questions from him and her other messmates. And she'd made it clear that she wanted no company. An hour after arising, she was down in the spaceport, checking out a flyer.

The agent, a wiry, brown-skinned man, was dubious of Carmen's plan to travel without a pilot. "Restricted zones, tricky air currents—dozens of things could trip you up. According to regs, you're supposed to have a qualified guide."

Carmen suppressed the urge to scream at the man. "I'm qualified to fly these things. I had the same basic training everybody gets. And I can read a map."

"Letting you go alone is barely legal."

"I can take care of myself. You just relax and forget about it." She peeled off an extra handful of credits to help him forget.

Grumbling, the agent ran her through the checklist on the light, two-passenger plane. He briefed her on the few sectors where outworlders were allowed and had her sign and thumbprint a waiver absolving his firm of responsibility for her fate.

Carmen felt a lightening of spirit as she rose from the ground and pointed the flyer northward. At last she felt that she was moving in the direction she was supposed to go. *Supposed? What does that mean?* Shaking her head, she turned her attention to the onboard computer and punched up the chart for the landscape below. The areas legally available for sightseeing were indeed limited. She laid in a course toward the Lake of Hali.

Within minutes she'd cleared the boundaries of the Trade City and was soaring over open country. The view confirmed what she'd been told about this metal-poor, underdeveloped planet. Outside Thendara, vast expanses of unpopulated land stretched beneath her.

A few hours later, she reached Hali. She considered landing to visit the town and the mysterious lake. One of Darkover's famed natural wonders, the lake was not filled with water, but with some heavier-than-air gas. A person could even breathe while submerged therein—if the lack of carbon dioxide didn't make him or her forget to inhale.

I'm supposed to be sightseeing, right? Why aren't I stopping? But she twitched with impatience at the thought. She had no time to waste; she had to hurry. *Hurry? Where do I think I'm going?* Irrational though the feeling was, she didn't stop. She had no need to land at all, since the flyer had an autopilot and a cramped but serviceable head. She turned northwest to the Plateau of Armida.

The computer beeped a warning when she veered away from the permitted zone. "Shut up," she said to it. When the noise recurred, she switched off the audio. "Idiot machine."

Well into the afternoon, the nagging of hunger

finally penetrated her consciousness. She ate absentmindedly. *What am I doing out here? Nothing to see but farmland and forest.* Furthermore, she knew she'd be put on report for this escapade. Yet she couldn't turn back. Whenever she considered doing that, a part of her brain screamed in protest.

She was into the foothills by dusk. Knowing she couldn't fly over this rugged terrain in the dark, she reluctantly set down on the first flat, open patch of ground available. She paced around to loosen her cramped muscles but soon retreated to the flyer. The evening air was too cold for her. After another uninteresting meal of freeze-dried rations, she made a nest in the pilot's seat, shut out the strange night noises, and went to sleep.

In the morning Carmen felt sorer than she had the night before. She woke with a headache and a stiff neck. It took her a minute to remember where she was. *What am I doing here?*

After she disembarked and stomped around to stir the circulation in her legs, she snapped wide awake. *Dios! I'm on watch at 0700!* Even if she took off instantly, she had no chance of making Thendara in time. Not only was she in trouble for leaving the permitted zone, she was now AWOL. Not to mention the fact that her rental for the flyer had expired the previous night, so she'd technically stolen it.

Munching a breakfast bar, she reflected that if she returned to the spaceport immediately and turned herself in, she might receive some measure of clemency. *No, I have to keep going! There's no time to lose!*

Despite her growing belief that she must be losing her mind, she couldn't shake the sense of urgency. She took off as soon as the ruddy sun rose fully clear of the horizon.

Would this bizarre compulsion drive her into the northern mountains, where even experienced pilots had been known to crash? She tested its force by turning southward. The result was a pounding in her head that nearly blinded her. With an inarticulate growl of protest, she corrected her course to the north. At once the pain subsided.

All right, I guess I'm stuck with this. Whatever it is, I hope it runs out before my fuel and supplies do.

Several hours after sunrise, the previously silent radio crackled into life. Flying in a near-hypnotic daze, for a minute Carmen didn't realize the voice was broadcasting her call sign.

"You are under arrest for violation of restricted zones and theft of a vehicle," said the disembodied voice. "Turn back and rendezvous at the following coordinates."

Carmen listened to the figures without replying. *If I obey, maybe they won't hammer me too hard.* But pain stabbed her between the eyes at the very thought. When the message repeated, she switched off the radio. Instead of reversing course, she increased her speed. With her head start, she should be able to reach her destination before they caught her.

What destination? Don't I get to know where I'm being dragged? Could this urge be some kind of psi power working on her? She had tested practically nil for psionics, though. There were rumors that Darkover did strange things to some offworlders' minds; however, Carmen viewed those rumors as typical spacer superstition and exaggeration.

She felt impelled to push the craft to its maximum speed. She no longer resisted, hoping that if she cooperated with the force acting on her, she would discover its purpose. A few minutes later, one of the dials buzzed a warning. Low fuel.

The flyer had been supplied with enough power for the legal day trip she'd planned, not this flight into the wilderness. *That does it, end of the line any time now.* A glance at the ground showed Carmen that the area didn't consist entirely of wilderness. A narrow road wound through the forest below her. Some distance ahead, she glimpsed cleared land and a cluster of buildings.

The flyer began to lose altitude. Carmen scanned the trees for an open space in which to land. Nothing. She would have to set down on the road. She cut her speed and glided in. Sweat broke out on her forehead as she maneuvered to avoid branches overhanging the track. *I'm an amateur at this, not a stunt pilot!* This narrow trail of pounded dirt wouldn't qualify as a road on any civilized planet. She managed to reach the ground without a collision, though. After cutting off the engine, she drew her first deep breath in fifteen minutes.

This is it, I'm stuck. I'll just sit tight until that Security flyer picks me up. The intruder in her mind insisted otherwise. It screamed, *Get moving, you're almost there, hurry!* So it wanted her to start hiking. Carmen shivered at the very thought of the cold air, even in daylight. She hastily bundled up in her thermal gear. Before disembarking from the flyer, she got the blaster from the pack and tucked it into her belt. She recalled that the briefing had mentioned large fur-bearing carnivores and vicious flightless birds.

She wasted no thought on where she should go. She started walking in the direction that felt right, northward along the road. Within minutes, the walk changed to a trot. An inexplicable need to hurry pushed her, although the altitude and the chill air made her gasp.

Shortly, she heard faint shouts ahead, around the bend. Human cries, mingled with inhuman snarls. She left the road to creep between the trees. Though the delay grated on her nerves, she moved slowly, silently, toward the noise of combat.

Moments later, peering from her hiding place, she saw the combatants. The animal growls emanated from fur-clad, taloned, fanged creatures that stood upright. Catmen: one of several nonhuman species indigenous to Darkover. She couldn't count them as they milled about—at least half a dozen, she thought. Before her eyes, one ripped open the neck of a man in green livery. He crumpled to the ground, dropping his sword.

None of his companions remained on their feet, except a dark-haired woman who stood with her back against the flank of a small, horselike, antlered beast. Another like it lay dead on the ground; the rest had apparently fled. The woman stabbed at one of the catmen with a stiletto fit only for ceremonial uses.

Carmen didn't wait to see any more. Her mind went blank as her Security training took over. She leapt upon the cat warriors in a whirlwind of arms and legs. She stunned the nearest one with a high kick. A blow to the nape of the neck snapped another's spine. Carmen spun around to deck a third lurking behind her. She had to deal hastily with the fourth, delivering a punch that only staggered it.

When it lunged at her again, she disabled it with a knee to the gut.

For the first time, she was able to glance at the Darkovan woman. Despite the limitation of the long robe she wore, the stranger managed to plunge her knife into the throat of one attacker. But a pair of unwounded catmen converged on her before she could wrench her weapon free.

Carmen sprang at them. In a fluid series of movements, she knocked both of the creatures to the ground. For an instant she stood face-to-face with the woman. *Why does she look familiar?*

Before either of them could speak, growls of challenge interrupted them. Whirling around, Carmen saw a second wave of cat warriors charging forward. Panic flooded her brain. *Too many—I can't take them—* Automatically she drew her blaster, set it on broad beam, and fired. The six catmen in the front rank collapsed to the ground. The aliens who remained on their feet turned and fled.

The Darkovan woman staggered to her mount and clutched the animal for support. Her left sleeve, ripped, revealed a bleeding gash. "*Z'par servu,*" she said, one of the few phrases Carmen understood. The woman added another sentence or two.

"I'm sorry, I don't speak your language," Carmen said. She felt dull aches in her head and ribs. Panting, dizzy with the pounding of her pulse, she noticed that the sense of pressure and urgency had totally vanished.

The woman spoke in stilted Terran Standard. "My profound thanks. Without your help, I would doubtless at this moment be hostage to the cat-folk. I am Doria Lanart."

Carmen introduced herself.

"That thing—" Doria's face looked winter-pale with strain. "Forbidden."

Carmen glanced at the forgotten blaster in her hand. Now, too late, she remembered the Darkovan taboo against distance weapons, which offworlders were pledged to respect. Well, if she'd honored the ban, the lady would now be dead or captured. Carmen returned the weapon to her belt. "You." She stared into the woman's dark eyes. "You called me here. You must have. I felt a—compulsion—and now it's gone."

Doria looked startled. "Impossible. I have no *laran* strong enough for that. I have been virtually head-blind all my life."

"*Something* called me." With the ebbing of battle fever, Carmen felt fatigue dragging at her. "Hadn't we better get out of here, before those creatures get up the nerve to try again?"

"True. You will have to ride behind me." Just before they mounted, Doria stared intently at Carmen. "Now I see it. Your face—it is the image of mine."

Carmen stared back. Yes, aside from the difference in skin tone, they could be twins. Though Doria's black hair was worn in a long braid, in contrast to Carmen's short, sleep cap, they were the same hue. Doria's eyes and the shape of her nose and chin were identical to those Carmen saw in the mirror every day. The two women were even the same height. "Impossible," she muttered.

Doria climbed into the saddle and helped Carmen struggle onto the animal's back. "Some *leroni* maintain that for every being in the universe, there exists one exact double. But I feel there is more at work here." She prodded the beast into motion.

"Let us go. My home is less than an hour's ride away."

A few hundred meters up the road, the noise of a flyer's engine broke the quiet of the forest. Carmen glanced up. "They're after me. I ignored a few rules to get here."

A moment later, a contingent of about a dozen men in the same livery as those killed by the cats rode into sight. "*Domna* Doria!" called the leader as soon as they were in shouting distance. He continued in his own language, and Doria answered him. Then, switching to Terran Standard, she introduced Carmen. The leader of the group, an older man with weathered features, offered a greeting in hesitant Terran.

Doria explained to Carmen, "A member of my escort, who had some measure of *laran,* broadcast a cry for help as he died. These are my household guards, who have come in answer to the call."

Engine noise interrupted her, as the Spaceport Security flyer swooped low for a pass above the group. It then turned around and skimmed to a landing behind Carmen and Doria.

The copilot stepped out, one hand upon his holstered weapon. "Specialist Delorien, I'm taking you into custody for unauthorized absence, theft, and resisting arrest."

Doria's eyes narrowed with anger. "This woman saved my life. She is under my protection."

"I'm surprised to hear that," said the Terran. "We found a lot of dead catmen back there, obviously killed by blaster fire. You people are supposed to have a law against firearms."

"True," Doria said. "But on my estate, that is a

matter for our laws. We shall decide whether the circumstances excuse her act."

"Delorien is one of our personnel."

"Must we settle this in the middle of the trail? Let us all go to Armida and discuss the matter in comfort."

An hour later, Carmen sat before the hearth in the great hall at Armida, behind thick stone walls that shut out the cold wind of the hill country. Bathed, wrapped in a heavy robe, she sipped from a cup of some hot, bitter drink. Doria occupied the chair next to her. The chief of her household guard stood a respectful distance away. Several members of Doria's family, whose names Carmen was too exhausted to keep in mind, sat nearby. The two Security men, though they chose to stand like sentries on either side of the fireplace, unbent enough to accept mugs of the warming drink.

"I was returning from negotiations with the Domain bordering ours," Doria said. "Since we have both suffered heavy losses from the cat-folk, I hoped to arrange a cooperative expedition against them. The nonhumans must have decided to take me as a hostage in hope of crippling our resistance to their attacks."

"Why are the catmen so hostile?" Carmen asked.

Doria shrugged. "Who knows? Perhaps they still consider this land theirs and want to destroy us, the intruders. Since I have no measurable *laran,* I have sharpened my ordinary senses, using them to read the subtle shadings of human behavior—as they say blind men gain extremely acute hearing. But I cannot read aliens."

An older man, taller than the average Darkovan

with thinning golden-red hair—Doria's uncle, Carmen recalled—said with obvious pride, "Doria has an almost magical sensitivity to human motives. That is why she is such a skilled negotiator and so well liked."

Doria blushed. "You exaggerate." She explained to Carmen, "I was fortunate to be born at Armida, which has a tradition of . . . unconventional philosophy. In most Domain households, a head-blind heir would be viewed with pity or contempt."

"If you insist you don't have any of this power you keep talking about," said Carmen, "how did you call me? I'm practically psi-null, too."

"There must be some link between us," Doria said. "We look too much alike for chance."

Her uncle said, "It's known that our people were descended from Terran colonists, though some of the Comyn resist admitting it. Perhaps, distant ages past, you shared a common ancestor."

That seemed farfetched to Carmen. "How could a shared heritage so far back make any difference?"

The Security lieutenant spoke up. Carmen gave him a startled look; she'd almost forgotten he was there. "I've heard that kind of convergence can happen," he said. "Random recombination of DNA could make you almost identical, couldn't it?"

Doria's eyes gleamed with excitement. "A likeness close enough to overcome our telepathic insensitivity—powerful enough to ignore the limits of time itself!"

"That's right," Carmen said. "I did feel the 'call' *before* you were in danger."

"This requires further study," Doria said. "Will you stay long enough to investigate this bond?"

Her uncle—Carmen remembered now, his name

was Kieran—said more sternly, "Such a proposal cannot be made without reflection. True, this woman saved your life, but if she becomes a guest among us, she must respect our laws. There are good reasons for the ban on distance weapons. You have not seen the blighted lands, child—I have."

Doria frowned at him. "Armida's tradition is openness, not rigidity."

"Openness to new ideas, but not an invitation to chaos."

The Terran officer broke in. "Wait a minute, you're forgetting something. Specialist Delorien is still under arrest. She has to stand trial under Terran jurisdiction."

Doria's turned to him. "Is it not true that your authorities want the favor of the Comyn? Most of our kin refuse to deal with you. Your Legate might prefer to have Carmen as a liaison with Armida rather than a punitive example."

The lieutenant said to Carmen, "Well, Delorien? Are you planning to desert permanently?"

"I didn't plan to desert. I didn't plan this at all." Carmen's throat tightened with tension. The fascination of what she'd discovered lured her. Moreover, to a loner with no family ties, the heritage itself beckoned, wondrous as well as strange. At the same time, her loyalty to her ship and career hadn't died. Torn, she gazed into Doria's eyes, mirroring her own. "I don't want to just abandon—all this. I want to test the limits of this bond. But I'm still a member of the Space Service."

"Then you'll have to return with us," said the officer, "as soon as flying conditions permit."

"All right, I'll take my punishment." She suspected that, as Doria had said, the chance for a continued link between them would supply a mitigating circumstance. "If there's any possible way to arrange it, I'll be back."

Ten Minutes Or So

by Marion Zimmer Bradley

Dyan Ardais has been very much more popular than I ever conceived when I first invented him; of course, the same is true of all good villains. I don't really want to recall all the stories I've read about him. (By the way, I still remember and regret a particular story about Kadarin which ended up in my wastebasket because the author had neglected to put his or her name on it, and I couldn't send out a contract to buy it. If the author of "In Hell, I am No One at All" will get in touch with me—if you're out there—I'd still like to print it. I'm sure the readers of Darkover would enjoy it.)

This story, obviously, takes place in a slightly alternate Darkover, and is the result of asking myself what would have happened if Dyan had taken the time to get acquainted with Regis before irrevocably destroying himself in Regis' eyes.

Dyan-Gabriel, Regent of Ardais, and cadet-master of the Castle Guard, sat behind a worm-eaten old desk in staff quarters below the Guard Hall. Behind him, his secretary was writing lists, and at the far end of the room, a giant youngster named

Hjalmar was testing a nervous cadet for knowledge of weapons. Dyan glanced up at the boy, noticing sleek, shining curls, and a lithe, agile body, but he had no time for the awareness now. At some other time he might have noticed the cadet's name, made a few carefully casual inquiries, marked the youngster for some attention at another time; even spoken a friendly, casual, not-quite-seductive word or two, just to let the boy know that Dyan was ready and willing to take a friendly interest in him, and perhaps a bit more.

But at this moment he had no notice for anything outside the circle of his own misery. He crushed the letter in his hand, as if he could annihilate both the Father Master who had written him this unwelcome news, and the news itself. *Amory,* he thought in agony. *My son. My only son, and I never even knew him.*

He knew the very place, under the cliff, where it must have happened. The students and novices at Nevarsin were forbidden to go there, but it was secluded from casual observation, and so of course it was a favorite place for the half-grown boys to go for private talk, confidences, or simply to heal the effect of being closely watched twenty-eight hours a day; and what boy of fourteen had ever cared for danger? Amory Di Asturien, called Ardais since Dyan had had him legitimated at twelve, certainly had had no thought for danger, nor for the rockslide that had ended his life in a great smashing of stone.

I am Heir to Ardais. I am forty-two years old. I have no son; and I shall never have a son. At that time, fourteen years ago, I could still demand it of myself, now and then, to ignore or overcome my loathing, hatred, fear of women. Not now. I know myself better than that. Amory, Amory! And I never came to know him well, because after the brief flare of passion when he was conceived, I had no wish ever to see Sybella again. I left him in her care, until I sent him to Nevarsin.

If I had known him better, if I had kept him with me and brought him up as my son. . . . Dyan strangled back a sob, thinking that Amory might at this moment have been among the young cadets down in the first-year barracks-room.

It is a judgment on me. I did not want to be bothered with the rearing of a son. I felt that if Hastur could send his heir there to be reared, Amory would be safely away. Was I only afraid that the boy would judge me, condemn my failure to marry his mother, think ill of my chosen way of life, the knowledge that I am a lover of men?

"Lord Dyan—" said Hjalmar, and with an effort, Dyan controlled his face, crushing the letter and thrusting it out of sight. He barked, "What is it?"

"Sir, Gareth Lindir had better have lessons in swordplay; he knows very little, less than the basic positions for defense."

Dyan raised his eyes, his chin grimly set, to the shrinking boy. "Where the hell were you brought up, that you didn't learn a damn thing?"

"At h–home, sir," the boy said, shaking.

"What the devil was your father thinking of not to have you properly taught?"

"Sir, my f–father died when I was three years old and my mother has seven daughters and couldn't af–af–afford to h–h–hire an arms-ma–ma–ma–"

"Arms-master? So you grew up a mollycoddle, then?" Dyan snarled, "Who in hell got you this appointment here?"

"L–l–lord Lerrys Ridenow, s–s–s–ir."

"Is that s–s–s–so?" Dyan mocked the boy, cruelly, "Damn it, stop that stammering, will you? What did he do *that* for? Are you his bastard?"

"N–n–no, sir, my m–m–m–mother—"

"What was she, his whore?"

The boy choked back a sob. He said, tears flooding down his face, "His cou–cou–cousin, sir."

Dyan felt a flood of rage but controlled it. He said, "Well, do you think you can learn enough to act in a halfway soldierly fashion, and not go running back to Mamma when it is a little hard? Are you going to work hard to learn swordplay and the manly arts?"

The boy swallowed. He said, "I'll t–t–t–try, sir."

"All right, then," Dyan barked. "Hjalmar, take the brat out of here and don't let me set eyes on him until he learns something! And you—" He glared at the sobbing child, "start by wiping your nose, and learning not to burst into tears and bawl every time an officer asks you a civil question! And stand up straight, damn you!"

Gareth fought to control his sobs, furtively wiping his nose on his sleeve. He said, swallowing and breathing hard before he spoke, "Ye–yes, sir."

Dyan scowled fiercely as Hjalmar sent the boy away. What material he had to work with! A year ago, seduced and attracted by the pure beauty of one of the cadets, he had taken an interest in one of them. *That* had been a catastrophe, right enough; Octavien, pretty and effeminate, simply hadn't had the stuff to make a soldier, and even Dyan's encouragement and help hadn't been able to harden him to barracks life; and when he stopped trying to encourage the youngster, and started insisting sharply that Octavien must share the hardships of the other cadets, the boy had simply grown hysterical and flung insane accusations at him; it had taken all of Dyan's influence to get him hurried quietly away before there was a scandal which would wreck the cadet corps.

Well, he wouldn't make that mistake again! If he chose a favorite in the Guards this year, it would be, first of all, a solid, brave, manly boy who would make a good cadet and a Guardsman some day, one capable of honorable behavior, not a girlish little crybaby, no matter how beautiful! He had long ago stopped making excuses for his interest in young boys, who were more attractive to him than any woman, or any man. A few years ago, Kennard Alton's older bastard son had reminded him so much of Kennard as a boy that it had been all he could do to keep his hands off young Lewis; but he had resisted the temptation to make a favorite of young Lew, had instead, out of a sense of obligation and long affection for Kennard, bent over backward to be particularly harsh and exacting with his son; if Lew survived the treatment he got in the cadet corps, Dyan felt, he'd *earn* his place as Kennard's heir, and he hoped Kennard would be equally exacting with *his* son.

He *had* hoped. He remembered, again, in agony, that all his hopes for his son were ended. The boy was dead.

He snarled at Hjalmar, "Are we almost through with this damned business? How many more of these wretched brats do I have to see today?

"Cadets Syrtis and Hastur, sir."

And then, Dyan thought, *I shall go and get myself*

blind drunk, and perhaps forget Amory. Find myself some handsome, compliant youngster to spend the night, and forget everything. His thoughts lingered a moment on Cadet Syrtis. What was the boy's name? Danilo. He'd thought him another of Kennard's handsome bastards. Although, Avarra's mercy, Kennard was so abstemious with women that Dyan couldn't be blamed for the mistake he'd made about Kennard in his own youth, that Kennard was one of his own kind, a lover of men and a wholesome abstainer from whoring and wenching. He still only half believed that young Danilo wasn't an Alton bastard; he looked enough like it. If he wasn't, if he was of commoner birth, so much the better, and the boy's resemblance to Kennard might give an extra fillip to whatever developed between them. Dyan thought, rather sorrowfully, of the only time of real happiness he could remember. His father had still been sane then—though precariously—and when he had married for the second time, his grandmother, old Lady Rohana, had sent Dyan to Valdir Alton for fostering with Kennard. Kennard, Dyan thought, was the only real friend he had ever had.

And then Kennard had chosen another *bredu,* that damned Terran, Lerrys Montray, and gone to Terra for study, and he had never been the same again, and Dyan had never forgotten, or forgiven.

But young Danilo was very much as Kennard had been as a boy; and if the youngster was a commoner, he would welcome the friendship and interest of a Comyn lord who could give privileges and presents—he had noticed the boy was so shabby he hardly had a decent shirt to his name. Yes, he would talk to young Danilo. Should he summon him now? Why not?

A few friendly remarks, a word or two hinting at his interest. The boy was a *cristoforo;* Dyan, who had spent years among the brethren, learning all he could of their techniques of healing, remembered their foolish prohibitions against such things. He knew the historical basis for this, of course; in the early days, when the ancestors of the Hasturs were crossing their blood with *chieri,* many men were born *emmasca,* sexually ambiguous, and the *cristoforos,* charged with their education, had had to enforce celibacy; there had been a saying in those early days; *if you lie down with a man, you may rise up as a woman.* That kind of thing had happened once or twice with an Heir to one of the Domains, and it could be awkward, at best, and so the prohibition had become absolute, and as with most moral prohibitions, the reason had been lost and had become a mere moralistic superstition.

Well, he could probably coax or flatter young Dani out of his superstitious scruples. If not, it might even be amusing to use a bit of—well, persuasion. He found he was enjoying the thought that Danilo might squirm a bit and try to resist him out of silly religious notions. That would be a bit of fun, to seduce the boy against his will, and watch him squirm. show him how foolish his scruples were. A bit of resistance made it more exciting. Octavien had been squeamish at first, too, shamed and shy, but Dyan had overcome it, quickly enough. Danilo would probably be so flattered at a Comyn lord's attention that he would put up only the most token resistance, a mere matter of form, and would really want to be persuaded, even if he made a big show of his *cristoforo* scruples!

"Shall I bring Cadet Hastur, sir?"

Dyan hesitated. Then he said, "Very well." He would keep Danilo for the last, a tidbit, a consolation, something to wipe out the agony he knew would come flooding back if he allowed himself, after duty was over, to think about Amory again. He said "Bring him."

Regis Hastur was taller than Dyan had remembered when he saw him at muster that morning. He was still wearing that absurdly ornate outfit, fit for a presence-chamber or Midsummer-Festival; why hadn't somebody told the youngster what it was suitable to wear?

"Cadet Hastur, reporting sir."

"Sit down," Dyan said with a jerk of his head. "What's the whole rigamarole they gave you for names? Regis-Rafael, is it?"

"Just Regis, sir," Regis said, and politely repeated all four or five names he had been given in Council. Dyan asked why he had not chosen to be called Rafael after his father, without much interest—he and Rafael had not been as friendly as all that—but the boy's answer, that he chose not to be judged as his father's son before he had earned it, touched a strong, responsive chord in him.

"It must be a good thing," he said, looking up into Regis' eyes, "to have a father's honor to cherish." Everyone knew about *Dom* Kyril, mad and dissolute. While he was telling Regis a few routine things about the rules of the cadets, the rules against drinking, fighting, gambling, whoring, he wondered about that.

Is this why I never had any love for women?

Whenever I set eyes on a woman, I saw myself becoming as lewd and lecherous as that old monster? The love of men, of comrades, seemed clean to me by contrast!

He directed Hjalmar, bored, to test the youngster in swordplay, and Regis took the sword. Dyan watched with swift growth of interest, for not only did the boy have startling grace to match his good looks, but he had, evidently, been well-trained in swordplay. The way he demonstrated basic fighting technique could hardly have been bettered, and within seconds he had demonstrated that he was more than a match for Hjalmar. Hjalmar had been chosen for that; so that he would not intimidate a raw novice.

''Give me the sword, Hjalmar,'' Dyan said, and taking the wooden practice-sword in his hand, fell into a standard dueling stance. As he parried the boy's deft strokes, he had time to wonder if he would disgrace himself; if a cadet could disarm his own cadet-master, it would be shocking. And yet it was pleasant to Dyan, to think that the Heir to Hastur, who could have been reared in idleness and luxury, had learned this strenuous art, and learned it so well. At the cost of savage effort, resolving that he would *not* be bettered by a boy of fifteen, he managed to drive down Regis' guard and touched him several times in succession.

Regis lowered his sword on token of being outmatched. He said, ''Captain, I'm very badly out of practice.''

Dyan wondered where he had learned to fight like that. At Nevarsin? He said amiably ''Stop bragging, *chiyu.* You made me sweat, and not even the armsmaser can do that very often.'' He saw the color rising in Regis' face, and wondered if his own son had been as shy and modest, or half as handsome. He would never know. He wondered, painfully, if Regis had known his son. Certainly Regis would never have thought of Amory as his son; he still wore his mother's name.

On an impulse he said, "Since you have already some skill at swordplay, cousin, I could have you assigned as my aide. Among other things, it would mean you need not sleep in barracks." It would be pleasant to have this young kinsman near him. A manly youngster, still awkward, unformed, but it would be a pleasure to see him grow to manhood, in a way he had never been able to do with his own son. This was no whining effeminate like Octavien Vallonde, but a strong, intelligent young man, and Dyan thought, *I could teach him so much* . . . even to himself, he did not consider overt seduction; if they came close to one another, there would be time enough to explore that, too, but Regis was his equal, even his superior; there could be no question of coercion or persuasion.

If he should come to care for me of his free will. . . .

But the youngster said, coloring, that such an appointment was a choice one, for an experienced cadet; he would prefer not to take it until he had earned it.

Touched beyond endurance, Dyan said "Well spoken, my boy. I'd have been proud of such a response from my own son!"

"I didn't know you had a son, sir," Regis said, and Dyan, unable to resist the impulse to confide, in this sudden closeness between them, said, "I *had* a son. He—he was killed in a rockslide at Nevarsin. . . .''

Regis looked at him in concern and dismay. Did the boy have *laran,* that he picked up Dyan's distress and agony so quickly? He said ''Kinsman, I did not know—I am very sorry! But, Lord Dyan,'' he went on, a little more formally, suddenly remembering that he was a cadet speaking to his commanding officer, ''You are not yet an old man, you could have many sons—''

Dyan raised his eyes and met the boy's. He said ''I fear not; I am not a man for woman, nor ever made any secret of it. I forced myself to do my duty to my clan; once. That was enough.'' He suddenly remembered where they were, and the presence of Hjalmar, waiting for him. He said, drawing a deep breath, ''This is no time for such talk, cousin. We both have duties, just now,'' and saw the boy snap back to attention.

This one will make a soldier and a statesman, better than ever his father did. Somehow, I will have to adopt an heir, for legal purposes, but there's time enough for that. I won't worry about it. Whatever my duty to Comyn, I can manage it.

He said ''Kinsman, I have a couple more of these young cadets to speak with. But we'll both be off duty in an hour or so. I want to talk to you.''

Regis smiled slowly. ''I would be honored, sir.'' And Dyan saw the hunger in him; a man of his own caste, one in whom he could confide, to whom he could say all the things he had never been able to say to a grandfather too old and indifferent to care. Lightly, he touched Regis' shoulder.

He said, smiling down at his young cousin, ''I have no son, and you—you are fatherless. But we are kin, close kin. In the Guards, I must treat you as any other cadet—''

Regis said, flushing deeply, ''I would not have it otherwise, sir.''

''But between us, apart from duty—well, we are kinsmen, and the Comyn will be in your hands, some day, as it is in mine, and Kennard's. I will consider it an honor and a privilege to guide you in the years until then.''

Regis held out his hands to the older man. He said, raising his eyes, smiling with that breathtaking smile which made Dyan's heart turn over with delight, ''Sir, I—Dyan, the Gods witness it; I will be a son to you, I promise.''

''And I a father to you,'' Dyan said, clasping the hands very briefly, ''and more, if I can.'' But at Regis' look of question, he only smiled and said, ''All in good time, you'll know what I mean. Go, my boy, I'll see you when the time comes. Walk with the Gods, cousin.''

Regis saluted him, formally, the moment of intimacy broken. Dyan watched him go, smiling, musing, thinking of the brief interview. Nothing, he knew, would ever dull the pain of Amory's death; Amory, whom he had never really known and now, would never know. But the warmth of Regis' response to him, made him realize that the boy was just as starved for close companionship, affection, as—*as I have always been myself.* He felt a flood of love and tenderness for Regis Hastur.

Hjalmar said ''You still have to see Cadet Syrtis, sir.''

''Syrtis.'' Danilo ridged his brown. Oh, yes, the handsome youngster who might have been Kennard's bastard son. But why should Kennard lie?

And Kennard wasn't a boy-lover; evidently, he was simply a protégé or poor relation. Oh, well, it didn't matter. He shrugged, thinking that he had been considering some kind of liaison with the boy. What the hell! Dani was a *cristoforo;* why bother? He preferred a willing lover, he supposed. Not even to himself would he admit to himself that he was hoping for some such relationship, eventually, with Regis, but he knew perfectly well that he had lost interest in anything less.

Regis desperately needed an older man to guide him, teach him, stand in a father's place to him—to love him, Dyan admitted. And he himself—all his life he had longed for someone who would love him, look up to him, admire him. Fiercely he resolved that Regis should never see him do anything less than admirable; he felt he would die of shame if Regis ever looked a him with disapproval. *In me,* he resolved, *he shall also have a father's honor to cherish.*

He said "Forget it. You have a look at him, Hjalmar—I imagine he has some skill at swordplay, if he's Kennard's protégé. And make sure the boy has decent clothes—tell him he has to be a credit to the guard, we can't have him going around looking threadbare. You can read him the regulations as well as I can; I'll have a formal interview with him sometime, I suppose, but there's nothing in the regulations says I have to do it today." He drew his hand across his brow, sighing, and took out the letter from Nevarsin. He said "I have had bad news, Hjalmar; tell my aides to handle everything else for me today."

"I'm sorry, sir," Hjalmar said, with gruff sympathy, "We'll take care of everything for you. I hope it will turn out all right, sir."

Dyan rose and went out of the Guard Hall. He had no idea that in ten minutes or so, he had altered the history of Darkover beyond recognition.

Victory's Cost

by Patricia B. Cirone

In addition to appearing in four of these anthologies, Pat has appeared in Marion Zimmer Bradley's Fantasy Magazine *and my SWORD AND SORCERESS anthologies. She has also sold stories to other anthologies, including CATFANTASTIC II.*

One of the things I've always been curious about is how a chieri *would relate to being in a Tower. This story attacks that question—and introduces us to some extremely intriguing characters. This, of course, is what writing is all about—a chance to live for a time with interesting and different people, and to live "more lives."*

The old, worn girth snapped, and with flailing arms, Grai fell to the ground amidst a welter of saddle, packs, and gear. *So much for entering with a flourish,* he thought, his eyes an inch from the ground and a flush mottling his cheekbones.

"Master Grai, are you all right?" Burly, kind-hearted Timmen jumped down off his horse and effortlessly hauled Grai to his feet. His big hands brushed at the dust marking Grai's clothes.

"I'm fine," Grai said roughly, pushing the older

man's hands away. Bad enough falling off his horse, he didn't want to look like he needed a nursemaid.

"Of course, Master Grai," Timmen replied stiffly. "Shall I attend to the horses?"

Ah, Avarra, now he'd hurt the man's feelings. One of the few who'd been nice to him all these rough, lonely years of growing up.

"I . . ." Grai started to say.

"That would be very helpful," a smooth voice interrupted. "I'm afraid we don't run to stable hands here at the Tower, so it's every man for himself, and young . . . Grai, is it? . . . will be quite busy."

The elegant stranger waved his hand dismissively and Grai heard the hollow clop of horses' hooves on paved courtyard as they started to move off. He forced himself not to cast a longing glance in their direction.

"So, you've come to be tested and trained in *laran,*" the stranger said. His eyes traveled slowly up and down Grai's body. "Well, you certainly have the *look* of it," he said at the end. Neither the tone of his voice nor the gleam in his eye seemed particularly friendly.

"Look of it! Bloody throwback!" Grai heard muttered from a window overlooking the courtyard.

"Bet 'cha it's *emmasca* as a rock," another snickering voice added.

Grai kept his eyes firmly on the one who'd greeted him, inwardly cursing his silver-white hair, six-fingered hands and slender, almost boneless body. He felt bruised. He had thought at least here. . . .

"Well, we'll see. Come. I'll show you to your quarters in the Tower. I'm Rudir, by the way. Keeper."

"I . . . I'm honored, *vai dom,* that you would greet me personally."

"It was my turn," answered Rudir. "Here at the Towers we share duties," he said haughtily. "It won't be what you're accustomed to. No fleets of servants, no lavish banquets."

He flung open a door. "No harem suites." Rudir, his eyes narrowed, waited for Grai's reaction.

Grai was grateful for once that the chieri face he'd inherited from some long-forgotten ancestor was difficult to read. Only those who knew him extremely well had learned to catch the slight changes that divulged his feelings.

Grai just nodded and carried his gear into the closet-sized room. The other sighed as if disappointed.

"It's not often we get young princelings here. They usually demand that matrix technicians drop their work and devote their time to following them up and down vale until they learn just enough *laran* to lob death at each other. Here, you leave your rank outside the gates. In a Tower only *laran* counts. And until you prove you have it in full measure and can manipulate it effortlessly, you're nothing. Doubtless a daunting change for you." The other turned on his heel and stalked away.

Grai felt like muttering after him that being the strange-looking, throwback seventh son of a third-rate king perpetually embroiled in others' wars, he'd felt pretty close to nothing all his life. But there would be no point. The man obviously resented the nobility; probably some unacknowledged *nedestro* son and still smarting from it. Protesting would only give him more ammunition. The only way to reach someone like that was to work hard and *show* him.

As he would. Grai wasn't here to learn mind-numbing and weapon hurling. Rudir had said rightly that he could have learned that at home. Grai wanted to learn *real laran.* The kind that built beautiful towers and smooth, flawless roads, the kind that summoned rain for the crops and nourished the land. It was why he had journeyed fifteen days to come to a tower, leaving behind family, rank, and his father's latest war.

The testing room was larger than his bedroom, but just as bare. Two tall windows let in the morning light—a welcome change from the barricaded windows of his father's estate.

"Why did you come here?" the man, after testing him, asked bluntly.

"To be trained in the use of *laran.*"

"Who told you you *had* any?"

"What? All in my family do. And the traveling *laranzu* . . . he looked at me."

"He told you you had *laran?*

"Well, he said it was probably blocked. That Tower experts could bring it out."

"We can't 'bring out' what isn't there," the man answered with a rather exasperated look.

"But he said I had energies."

"*Everyone* has *energies;* all that means is you're not *dead.*" The *laranzu* stood up and brushed off the front of his robe as if it had been dirtied by his proximity to Grai.

"Does that mean I'll be sent home?" Grai asked in a small voice, bracing himself. No good on a horse, no good with a sword, no good even with studies. He tended to latch onto stray paths and follow them to ends no one else had dreamed of—or was interested in. He had never thought he might not have *laran,* either, even if he had never had the agonies of threshold sickness most nobleborn went through. He and the nursery mother had just thought, well, his looks. . . .

If he didn't have *laran* either, he might as well disappear into the bottom of Hali Lake. His father didn't need a seventh son; as he had made clear many times, he especially didn't need one that was useless.

"No," the *laranzu* sighed. "You might as well stay here until Louro is back. He usually does our testing, but he's out babysitting some precious princeling. It's rare, but occasionally there *is* someone whose *laran* is blocked behind natural blocks—not *laran*-induced ones—they can be spotted by rank amateurs—but natural ones: psychic, developmental, what have you. I'm not very good at perceiving natural blocks. I doubt you have them, but since you've come all this way, we might as well be sure."

"When. . . ?" Grai asked, but his tester was already out the door.

Grai sighed. He had thought Towers would be different, that being open to other's emotions and working intimately mind-with-mind, would make people more gentle, more . . . well, nice. But they treated him here the same as he had been treated for long stretches in his father's house—as another inconvenient body in the way.

He wandered down to the stables and whiled away two hours grooming his already groomed horse. He might not be adept at riding them, but he loved the feel of horses, of all animals, really. They were soothing to the touch, they felt . . . "right."

He could never describe these feelings he'd had

all his life; some things, like animals, and trees, and hand polished wood felt ''right'' while others like weapons and loud voices and, well, sexual things, the things young boys were supposed to giggle over and want, felt ''not right,'' or at least ''not right for now.'' He sighed. He had tried to explain it to his older brothers once, and had been laughed at and called a big baby. Maybe that's all he was, still. A baby, all feelings and no abilities.

Grai turned around and glumped back up to his room.

No one called him for dinner. Maybe the matrix workers were busy doing something important. Maybe he had just been forgotten. Maybe he wasn't supposed to wait to be summoned. Grai didn't feel like venturing out to ascertain which. He never ate much anyway—another of his oft mentioned failings. It was easy to make do with what was left of the trail food in his packs. Soon he was going to have to find out when and where to eat in this Tower.

After munching the last crumbs of his trail bar, and washing it down with some stale water from his travel-skin, Grai curled up in his room's high, skinny window and daydreamed himself off to sleep. He regretted it in the morning, when he woke up bleary-eyed and stiff, with vague, confusing memories of having wandered through snow drifts the whole night. He stretched as well as he could within the window's embrace, and looked down into the courtyard. There was none of the bustle he was used to: no horses or formations, no sword practice or bantering talk, no rough voices shouting commands at scurrying servants to speed up the unloading of war supplies such as scrap-shatter and the new *clingfire*.

Here, everything was quiet and peaceful. Two figures crossed the courtyard, talking intently. They had none of the anxious hurry of his father's soldiers, and something about the way they moved suggested they were discussing very important matters. Not just boasting of war prowess and exchanging lewd jokes.

Grai wanted to belong here so desperately he could taste it in his mouth. Here, where *laran* was an art, not just a means to kill someone; here where peace and harmony would rule his days, and crude voices didn't fill the air with talk of war and killing.

Maybe if he found where everyone ate breakfast, he could talk to some of the others, start to make friends, start to experience the heady excitement of living at a Tower.

But breakfast, when he found the kitchen (no dining hall!), was a solitary affair.

"The circle be too busy to be sitting down to a formal breakfast, lad," the server scoffed. "Why half of them be up before dawn working and others worked till midnight on the relays and be sleeping."

Disappointed and embarrassed, Grai downed his bowl of grain in silence.

It was the same for his other two meals. The circles never ate at ordinary times, it seemed, and when they did, it was food snatched and carried to where they were working, or the rooms where they were waking or getting ready to sleep. Despite Rudir's comments upon greeting him, the Tower *did* have servants, and the matrix workers *were* waited on. But Rudir had been right about one thing, *Grai* certainly wasn't.

In fact, he found out the next morning, he was

supposed to pay for the food he consumed by working as a servant himself!

"Come with me," a towheaded, knock-kneed youth named Foran commanded.

"Has Louro come, then?" Grai asked eagerly.

"Louro won't be here for weeks—months, perhaps. You don't think you're just going to loll about eating your head off and doing no work in the meantime, do you?"

"No, of course not. But what. . . ? If I don't have any *laran*. . . ."

"There's plenty to do, princeling. Work that will free those of us that are more important to do *real* tasks."

Grai sighed. He was tired of being called princeling. Rudir's "nickname" seemed to have stuck, and that was all he had heard himself addressed—when he was spoken to at all. "I could help in the stables," Grai suggested. He liked horses, and besides, he'd get to talk to Timmen.

"Do'in what?" Foran snorted. "Polishin' the empty floor? You don't think we kept those animals around eating their bone-filled heads off, do you? Sent home yesterday."

"But . . . why wasn't I told?"

"Who'r *you* to be told? You're not in charge here, princeling."

But I would have liked to say good-bye, Grai thought silently.

"But what if I have to be sent home?" he asked, dreading the possibility, but realizing it would happen if Louro found him wanting.

"Then a message'll be sent out from Tower and you'll just wait for 'em to come fetch you," Foran replied smugly. "Meanwhile, *here's* where you'll be working.'' He brought Grai out into a rear section of courtyard he'd never seen before. Several heavily-furred beings were packing bundles and hoisting them onto carts.

''Ktel will show you what to do,'' Foran said with a gleam of pure malice. ''You sh'd be able to do this.''

Foran turned around and left. Grai stood, blinding, wondering where Ktel was. He didn't see any humans in the courtyard at all.

One of the small, furry beings approached him. ''Come,'' he said in thickly accented speech. ''I show.''

''I'm supposed to wait for Ktel,'' Grai said politely, blinking in surprise.

''I Ktel.''

Grai looked closer at the small being. ''But . . . but you're a trailman!'' he said in astonishment. He had heard of such creatures living high in the mountains, but had never seen one before. He thought they couldn't live in the lowlands.

''Nah,'' the other said with a grimace. ''Mothers were People, but us . . .'' he shrugged his small shoulders, ''we just workers. Adapted. The *leronis* what designed us calls us crailmen, but 'jis usually shorted to cralmacs.''

He squinted his large eyes against the sun and turned back toward the stack of bundles. Numbly, Grai followed.

The day became a hot, sweaty torture of bending and lifting, packing and shifting. The small packages wrapped in a thick oily cloth had to be cushioned in yet more layers of the strange cloth and packed into large metal containers. When one was full it was sealed, then lifted—it took Grai and at least seven of the little beings—onto carts.

They didn't even break for lunch. It seemed crail-men, or cralmacs, or whatever they were, didn't require lunch. Or at least that was what Ktel seemed to say when Grai asked. There was something in the phrasing that made him suspect it was just that *Tower* people didn't think cralmacs required lunch. Grai ignored the rumble in his stomach and simply bent his back to the task.

When the red sun set sullenly over the walls surrounding the tower, they were allowed to shuffle in, eat some bread and cheese, and stagger on up to their rooms. At least Grai staggered. Ktel and the others seemed used to such hard labor.

Grai fell asleep before his head reached the pillow.

. . . Cold thin air slid down his throat like iced knives, and the wind bit into him as if it had jaws, sharp toothed through the rents in his clothing. Carefully he put one foot in front of the other, two breaths per step, always upward. There was a rock face up ahead. It might provide some protection for the night. If he could make it. Two breaths, step. Two breaths, step. He could spare no energy to warm himself, none even to call. The banshee had gotten the food-sack hurled at it in desperation. Lucky not to have gotten him. Maybe not so lucky. Two steps, breathe, air like knives of ice, two steps, breathe.

The rock face was here. . . .

He woke muddleheaded and feeling tired. He had had some strange dream . . . but it was already gone from his head. Zandru's hells, he was tired. As if the sleep had drained more energy out of him rather than replenishing what he had used the day before.

When Grai went out to the courtyard that morning, he felt a grudging respect for the little furred beings. They were already hard at work with no sign of the lassitude that seemed to pull him downward. Ktel eyed him and motioned him over to a corner beside him. They worked side by side, falling into a rhythm that seemed a bit easier than the day before.

At noon Ktel turned and handed him a small bundle wrapped in white paper. "Sit," he said, motioning over to a corner in the shade.

Puzzled, Grai went over and sat down.

"Eat," the other said, motioning toward the white-wrapped parcel he had handed him, and bent back to work.

Grai unfolded the stiff white paper to find a square of *jalap,* a spicy blend of crisp vegetables and cheese baked in a flaky, light crust.

"But what about the rest of you?"

"Cralmacs no eat lunch."

"Then I won't either."

"Be foolish. We be small, but we be grown. You be young, almost baby *chieri.* Why humans capture you we not know."

"I'm not a baby. And I'm not *chieri,* either. I'm human."

The crailman flicked him a disbelieving look. "Eat," was all he said, and bent back to work.

Grai gave up. The *jalap* was making his mouth water, and his hands were practically trembling from wanting it. He ate it in about three bites, and took a swallow from his water skin.

"Thank you," he said gratefully as he took up his position next to the little furred creature. Ktel just grunted.

Over the course of the day he got to know them all better: Tig, with the grayish fur and a wry sense of humor; Loj, who hummed trailmenish songs to make the work go faster; young Xir who bounced when he walked and was always asking questions . . . Grai felt more comradeship among these furred, genetically altered beings than he ever had among his own kind. It wasn't just that they accepted him as he was, white-haired, six-fingered, and all, without comments behind his back or suddenly averted stares. A lot of it was just the way they lived, with joy for the day and no hatred or schemes for gaining power over each other.

He hoped it would be the same among the Tower people, once they got used to his looks.

He had had very little contact with the Tower's circle, however. Most of what he knew of them was from overheard snatches of conversation, bits about formulas, whatever they were, and heady references to reaction times, maximizing potentials, and increasing range. He longed to have the knowledge to enter into conversations like these, and his mind took wing and followed the elusive words to the edge of the world, imagining the great uses of *laran* and wanting to be part of it.

Yet his night-dreams were not of *laran*, but of cold. Cold that ate through his clothes and numbed his long, narrow feet until his very bones ached with it.

He had to go on. They were waiting for him, his

family, his friends, waiting to gather him back amongst their fold. He had been too long on the wrong side of the mountains, too long wandering hidden among the human peoples, trying to repair the damage to the land their hatred and greed had wreaked. He had been separate for so long he was weak, could no longer reach out and touch his family, draw strength from their presence. He was so weak, he could not even cry for help. So cold . . . so cold.

I will help you, *Grai whispered in his dream. He reached out, putting an arm around the other—or was it himself?—to guide the faltering footsteps up the icy path. Startled, the other turned to look at Grai, stumbled and fell, fell away in a swirl of mist and snow, and Grai was floating in the sky, looking down through clouds at a rugged snow-capped range of mountains whose icy patches glittered like polished knives next to the bare bones of rock they had carved.*

He fought his way downward, found the small figure struggling, floundered through the snow to its side and scrambled up rock after rock, pulling the other up behind. He wasn't sure who he was, himself or the figure at his side—he seemed to slip in and out of both. The enemy was the snow, and the cold. That much he knew.

Grai woke huddled at the foot of his bed, his arms cramped from hugging his knees, tears frozen on his face.

No, not frozen, merely sticky and dried. His legs ached as if he *had* scrambled up a mountainside during the night, and deep inside of him, he still felt cold, frozen cold. Grai shivered in the warm, humid, early spring air.

He received funny looks when he asked for hot tea at breakfast, but it felt good, reaching into the coldest recesses of his body and warming them to normal.

That day one of the oilskin bags dropped.

It happened in an instant. Xir, laughing over a joke Tig had made, reached down, lifted one of the bags, and turned to carry it to the packing crate. Out of the corner of his eye, Grai saw the wrapping give way, an inner bag tumble out, turning over to land with a flat sounding thud. The next moment Xir was a torch of flame.

He didn't have time to scream. The nauseating smell of burning fur deadened the air.

Grai started to run forward. Ktel grabbed his arm, jerked him back.

Tig grabbed an end of the sack and swung it away from the burning lump.

"Xir!" Grai cried.

"Too late," Ktel said. "Too late."

"But . . . but what *happened?*"

"*Clingfire,*" Ktel answered, surprise in his voice. "Haven't you ever see *clingfire?*"

"*Clingfire?*" Grai whispered, appalled.

"What think you in oil sacks?"

"I, I never thought at all . . ." Grai whispered, realizing it was true. He had loaded and stacked and joked and talked and never once had he wondered what it was he was doing. What might be in the little wrapped bags.

He turned on his heel and ran into the Tower. He grabbed the first person he found. It happened to be the trim-bearded man who had tested him.

"Xir just burned up."

"Who?"

"Xir. One of the crailmen."

"Gods, what now! Well, be careful when you clean it up. Use the oilskin and make sure you don't get any on your hands. I suppose Riori will want to take two or three days out of circle, now, to start a new one of 'em gestating. What a nuisance."

"That's *clingfire* out there!"

"That's why I told you to use oilskin."

"I mean you're making *clingfire.*"

"Of course . . . who did you think made it?"

"But I thought only war *laranzus* . . . "

"Don't be ridiculous, child. Wandering *laranzus* aren't powerful enough to make *clingfire.* It needs highly trained matrix technicians, working in a circle. All *clingfire* is made in Towers."

"But how *can* you? How can the Towers make something as awful as *clingfire?*"

"The kings want it, we make it." He shrugged.

"But you could just tell them you wouldn't!"

"Why would we want to do that? We've got to eat, you know. You don't think we've got the time to dredge fields and herd cattle, do you? We have to buy our food, and pay for it with services."

"But the Towers are supposed to be apart from war!"

"Who fed you that nonsense, boy? Not your father, to be sure. *Laranzus* die just as easily as nullfolk, if you stab them or burn them. It's up to us to see we don't get killed, and we do that by supplying the best weapons we can to whoever it looks might best protect us. Oh, we pay very close attention to wars, princeling. Even to taking in their worthless sons, when asked."

Grai stood there, scattered thoughts swirling around a numb core, as the other walked away. By the time he stumbled back to the courtyard, Xir's remains had already been swept away and work had resumed.

That night, as he slipped into troubled dreams of pain and death and fire, his body burned, each nerve, each pathway liquid with pain. He carried it with him into the snow.

The pain surrounded him like a glowing ball, splashing bright patterns on the frozen whiteness, ruddying it with reds and oranges.

Little brother, you are in almost as much pain as I, *a voice whispered through his mind, and in the glare of his ball of pain, Grai could glimpse the shadowed angles of a figure hunched against the wall of snow, its long white hair frosted with ice, its skin deathly pale—only the intense glitter of blue eyes peering from beneath pale snow-crusted eyebrows a clue that it was still alive.*

For a dizzying moment, Grai was that figure, seeing himself through its eyes, remembering the long, aching trek through the wind devastated pass. Then he snapped back into his own body, his own mind again. He shook his head; waves of pain coursed down his veins, felling him to his knees.

You are sleeping, little brother, *the other whispered.*

No, Grai thought. That didn't seem right. This didn't seem like sleep. This figure was real. This figure had walked through the mountains, night after night in his dreams, but it was somehow real, too.

You are in threshold. It thins your barriers, and your spirit is flying free.

No. It's not threshold. I never went through

threshold, *Grai protested, his voice as much a whisper of pain as the other's.*

A dry, rasping chuckle traced delicately over his mind. You are now, youngling.

I'm too old!

Old! Why you are the veriest babe, not even old enough to sexually awaken! But go, now, little one. You do not want to be with me when I die.

You are not going to die!

But of course I am, little one. I will not make it through the pass. I have no food, and no reserves left to make warmth, let alone the energy to walk on.

I have warmth. I am burning up with it! *Grai's spirit moved forward toward the snow-encrusted figure on the ground.*

No, little brother, it could kill you!

Better to die warming someone than packing *clingfire* or shooting down lightflyers.

Ah, little brother, you are swept up with the humans, then? *Pity etched the thin lines of the other's voice.*

With the humans? I *am* human.

Human you may be born, but *chieri* you are, *the other thought to him.* Come close, and let me show you.

Grai moved forward, and as his warmth enveloped the other, pictures of chieri *life flooded his brain. The laughter and the joy, the searching for truth, the love and compassion. Here were the workers of weather, the guardians of the bees, the seekers of light he had thought the Tower* leroni *were. They were so few in numbers, but so loving, so mystified why humans insisted on growing in such numbers that overuse and downright destruction poisoned the land until its ugliness matched that which festered in their minds. Grai saw how the* chieri *had shrunk in reaction to such ugliness, their numbers growing desperately less in an attempt to restore the balance of sentients to overburdened land, and then finally drawn into trying to repair the very world itself, slipping down shadowed pathways amongst the human settlements to try to bring life and fruitfulness back to the land, to repair the damage done by their careless, greedy cousins.*

Grai felt his yearning and despair grow as the other gained strength from his warmth, bleeding off energy from the traceries of fire in his veins, working as delicately as a surgeon, healing and helping even as he took, even though it exhausted him more.

Take as much as you need, *Grai insisted.*

No, you have given me enough, little brother. I should make it now. And even if I don't, I will go to the all-maker knowing I have not carried you with me before your time. *SLEEP,* little brother. *And it was a command that plunged Grai down into blackness despite his protests.*

He woke aching, but well. Cautiously he reached out with the *laran* that was just waking, but he could catch no glimmer of the *chieri's* spirit. Had he made it? Was he still struggling down the other side of the Wall Around the World? Or was he dead, his spirit scattered before the wind?

Grai felt like crying. He didn't want to be among people, with their crass and greedy ways. Even the Tower workers, whom he had adored from a distance, had proven to have spirits of clay and coin. He wanted to escape, but where could he go? Whether he went to castle or Tower, to field or forest, he would find himself swept up in the wars, pressed into service, commanded to kill others with his hands or his mind.

He sobbed and buried his head in his pillow.

"Come on, sleepyhead. Get your princely butt down to the yard and start loading. Yesterday's carelessness put us behind schedule, so it's double time for coddled princes today." A sharp slap came down on his backside.

With a stifled yelp of surprise and a set jaw, Grai rolled out of bed and stood up. What would happen if he refused? Would they kill him? He'd almost rather that, than live in this world of cruelty and pain.

"Come on, MOVE it!"

Grai found himself walking automatically. With despair he found himself handling the hated *clingfire*, loading it into boxes, hoisting the boxes into packs.

"This load's got to go to Keriton," a voice declared. "What a nuisance."

"What's-your-name! Princeling! Throw your belongings in a pack and saddle up one of those chervines. You'll have to lead the pack train out to Keriton with his order of *clingfire*. He's buried too deep in the mountains to get it to him any other way."

"But I've never done that before," Grai protested.

"First time for everything, princeling," the other said dismissively, too busy to add his usual sneer.

His protests drowned at every turn, Grai found himself leading a train of twenty chervines toward the foothills by nightfall. After the initial shock, he decided he liked it. He liked being by himself, away from people who thought of nothing but "better" ways to kill each other. If only he could always be alone!

But that would pall before long, Grai realized, as he sat by his campfire the second night out. Already he longed to talk to someone other than a chervine—or maybe he just wanted to hear someone talk back. It didn't have to be a human. One of the crailmen would be nice . . . or a *chieri* . . . like the one in his dreams.

The thought of the *chieri* stayed with him the entire next day. He remembered the other's warmth, the community of friendship he had shown him, the promise of beings who were still gentle, and sought goodness instead of war and destruction.

What if. . . ?

He would never see his family again. The thought gave him pain. For all they had kidded and ignored him, they had still, in their own fashion, loved him. And he loved them. But he didn't belong.

It would not grow easier with the years, but harder.

The older he became, the less they would understand his continuing to act "like a child," refusing to lift sword or throw *clingfire* for the reputed honor of his family. What love there was would turn to disgust, maybe even to hate. And not just on their part. Despite his looks, he was human. He would learn to hate back.

Unless he refused to do so.

It would be better to lose while still loving, than to learn hate.

He changed the course of the pack train and led them deeper into the mountains, beyond the foothills. He wound his way ever deeper, and higher, heading toward the Wall Around the World, visible, even in high summer, as a haze of towering whiteness.

Would he ever manage to cross it? And if he did, how would he find those elusive creatures that held his last hope of sanity in this world? Would they even accept him, gross and tainted as he was, his humanness clinging to him like an odor, despite his looks?

He lived off the land, and the delicacies packed for Keriton's enjoyment, tidbits of civilization packed cheek by jowl with the deadly and disgusting *clingfire.* He would have gotten rid of *that* if he had known how. But he didn't dare bury the oilskin pouches for fear they might rupture and cause devastation now, or even years down the line. Maybe *they* would know what to do, if he ever reached them.

So, packed as if going to war, Grai traveled on, climbing higher, knowing instinctively how to head for the trail taken by the other. It was etched on his mind like heartfire.

Better to die trying, than to be a part of that world down on the lowlands, he thought, as ice and snow started to surround him, and the chervines huddled closer for warmth. He pressed on, starting to live for real what he had only experienced in those dreams: the cold, the numbness, the exhaustion.

Better I should die, he thought, placing one foot carefully down in front of the other, pulling the lead chervine up behind him, putting the next foot down ahead. *Better I should die.*

But why would I let you die, little brother? You gave me life when I was crossing the pass. It would be poor return if I did not do likewise, a strong, loving voice spoke through his mind.

Grai looked up, and framed against the rocks and snow ahead stood a figure with snow white hair and vivid blue eyes.

You are, and will always be welcome, little brother, it said, and smiled. *Come join our work.*

Grai felt a community of love and hope surround him.

Kefan McIlroy Is Snared

by Aletha Biedermann-Wiens

Aletha Biedermann-Wiens is a newcomer to these pages. In mundane life she has worked as a librarian for a television station—which, come to think of it, isn't really so mundane. She has also been a jewelry designer for a store in Oakland, California, and now works at a business service in Concord, where she is learning Arabic on the job. Did it ever occur to you to wonder why budding writers have so many and such peculiar ways of making a living? It's because writers, like everyone except the independently wealthy, have to do anything which will keep body and soul together while learning their craft. The arts are notoriously poorly paid, especially in the United States at the present time.

This story answers one of the questions which has surfaced in my mind at times, and may resurface one day in a Darkover novel: what if someone had a laran *which manifested itself with computers? Being a technophobe myself, I'd call it a technophobe's nightmare. But I'm always interested in other people's solutions to questions I've been puzzling over, especially if their solution is different from mine. . . .*

He was escorting his sister Megan to the seamstresses' for what seemed the thousandth time that spring as she prepared to be wed. Father was in the south on business, his older brother was managing the business in town, and he was stuck with Megan. She found the little rectangle in the street; pointing as if it were dirt she said how typical it was of the Terranen to make something so ugly.

No one commented as he examined it. He sat in a chair at the seamstresses', too bemused to say he was going out for a cup of *jaco,* and watched the zero turn on as he tilted it into the sun. The Standard numbers on the little instrument's buttons were legible. He had learned some Standard at Nevarsin, and some mathematics. A lot of mathematics; he had enjoyed it. He found the crisp logic soothing. But this little machine could do more than he could. The worn instruction booklet was still inside the thin leathery pocket of the case. He sat there, oblivious to the women, and tried to puzzle out the instructions. π he knew, but—Σ?

He began to look inside the case, behind the buttons, with his *laran.* He never had much *laran;* nothing worth training, the healer had said, when his agitated mother had summoned her, impatient that her son had not become ill from threshold sickness. His father had grunted that one Comyn ancestor out of eight great-grandparents was hardly grounds for expecting the boy to have *laran.* But he could follow the path of least resistance in the foreign materials without needing to look into his starstone. The foreign materials themselves seemed to speak to him as clearly, no, more clearly than the stone ever had.

He could follow the architecture of a path as it met with other paths and they divided into precise branches. He could punch in "6" and feel what happened inside the paths throughout the system. "6, √." Amazing. "9, √." Zandru's hells, was that what the first number was?

The machine's binary language was a revelation. He escorted his sister home, and then went out to buy a mathematics book, and worked until his eyes were sore. Annoyingly, the machine would not stay turned on after the sun went down, so in the evenings he worked out of the book, and during the days while he waited on his sister he traced out the paths in the machine. The paths felt like tunnels, and in them he was free, hurling exuberantly down the tunnels with the other impulses, switching at the gates, combining and furiously bouncing around in a flurry of computing that ended with an inhuman suddenness and correctness.

If a small one would do this, one so insignificant that the Terranan who had dropped it had not set up a hue and cry the minute he knew it was lost, what else did they have on their base? How could he find out? His father would . . . his father would kill him, most likely. Father expected them to stay away from the Trade City, much less the Gate Plaza.

He struggled with the decision for two nights, and the third he quietly left the house and walked to the Gate. When uniformed guards ignored him, he leaned against a pillar, as if he were waiting for someone, and began to investigate the machines. The recognition machines were wonderful, and he was beginning to understand a few of their instructions when he heard the Castle bells strike one, and realized how late it was.

The next night he was back, and the next, and after a week or so, he began to try to talk with the machines, to send them impulses. Occasionally, they would respond by opening, but they also responded by buzzing loudly, startling him. A week later, to his horror, he jammed all of them. He stood there, his back to the pillar, stiff with fright, and the guards called in to report; he could hear the annoyance in their voices. They switched to a manual system, and just as he was relaxing enough to trust his legs to carry him away, a gray-haired man stepped through an access door and stood in front of him.

"Out a bit late tonight, aren't you?" he asked in the townspeople's language.

Kefan, dry mouthed, couldn't answer.

"Something bothering you, son?"

"No, Lord, I just, I'm . . . just waiting for my—my uncle." He stared at the man, wide-eyed. But when he twitched, preparing to run, the man bruskly put a hand on his shoulder. "What's his name? We'll look him up and ask how much longer he'll be."

"No, no, Lord, I just . . ."

"The repair crew is beginning to plan their schedule around you. Every night you're here, the gates go on the blink. When they told me you didn't have red hair, I didn't believe them."

"I'm not . . ." Kefan protested.

"No?"

"I'm NOT!" They gazed at each other, and Kefan dropped his eyes.

"I just—feel them."

"You've been hanging around the Gate for three weeks. What else would you like to inspect?"

"Two weeks."

"Three of our weeks; two of your weeks. What are you after?"

"How do I learn Standard, better than at school? Lord?"

"Do you have your father's permission?"

"I'm fifteen. My father's in the south, on business."

"Fifteen isn't old enough for Terranen. Could you get your mother's permission?"

"My mother's permission!" Kefan said scornfully.

"Yes." said Jovin, masking a smile. "A written note, signed by her, saying you can take classes at the Spaceport."

Kefan glared at him.

"Terranan rules." said Jovin, mildly. "Come back with it and I'll let you in."

Kefan went home and thought about forging the note. He wasn't interested in upsetting a household already in turmoil. His brother caught him brooding the next day and asked what was wrong.

"Would you sign a note letting me study Standard at the Terranan Spaceport?"

"Hell, no. What do you want to do that for?"

"To find out how this machine works. I can't figure out what it's doing from the books I bought."

"You're crazy."

"Maybe. Maybe I'll go ask Mother."

"Don't you think of getting her all rattled. Father would give you such a thumping when he gets back, if you provoke her now. What do you need a note for?"

"They think I'm a child, I'm only fifteen."

"Oh, Terranan are such asses, how could you stand to be around them?"

"Are you going to pound me if I go?"

"You upset Mother, you'll get it."

"What does her handwriting look like?"

"How in Zandru's hells would I know? She never wrote me a letter. How would any stupid Terranan know, anyway?" Kefan's brother stomped away, muttering, and Kefan forged the note.

That evening he walked up to the guards. They pointed at him, quite rudely, and quickly opened the access door and escorted him into their glassed-in booth. He would have been in heaven, if he hadn't felt a prisoner. But the gray-haired man he had met before arrived, introduced himself quite properly as Jovin McEnerny, accepted the note, instructed the guards to make Kefan a badge, and escorted him to a building he called the Learning Center, a short walk from the gate. They sat him in a chair. Jovin warned him that he would feel woozy, and that when the tape was over he should go home.

When it was over, he was dizzy and nauseous, but the attendants helped him recover. As he was leaving, he saw people in some of the other rooms of the learning center watching moving pictures, playing musical instruments, and, wonder of wonders, studying mathematics. And their calculators continued to operate in the harsh brightness of the artificial Terranen lighting. He went back to ask the attendant how he could study the mathematics, and the man chuckled.

"We've actually got tapes for it, brain stimulator tapes just like you've been using, but it's a wild and crazy ride, and most people can't stay in the saddle."

"I'll take one."

"Only one a customer a night. You come back tomorrow, and we'll set you up."

Kefan came back and tried the tape, but the language defeated him. He pulled out from under the headset, agitated, but the attendant smiled, and motioned calmingly with her hand that he should stay in the chair. She checked his badge in a machine, and brought back a Standard language tape. It took another two weeks of language lessons before he could grasp the ideas on the mathematics tapes, but then he was surely in heaven. He escorted his sister peacefully during the day; he slipped out of the house in the evening; he came back reeling with new ideas two hours later to make notes before falling to sleep, where x's and y's wove curves through his dreams.

His father came home, and the wedding went well. It took several days before his father noticed him coming home late and followed him upstairs. He was too enraptured to care, and stood at his desk, writing in his notebook by the light of a candle, as his father opened the door.

"Kefan . . ."

"Just a minute, please, Father . . ." His father walked over to him and looked over his shoulder at the notebook page: "$x^2/a^2 + y^2/b^2 - z^2/c^2 = 1$." After a while, he realized his father was quiet, and looked at him, apprehensively.

"What is that?" his father asked, without menace.

"It's a—" Kefan wondered how to translate "hyperboloid of one sheet" into any Darkovan language. ''A shape, like this,'' and he began to sketch the waisted form.

''Your brother says you've been hanging out with friends and not getting into too much trouble, your mother says you've been remarkably decent; what misconduct are you concealing?'' His father sat down on the bed. ''And where did you learn this?''

Kefan eyed the man, trying to keep his nervousness from showing. ''With my friends.''

''Nobody in Thendara knows that much algebra.''

''Well, we just get together, and. . . .''

''I studied mathematics at Nevarsin, too, boy, and I was good at it. I had to graduate with the rest of my class and help my father, but I knew there was more, and I wanted to stay and learn it. You are drawing me a three-dimensional shape with a z axis, and we only worked with two variables in our equations.''

Kefan looked at his father, the man's shoulders slumped tiredly, his brows worried. ''From the Terranan, Father.''

His father squeezed his eyes shut, and put a hand to his head. ''They let you?'' he said with his eyes closed.

''Yes, Father.''

''Don't tell your mother.'' His father left the room.

Kefan continued his mathematics and language lessons; there seemed to be an endless well of tapes, and he could use the computers to practice the analytic geometry. But sometimes the computers were in use, and he couldn't wait for them to be free. He found that his *laran* would operate the cardlocks on the doors of the offices in the Learning Center, and he began to make use of the computers in empty offices, eyes closed, slouched in the chair, not touching the machine, joining in the rush of the impulses through the optical and magnetic systems.

They caught him, of course. It took a while, for Security didn't believe who they were after. Jovin insisted that he existed, and the files at the Learning Center showed when he came and what he had studied; "He's getting into upper division," said the attendant, smiling. The night they caught him, they let him complete a tape, and followed him on the guard's vid before they walked in on him, weapons drawn.

"Good thing the bank isn't between the Learning Center and the Gate," said one Spaceforce as they escorted him to Jovin's office in the Legate's Building.

Kefan was almost relieved to be caught. He knew he wanted to go where those computers were designed, he wanted to make the gates answer to his desires, to follow his paths.

"You know what we do to hackers?" asked Jovin. The name plate on his desk read "Deputy Asst. to the Legate."

"No, sir."

"We give them two options. One, parole themselves to become responsible members of society, to pay for the down-time and the repairs they have engendered, and to refrain from damaging any more Empire equipment; two, go where there are no computers, and not much else, either. But since you have not caused any serious damage, and you have reached upper division math courses, there may be a third option for you."

"Yes, sir?"

"The Learning Center attendants suggest that you be sent to Terran schools, and the principal here insists that his school is not adequate; that you be sent to Terra. There is money in the Legate's Scholarship Fund; there are schools near the centers of computer design on Terra where you could find employment during the school holidays.

"You cannot afford to repay the Port for the down-time you have created; the bill so far comes to more than your father makes in five years. You would not enjoy the Youth Authority. We will give you a college placement test and a TOSFL, and help you fill out the application forms to various colleges, and we will give you a job in the computer repair shop until you are accepted by some college."

Kefan stared at the man, and when Jovin raised an eyebrow at him he smiled and looked away, too nervous to speak. He felt like a *klaedis* bud, the way the expanding flower snaps the calyx cover off with an audible "pop" and falls open, the bright red petals appearing as if by magic at the first touch of warm sun in the short Darkovan summer. He looked back at Jovin in wonderment.

"Yes, sir; thank you, sir."

"Will your parents let you go?"

"I'm fifteen."

Annoyed, Jovin repeated; "Will one of your parents sign a form in person, here at the Port?"

"I think so, sir."

"Here is a Terran chronometer. You must adapt yourself to Terran work schedules immediately—do not expect any preferential treatment from the repair shop. They are very curious about you, but you have caused them a lot of trouble, and if they suggest you be sent to the Youth Authority, their suggestion will carry weight.

"The alarm is set for 7:30 in the morning. Be here at 8:30 tomorrow morning. And don't hack any more of our machines."

The rest of his life, well-paid and rewarding as it was, he rarely could resist reaching into nearby computers and leaving the tag and a tiny flower shining red on the screen; MCILROY WAS HERE.

Rosa the Washerwoman

by Mary Ellen Fletcher

Mary Ellen Fletcher says she has been writing since she was in fourth grade, but would never have actually submitted anything if it were not for her sister. "It took her about three years of reminders and encouragement, and even then she had to retype it for me."

Seems obvious, doesn't it? We can't buy your story, no matter how good, if you don't send it to us. We're glad Mary Ellen got her courage up. It would have been a shame if this wonderful story had never seen print.

On the sheets which I assign to these stories when I'm first reading for the final line-ups, I often scribble little notes to myself to tell me if I want to use a given story. What I wrote on this one was "unusual use of laran.*" This, of course, is one of the things I'm always looking for—and I don't get it nearly often enough.*

Welcome, Stranger.

I am the tavern keeper in this little settlement of Lonolrrey, and I can tell you it is true that a tavern keeper sees nearly everything there is to see of life including birth and death and most things between. Since you are a stranger here, I can guess that you are about to say something which will lead to knives and broken dishes, so I thought I would just set you straight and save myself the trouble of replacing the crockery.

You were about to make some unkind remarks about Rosa, there. She may be fat and fifty, but she is still willing to defend her *kihar* with any weapon to hand, including my good ale. But even worse for you, at least half the men in the town would probably stand by her, and the only thing that would keep the other half in their places is that they are too drunk to move. Now, I can see that you can care for yourself, and you have your own friends by you, but only a fool or a drunk would want to take on so many unless there is a real need, and I would think you are too smart and too lately arrived to be either. But I can tell you wonder what we are about here, so let me tell you a little about Rosa

First, she's no employee of mine. If I could have hired her to company men I would have, but when I dared to mention it once many years ago, she held a knife to my throat and told me what I will tell you, that she's never let any man pay her to share her bed, but she owes no one loyalty and may do as she wishes. She's a lusty female, but she has her work. As she'll tell you herself, she's the best damn washerwoman in all the Domains, and any money you see them give her is money for washing, not for bedding. This talk about being a lowly washerwoman is beyond me, but Rosa even showed me a little keepsake that she says had been handed down from mother to daughter in her line since time began. She showed it to me, that time after my wife died and she let me come cry on her shoulder. It was a little piece of glassy looking stuff, but so hard you couldn't smash it with a hammer, and it had a place on the back that Rosa says used to hold a metal pin, although that was gone before the little thing was ever passed down to her own mother. Inside the glass were some squiggles that Rosa says prove that her ancestors were superior washerwomen. She even traced the squiggles out on this bit of slate for me, see:

ROSALEEN MAGYAR
HOUSEKEEPING STAFF

What such a thing can mean I could not say, but Rosa sets great store by it.

See that man drinking at Rosa's side, the one who won't keep his hands to himself. I'll bet all you noticed was the way he leers in her direction. Look carefully at his clothes. Sure, Rosa took him home, and I am just as sure that she took him to bed, but what he pays her for is the shave and haircut and bath, and you'll see that his clothes are laundered and even mended, and except for the ale on him, he smells of clean winter air. Last night he was shaggy, filthy, and smelled strongly of chervines. Rosa also changed him from a nasty-tongued, short-tempered bastard into the fairly pleasant drinking companion he is now.

When the war brought so many strangers here, I used to wonder why Rosa would pick the worst man here to take home with her. Either he was vacant-eyed and grieving, nasty and quick-tempered, or the scum of the earth. Rosa can do so much better, for in spite of the fact that she's getting long in the tooth, she's all woman, and any man around knows it. Maybe she has some Aillard blood in her, but she says if she does it's from some male ancestor and her family has never been interested in the male lines. Anyway, by the time she gets done with him, the fellow is someone you wouldn't mind sharing a drink with yourself. Rosa says it is all part of cleaning up and getting a good night's sleep and a good meal, but I have seen plenty of people come to stay with *Dom* Corril at the big house, and they can wash and eat and sleep up there as well as anyone, but it doesn't change them any, not the way staying at Rosa's does.

Certainly, I have seen Rosa do some amazing cleaning jobs, but one sticks in my mind the most because it was such a sad occasion. Early this year, before the thaw, young *Dom* Edric was brought home on his bier. I was there to help, for someone strong was needed to transfer his body from the wagon to the parlor. *Dom* Corril and his wife were so broken up at the loss of their only son that they weren't a bit of use, and it was me that sent for Rosa to come lay out the body. So late at night, I carried the kettles myself for water hot and cold, like Rosa always wants, and I stayed by in case I was needed.

The tears were running down Rosa's face, and she was fingering her little talisman when she came in. Young Edric had been a favorite of hers, and her oldest daughter was big with the boy's child, though of course there was no chance of a marriage between those two. She got his clothes off him and washed him as tenderly as if he could still feel what she was doing. Sometimes she needs to sew wounds together, but there wasn't a mark on the boy, just an expression of incredible pain on his face. She smoothed out the lines on his face, so that he looked a little more like himself, and tied some of his hair back to keep the expression of pain from returning. Then she dressed him up again in the fancy clothes his mother had picked out. The boy would never have worn something like that of his own choice, but once you're dead your wife or mother can dress you up any way they like.

Rosa was gathering up the clothes she had taken off the boy, when this little stone fell out and clattered on the floor. I picked it up first, then suddenly I recognized it. When the visiting *leronis* gave it to *Dom* Edric, the boy was so proud that he showed it to everyone. Back then it was a clear blue and sparkly, but when I picked it up it was a dull dark gray.

How can a rock change color, you ask? Neither Rosa nor I knew, but we both knew how much the boy had valued it, always keeping it in that little pouch around his neck, even after he was a man grown and swinging his own sword. We both talked a little about the way he loved it, and Rosa took the thing in her hand, and, while the tears ran down her face, she vowed, "I am going to make it clean again. There has to be a way."

So she took it from him. When I saw her the next day I asked her about it. She looked real frustrated. "I tried it in my regular soaps first," she said, "then I tried it in hot water, and I tried to dye it. There has to be a way."

It became a regular thing for us. For about two weeks, every day I would ask her how the rock was, and she would tell me that she had tried to bleach

it, or that she had put it in the sun or that she had polished it, or something.

One day she said to me that she had seen some *kireseth* plants growing out of the snow, and she was going to make a stew of their blue blossoms and her best soaps and herbs and soak it in that. See, she was willing to try anything, even those poisonous little plants. Then the thaw came, and we were both too busy to worry about that little stone. The Ghost Wind blew, and some of the low-landers were not used to its effects. I was somewhat affected myself, though only to drawing eighty mugs of ale and not asking a single customer for a penny. But the army was camped near us then as it is now, and there were fights and rapes and people wandering away into the wilderness, and in the middle of all that the enemy struck and they were affected, too. When the freeze came again, there was a lot of cleaning up to do, and we were all busy caring for stragglers and wounded.

Then one day Rosa came to show me the stone, and it was as blue as could be again. It had soaked in that mixture all that time, and finally soaked clean.

I offered to take it to *Dom* Corril, but when I told him that I had Edric's stone he grew pale as death and said he never wanted to see it again, that if Edric had never had *laran* he would still be alive. Well, who knows what would have happened, but plenty of men died in the army who had no blue stones, so I don't blame the jewel. I didn't like to just toss it away or sell it, either, so I put it in the jar up there on the top shelf.

Now that Rosa knows how to clean the things, she is content. Now and then she brings me another

one, as blue as the rest, that she gets from laying out those nobles that die in these parts. I think there are five in the jar now, and I can't think of any other washerwoman who would have gone to the lengths Rosa did over a little stone that no one expected her to clean anyway, so I really do think she is probably the best washerwoman you and I are ever likely to meet, anyway, and who does she hurt by being comforting to strange men. As she says, she owes nothing to anyone.

So, stranger, let me order you another round on the house, and remember, unless you are contracting for cleaning services, address Rosa there with due respect, and keep your other thoughts to yourself.

Like a Moth to the Flame

by Emily Alward

Emily Alward is not a newcomer to our anthologies; she had a previous story in RENUNCIATES OF DARKOVER, and works as a reference librarian. It's surprising how many people find library work compatible with writing. She says there's a lot of patron interest in science fiction, and she'll now have the fun of ordering novels to fill the demand. I never found library work possible. Maybe I'm just lazy; I'd always rather read than write, and must discipline myself to ignore all those many tempting books to get around to putting my own words on paper. I think that's one reason I became a writer to begin with. No one wrote the stories I wanted to read, *so I started frantically writing them myself.*

Emily has moved from Kentucky back to Indiana, and has a new house on a small lake; she adds that "my dogs think this place is heaven, what with the possums and deer in the woods, and the frogs and ducks at the water's edge." Just make sure they don't hunt out any skunks or porcupines, or their perceptions may change suddenly from Heaven to 'tother place!

She has sold to STAR TRIAD and to HEROTICA.

Melisendre stood on an outcropping above the murky Wind River and listened to the air crackle. Orange fire flared behind the distant mountains. She could feel the resin boiling in the evergreens' limbs on the nearby hillsides. Then they burst into flames, too.

Alarm and horror filled her, for in the mountains no danger was more feared than forest fire. She fumbled at the little bag which held her matrix, finally pulled the blue stone out, and held it in shaking hands as she concentrated on relaying the image.

But as she reached out through her matrix she could not connect at all, even though she was a strong telepath and the Tower could not be far away. Her panic flowed into her crystal, sending random jolts of energons through her already shaky nerves. The mountains before her blurred, but the red and orange of fire still burned inside her eyes. The evil wind of the river's name swept up, heated and cloyingly sweet from the ashy residue. She reached out to steady herself by clinging to a rock.

Cold metal met her hand.

"You can hold the fire." Words came to her on the wind. She heard a woman's voice, soft as a cloud of *kireseth* blossoms, strong as the steel forged in the caves near her family's lands.

Melisendre poured determination through her crystal. Her vision cleared. Looking around, she saw no one. Without her will, her fingers closed over the metal. Her hand raised it up. She stared in wonderment at a shining sword. Blue fire like the light within a matrix crystal danced along its blade.

She could lift it easily, yet she felt its immense weight. She flourished it, as she had seen her brothers do with their short fighting swords.

One portion of the hill fire died down, then surged up again and leapt across the river.

I cannot use this sword! she thought fearfully.

"Of course not. It is not an object suited to you. I will give you a better tool." The voice came back to her out of the wind and fire. Unseen hands slid the sword out of her grasp.

It dropped to the ground and shattered. Melisendre stared at the pieces, drained of their blaze of magic. Dulled and empty as they were now, the shards were still more pleasant to her eyes than the earth beneath them. The ground lay caked in dry clods, waterless for months. Nothing could grow in it. Beyond, a sickly gray marked areas where the World Wreckers' poisons still infected the soil. Scraggly plants spread out there; they bore thorns and noxious saps. Melisendre's circle had tried curing people sickened by touching those plants, but *laran* could not heal them.

Melisendre trembled. Her hand reached toward her starstone again, but before she could touch it, the other hand flew up involuntarily. A copper bowl fell into her hands. She gasped to see so much precious metal in one object. Intricate designs were etched around three-fourths of the inner rim. She saw mountains and waterfalls, stars and moons and lightning bolts. In the unadorned space, a circular indentation had been carved to receive a large stone. It was empty, but Melisendre visualized a lovely gem set there, blazing red incandescence to represent the sun.

A fragrant minty scent rose from the liquid at the

bottom of the bowl. Melisendre raised it up to drink, to comfort her parched throat. All at once the metal she held changed from cool to warm. The lovely liquid evaporated into the dry air. Glowing coals materialized in the bowl's interior.

"Refreshment *after* work." Melisendre could almost hear the Tower workers' adage repeated to her, and in the tone of a reprimand. The voice was nearer now, soft as ever, but edged with the sureness of absolute authority. "You have not yet completed your task."

Strangely, although the coals burned steadily, Melisendre's hands were not hot from holding the bowl. She felt a prickle, and then a great stream of energy flowed into her body. It sang silently through her hands, then up her arms and into every nerve and muscle. The bowl tugged at her will with the insistence of an impatient lover. She held it out toward the distant mountains as it demanded.

On the horizon, the angry orange flame vanished into a rosy, fair dawn. The fires on the nearer hillsides sputtered and died away. Melisendre watched, unbelieving, as the cracked ground under her feet blossomed with a carpet of yellow and violet wildflowers. The gusts from the river lost their evil taint and brushed across her face with the pleasant mint-like scent of the vanished liquid. In the poisoned meadow, trees miraculously appeared. A rabbit-horn bounded out, then a wild chervine. She sighed with a relief she hadn't felt for many months. Nature was finally righting its balance.

She was physically unable to let go of the bowl, to break the link to the rare metal and the glowing coals. Power still poured into her body, filling her with a pleasure beyond comparison. Yet terror fought with the exaltation within her soul. She was a tool no less than the copper bowl or the sword, used for the purposes of an unknown being.

Then the bowl allowed itself to be lowered to the ground. Around its rim red and blue flames flickered. Scenes played within the fire—great natural cataclysms, earthquake and storm and exploding mountains; scenes of captivity and suffering. Melisendre tried to wrench herself away from the metal. Her hands were beginning to burn.

But not until a figure rose up in the flames, wrapped in golden chains, wearing them proudly as a badge of office, was the young woman able to let go of the copper bowl. She backed away slowly, suddenly wanting to distance herself, but afraid to anger the Form of Fire.

It was only a dream, Melisendre told herself when she awoke, shaken.

Like the hound to the rabbit-thorn. . . ?

Like the bear to the honeycomb. . . ?

Unsummoned phrases drifted in Melisendre's mind as she climbed the worn staircase in the Terran Headquarters building. She batted them back, not sure where they were coming from, unpleasantly reminded that if her fellow Tower workers knew of her visit here they would taunt her with exactly such thoughts.

Like a flower seeking lifegiving rain. . . ?

That was better.

Tad's was the office at the very end of the half-lit corridor. Spaceforce had its own ways of signaling disfavor.

Melisendre knocked twice; heard a muffled "Come!" She slid through the door and latched it soundlessly. There was no need for stealth, but the very atmosphere of the building seemed to forbid her, an outsider, from calling attention to herself.

Half-circles of fatigue lined the man's eyes. His sandy hair was rumpled and stubble dotted his cheeks. He slumped over a desk, touching up diagrams on an old-fashioned sheet of paper, oblivious to the nest of Terran technology which surrounded him.

He was still the most attractive man Melisendre had ever known.

She crossed the room quickly, shaking the crimson hood away from her face to be ready for his kiss.

"Thanks, Melisendre," he said as she set the basket of cheeses and spicebread on the desk. "I haven't had time for anything but a cup of coffee. These blasted reports—" He stood up groggily, and leaned over to touch her lips with his own. "But I'll make time for this."

Melisendre felt the touch of uncertainty that rippled through all of their conversations. Did "this" mean her, and the chance to share some confidences along with the caresses? Or did he merely mean he would take time out to eat?

Never mind, she told herself. *You don't have to know all his thoughts.* It was one of his attractions, that his mind was opaque to her. That she didn't have to deal with all his passing thoughts and moods. That he might mean several things at once; that she never knew just what twist of perception he might surprise he with next. It was one reason she felt she could "fall in love" with him, as his people said.

But it was so different from her everyday life in

the mental hothouse of the Tower that each of their meetings also felt slightly like a trip to the overworld.

She smiled slightly and began to unpack the food. He watched her, then shrugged the fatigue from his shoulders and smiled back.

"Sorry I didn't greet you better. Here Little Red Riding Hood brings me a basket of treats, and all I can do is grumble about paperwork."

"An unlikely wolf," she said lightly. She had heard the Terran legend some weeks ago, when Tad took her on an outing that included the Coordinator's family. It sounded like the stories told to keep lowland women from dancing with unrelated men, but the Terrans apparently thought it a tale for children.

"A tired one," he added. "But we'll overcome that. It's been a long time, Meli."

She sighed. "Yes. I've missed you too, Tad. But we've been working frantically in the circles, trying to bring some life back to the dead lands. And I knew you had problems here you needed to work on."

He groaned. "Maybe it's time to forget them for a few hours. Come here." He held his arms open and Melisendre snuggled happily against him. She was still amazed that his touch brought comfort, rather than the sense of violation she'd been told to expect from a head-blind man's embrace. *Maybe there's something wrong with me,* she thought as she often had before. At the moment she didn't care. She only wanted to bask in their shared affection after so many days apart.

Tad fumbled in an airtight cabinet and brought out two bubble-spheres of a frosty Terran drink.

They sipped them as they ate and caught up on events in each other's life. Melisendre could not explain to Tad what working in the matrix net was like. But he was interested in the circles' discoveries about the condition of the wrecked lands. His own work—at least the work he was *supposed* to be doing—also dealt with planet-wide changes.

"Not that there's been much done on it lately," he said, more cheerfully than Melisendre expected. "Every time I try to set up the instrumentation something goes wrong. Might as well stick to administrative busywork like this," he glared at the flow-chart he'd been drawing, "and keep the big-shots happy."

"Tad, *caryo, anyone* can do that sort of puffery! You should work on your science!" She gazed at him fondly but in exasperation. "Can't you get your experiments set up right? Oh, I suppose that'll just give fuel to the people who want you out of here altogether."

Melisendre raged inwardly when she thought of Tad's predicament. Trouble had shadowed him when he was stationed in Thendara. He'd explained to her that his theory of planetary disturbances, presented at the meeting of the local chapter of the Empire Academy of Sciences, had alarmed some Terran leaders. It might be good science, they told him, but it was bad politics and would offend their Darkovan hosts. Melisendre couldn't understand why it should. Everyone knew that Terrans liked to use gobbledygook words like "nuee ardente" and "pyroclastic." And his comparison of Sharra to the Terran volcano-goddess Pele sounded reasonable. In any event, he had been banished to Port Chicago, where he was out of sight of his superiors.

Melisendre couldn't entirely regret his exile, for otherwise she would never have met him. But he'd been warned that with one more mistake, he would be shipped away to a planet that was even more of a hardship post. Melisendre couldn't stand to think of it. Tad was the first man she had ever—haltingly—begun to love.

"Let's take a look," she said, walking over to the apparatus. It was a maze of tiny power-packs, wires, and plasticene sensors. She almost shrank away at first. But then she began to grasp its connection to the planet's mantle. She was able to trace the intricate paths which revealed the ebb and flow of forces beneath the surface.

She looked up at Tad and smiled. He whooped for joy when he realized that she intuitively understood the machine. Melisendre began to adjust tiny wires as her *laran* perceived the planet's force-fields. It was not so different from the operations she'd been leading in the Tower. Tad followed her on his monitors and reprogrammed his experimental protocol to match the changes she was making.

Tad's weariness had vanished; Melisendre felt her skills expand with each new circuit they linked up. Only when the night's work was almost done did she realize that she felt closer to Tad than ever before. Through the machine they had shared a mental unity they could never experience directly.

They left the apparatus set up to record its data. Strolling hand-in-hand through the first wisps of dawn-light, they went to Tad's modest quarters and made love.

The next day, Melisendre sat staring glumly at a tableful of food. Her group had not been able to find the two children lost berrying in a nearby forest preserve. She had picked up tiny glimmers of their energy fields in the circle's search, but it was impossible to focus on a direction. Now she silently retraced their work, trying to discover where they had gone wrong.

"If we had dedicated people in the Tower, there wouldn't be so many failures." A grating voice interrupted her thoughts.

"Why, what do you mean?" Melisendre looked searchingly at Justin. He was a pessimist, but she had never known him to criticize his colleagues before. "How can you say that when Gabriela is pushing herself so hard?"

"As a Keeper should," he shot back. "There's more to the song than the notes."

"If you are implying she should live like an old-time Keeper, ignoring human contact and the outside world, I cannot agree," Melisendre said sharply. In her opinion Gabriela had always been an exemplary Keeper: a confident middle-aged woman with both concern for her Tower members and the objectivity needed to handle high-level matrix forces.

"Nay, I did not mean that." Justin shrugged and reached for a loaf of hot bread. He deliberately filled his mouth so he could not talk further. But long-concealed resentment rippled through Melisendre's shields. She caught Justin's unhappiness that Gabriella sometimes joined the rest of the Tower in their leisure hours, and kept apprised of the efforts in Thendara to develop a new government. But stronger than his dismay with the Keeper was his fury at Melisendre.

How can a technician with divided loyalties lead

a circle? No wonder we can't find the children, when half your inner life is outside the Tower! Do you even know us well enough to focus our gifts?

Melisendre's first impulse was to slam back through his shields; to tell Justin that her life outside the circle was none of his business. He had always subtly questioned her competence, she recalled, ever since she had rejected his invitation to bed. But she stopped herself. Bigger issues were at stake than her own or Justin's anger. Discord within a working circle was dangerous.

As she ran a small probe over the thought-strands in the room, she realized the others shared Justin's doubts. Melisendre *did* block off the constant jangle of their everyday emotions. It was easy for her colleagues to mistake her self-protective shielding for unconcern. Most of them liked her regardless, but a liaison with a Terran was beyond their understanding.

Her self-assurance shattered as the messages came through. She still had enough pride to flee from the dining place to her own quarters before asking herself if the accusations could be true.

After a while, still bereft at the thought that she might be responsible for being unable to locate the children and tearing apart the circle's rapport by her own willfulness, she sought out her Keeper.

Gabriela's apartment reflected her own virtues; it was capacious, cheerful, and serene. She beckoned the door open before Melisendre had even knocked, and asked, "How may I help you, *chiya?*"

Melisendre's worries poured out, half in words, half in unspoken images. The Keeper listened to both, looking thoughtful but saying nothing until Melisendre had finished.

Finally she spoke. "In some ways Justin is exactly right."

Her words jolted Melisendre, who nevertheless had enough sense to keep quiet for the moment. Gabriela went on. "Do you think I do not know why you have to barrier yourself? *Especially* here within the Tower, where tradition has always said the members share so much?"

Melisendre said nothing.

"Just because someone survives threshold sickness and learns a few tricks does not mean he is a strong person. People have fears and needs. If they cannot manage them adequately they reach out, grasping for help. Even through another's mind, if that is within their abilities. You are very sensitive, Meli, you *want* to help when their plea reaches you. It can tear you up, being called on to give so much."

Melisendre suddenly wondered if part of Tad's attraction was that his demands on her sympathy were limited to whatever he specifically chose to tell her.

Gabriela sighed and went on. "Justin is right that tradition has certain virtues. The training of Keepers—before Dorilyn of Arilinn—taught methods of distancing oneself without losing any sensitivity to Power. You would have benefited from it in that way, Melisendre, I am sure. Though I would not like to see that regime imposed upon any woman."

Melisendre shuddered, imagining the pain of renouncing love forever. "Do you think there is truth in Justin's idea that my divided loyalties are interfering with my circle's work?" she asked.

"No, dear. I think there are other forces involved. I also think you've needed your friend Tad Casley as a respite. Nevertheless—" Gabriela lifted herself out of the chair and paced back and forth before the narrow windows. "Nevertheless, I am going to ask you to consider giving him up. Not because there is anything wrong with your relationship. But for the sake of the Tower and our world."

Melisendre's breath caught. Even before she heard the next words she knew what Gabriela was going to ask. A sweet exaltation filled her. Everything seemed to be settling into a plan the deities arranged long ago. From her dream she recalled the heady flow of energies channeled through her body, healing the world's wounds. While technically there was only a small degree of difference between her technician's work within the circle and a Keeper's tasks, the gap in respect and access to power was immense. Ever since the first faint stirrings of her *laran,* she had dreamed of becoming a Keeper.

"You are the only one here who can do it," Gabriela was saying. "I intend to lay down my office once I can find a successor. Oh," she laughed, catching the inquiry in Melisendre's mind. "No, I have not found someone I want to marry, at least not yet. But Lord Regis has asked me to come to Thendara, to set up a training program for the new telepaths on the council. Many of them have more *laran* than sense, as you can imagine, and it's not practical to expect the few remaining Towers to train them all. It's important work. But keeping the Towers open as a refuge from politics is important, too."

Melisendre smiled, feeling sympathy as well as admiration for this energetic woman. She wanted to give Gabriela her wish, to agree to be her successor so both of them could do important work that they wanted to do. Melisendre knew that with only a few weeks of intensive training, she would be able to carry out the responsibilities of a Keeper. She started to say yes.

Then she thought of Tad: his half-funny quips when they met after the stretches of time apart; his intense concentration on his scientific puzzles; his steady affection for her. While Keepers were no longer required to be virgins, a woman could not perform the work unless she remained apart from love during the time of her office. She did not think she could bear to give Tad up.

"I'll have to think about it," she murmured to Gabriela. Her soul was tearing apart with contradictory desires. Deciding between them would not be any easier later, but perhaps the Goddess would guide her.

Gabriela nodded, unsurprised. "Let's try to find the children," she said matter-of-factly. She took out her dazzling matrix stone. Melisendre reached for her own. Together they called up a picture in both crystals, matched them, and magnified the faint quivers of life-force which shone out. In a few minutes a jumble of boulders took shape in the background. Melisendre recognized the area; it was not far away. Gabriela sent the message with a *kyrri,* knowing townsmen would bring the children home safely within the afternoon.

It was a good omen, Melisendre thought.

A *kyrri* padded up to her room later that evening. He gestured in the unexcited way the creatures approached all things, but Melisendre caught a hint of trouble behind the call. She quickly dressed for the autumn night's chill and hurried to follow his summons.

Tad was waiting just outside the Tower, pacing and staring at the ground as if he wanted to curse it forever. It took no *laran* to see his distress. He looked up when Melisendre walked through the veil, but for the first time since she'd known him he didn't smile at her approach.

"We have to talk," he said glumly. She fell into step with him and they walked silently down the path to the town. She found herself wishing desperately that she could enter his mind with a tiny tendril of rapport, if only to comfort him. It must be hard to have to stay alone in your own mind, she thought, until you could summon the words to tell about some terrible event.

At the edge of town they found a dingy tavern. It seemed as good a place to talk as any; the few other customers were too far gone in their cups to goggle at the presence of a Terran Spaceforce man and a flame-tressed Tower technician. Melisendre asked for watered wine. It was something to play with, at least, until Tad could tell her what had happened.

"When we set up that apparatus," he began, talking barely above a whisper, "did you notice anything worn or unstable about any of the connections?"

"No," she said. "Everything seemed pretty solid to me."

"Did anything just plain feel wrong? I know that's not scientific, but I trust your perceptions."

"No," she said again, wanting to say how right everything had felt that night. Knowing she didn't dare say it, now, because obviously something had gone very wrong, afterward.

"That's what Michaels said, too. He checked out the setup yesterday. If anyone on this forsaken planet should know, it's him. He said it was perfectly calibrated, no faulty sensors, nothing that should have malfunctioned."

"And?"

"It exploded this afternoon. Blew the whole room up."

The images came directly into her mind as Tad spoke. She saw glass and plasticene shards and twists of metal lying everywhere, charred floorboards, shredded paper, and melted disks. Whoever or whatever tore the machine apart spared no fury in the attack.

"Oh, Tad, *caryo*, I'm so sorry. You weren't hurt? Or anyone else?"

"Not—" Tad swallowed, looked down and refused to meet her eyes. "Nobody's hurt, thanks. I—I have two days to get off-planet."

"But it's not your fault," she protested. "How can they punish you for having bad luck?"

"Spaceforce doesn't have room for habitual goof-ups. Or so the Coordinator tells me. He was fairly decent about it. Offered to set me up in a job with a mining contractor on Achterrein Five. Or there's always the Nucidian asteroid belt where they're desperate for personnel. I could stay in the Force that way, maybe earn a promotion back to some decent posting after five years or so."

"They can't treat you that way!" she said. "It's unfair and unfeeling. Gabriela knows Lord Regis himself; surely if he speaks to your Terran Legate they'll reconsider. Let me see what I can do."

"*Carya,* it won't make any difference. Terran bureaucracy *is* unfeeling. I'm not important enough to win against the system. I'm just an ordinary guy who seems to have messed up on everything, ever since I came to this planet."

"No you haven't. You've made me happy," Melisendre said. She reached across the table and put her hand over his. For the first time in the whole dreadful evening he smiled.

"Then I won't be sorry for the time I spent here. I'll just get out of here before I mess up your life, too."

"And if I don't want you to?"

"Then you can come with me. I won't ask you to, Melisendre. You have your work and your whole heritage here on Darkover, and I have nothing much to offer. But if you want to come along, I will love and cherish you."

There was nothing more to be said. They paid for the wine and left. Parting at the crossroads, they exchanged a bittersweet kiss and agreed to meet for one last time the following evening.

As she walked back to the Tower, Melisendre pushed away the unwelcome thought that fate had made her decision for her. With Tad sent off-planet she would be able to fulfill her lifelong dream of becoming a Keeper.

It was snowing in the Hellers.

It was always snowing in the Hellers, so Melisendre paid no attention as she went about her morning chores in the courtyard. Thistlewaite was a small and unprosperous holding, which was why Melisendre was up at dawn feeding hens and sweeping, rather than snugly asleep like a proper young Comyn lady. Not until she tried to shrug the little white mounds off her cape, and couldn't, did she notice the weather.

An intangible charge crackled in the air. The snow clung like white syrup to surfaces. The hens, who earlier had been clucking cheerfully, fell silent and huddled together in their small hutch. A thick curtain of fog and heavy flakes blotted out the nearby mountains. The silence was deafening.

When Melisendre was leaning over to pick up the last egg, the world exploded. Thunder volleyed across the valley. The ground wobbled like jelly under Melisendre's feet. She grabbed a post and held on desperately while earth and sky and horizon spiraled around her. Bells in the tiny lady chapel began to clang, their raucous peals picked up and carried by the suddenly shrieking wind.

Diamond white ice and charged air played off each other. Lightning flashed through the veil of fog and snow, suffusing the world in frosty light. Pain shot through Melisendre's eyes from the brightness. It was like looking into the heart of a high-level matrix.

A wall of flames flared up on the peaks which ringed the holding. The manor house crumbled all at once.

Melisendre screamed. She ran for the uncertain shelter of the village at the end of the valley.

"It's the end of the world, isn't it?" Melisendre asked.

The old woman wore the rough starstone and herb pouch of a folk *leronis*. Her eyes looked through Melisendre as she replied.

"It's just the Goddess raging at being torn from her world. She's grieved ever since that madman loosed her chains and the Comyn lord took her away, but now— Mark me, *chiya,* the world *won't* work right until she can find a way back.''

Melisendre squirmed uncomfortably. The old woman must be raging, unhinged by the storm. Yet her house was the only one left standing in the village. Melisendre nodded a thanks to her and walked away.

For a moment she thought she had walked directly from the village to the Tower. She stirred as she came out of the dream, burrowing into the warmth and shelter of the covers on her bed. But she could not sleep. A pearly streak of light played across the stone floor. She got up and followed it to the window, looking for Mormallor's familiar face.

Snow filled the air, blotting out the town which Melisendre could usually see from her window. No moon peered through, but streaks of lightning played fitfully in the distance.

She was not back in the dream again, she knew. The dream was built of events from her girlhood, of fears she had put behind her when she came to the Tower.

Yet something was calling to her from that time.

An uncompleted task.

Something she must do to heal the land, to put the world to rights again.

The stone steps half-froze her feet as she crept down the long, spiral staircase that lead to the little cave beneath the Tower. She had not put on shoes because she knew she needed to be grounded directly in the earth.

The rough-hewn walls were damp with water that had been locked in the rock. The water would flow out soon now, healing the cracks in the parched soil and bringing life back to the ruined forests and fields.

She turned a last sharp corner and came to a split in the tunnel. Energy streamed from the stairwell on the left, pulling her smoothly into its current. She had no doubt which way she must go, although she had never been this far down the steps before.

Like a moth to the flame. . . .

She had heard other phrases in her head when she climbed the steps to Tad's office. They were the weak shadow-images of this call. It sang in her veins, promising completion.

Promising power.

The ancient hinges creaked when she tugged open the door. A honeycomb of stones lined the tiny cave. Pale blue light seeped from the walls. Natural matrix crystals shone dully amidst the ordinary rocks, awaiting the quickening touch of a Keeper.

Melisendre walked straight across the cave, to the largest crystal embedded in the rocky wall.

She pulled tentatively on it. The crystal fell into her hands. A ribbon of light flared through it. Her hands turned luminous. A pulse of energy soared through her body, a reassuring impulse exactly like the merged *laran* she controlled within the circle.

With the next surge she felt herself shaking. Light blue and diamond white flames hovered above the crystal. She held it out at arm's length. Fire flickered across her skin, but she felt no pain. Instead, a sweet, melting warmth suffused her.

The beautiful copper bowl she had seen in a dream appeared in her mind. She pictured herself leaving the cave, going to the closet where she knew she would find it, fitting the blazing starstone into the hollow where it belonged. She would hold the bowl and send out great pulses of healing across the land.

She stared at her arms and hands again, at the lovely rainbow of colors in the fire which surrounded them. For a moment she saw two pairs of hands and arms, almost as if another woman's form was fitting itself into her body.

Melisendre opened her hands to drop the crystal.

It didn't drop.

A scream tore at her throat. Melisendre choked it back because Sharra's songs were riding on the scream.

The ship took long minutes to pull out of Cottman IV's gravity well. The Terran passenger mumbled that the planet was trying to throw one last complication into his departure.

"It's not you she's seeking, *caryo.* The Goddess has her own purposes. I'm sure things will go much better when we're in the asteroid belt, beyond Her reach." The red-haired woman sighed and shifted in her seat harness, wishing they were already on the interstellar part of the journey. She wanted to lean against Tad's shoulder, to reassure both herself and him.

Her hands itched fiercely inside their bandages. The Terran doctor who had treated her had said her injuries would heal. Melisendre herself was not so sure. She had torn strips of flesh from her hands; it was the only way she could release the matrix stone which was bonding to her. Terran medicine could repair ordinary burns and cuts, but Melisendre knew her injuries were different. She would be lucky if their outward appearance returned to normal and only the pain remained.

The pressure fields within the cabin shifted. She glanced at the viewscreen and saw that the ship had turned. Darkover was falling rapidly out of sight and the great red disk of the sun shrank even as she watched. The questions she had ruthlessly pushed out of her mind for the past two days flooded back in.

Was it true, as the old woman had said, that the planet would never prosper until the Flamehair could find a way back? Should she have let the Goddess overshadow her?

Melisendre shuddered when she remembered how close she had come to having no choice.

If the warning is true, some other leronis *or* laranzu *can have the glory of enchaining Her. I do not have the strength to control Sharra.*

The all-clear button was flashing, so Melisendre unfastened the seat harness and walked over to be near Tad. Their new life together was beginning. She would show him as much love as he had offered her.

He thought her hands were burned from an accident with the Tower's cookstove. She vowed that he would never know why she made the decision to go with him.

A Change of View

by Judith Kobylecky

Judith Kobylecky begins the letter updating her biography by the hope that we were missed by the Oakland Hills firestorm.

Everybody here and at Greyhaven was safe; but we could see and smell the fire. While it was raging, we felt as if we were living on Darkover, with the smell of fire in the air. The fire itself, quite literally, missed us by a mile; they contained it a little more than a mile away.

Judith adds that her biography has not changed very much since her last appearance in these pages. "The children are two years older . . . and they do seem to get bigger overnight. Anna is now eight, Ian five, and the baby, Emma, is two. For me one of the best things about having kids is the chance to show them things of interest, as much as you can teach them they are always ready for more." (Ah, a girl after my own heart—a born teacher.) "We have to scramble to keep up, but it's great fun."

Judith also has "a polite but benignly crazy dog who is so far removed from her fierce predator ancestry that when she and I literally stumbled over a mouse in the middle of the stuffed animals we both almost fainted." I have a dog like that; Signy is more wolf than dog, and like all wolves she is very timid. The usual fierce wolf of fiction doesn't turn me on much; my fierce, feral Signy spent most of her first obedience class hiding between me and the wall.

There haven't been too many Darkovan stories laid among the Terrans; few such stories, in the opinion of our late editor Emeritus, Don Wollheim, preserved the real flavor of Darkover. This one, I think, preserves it very well.

Mhari watched as the latest group of tourists came through the low carved door from the street. Each entered with bitter complaints about the freezing rain outside, yet not one had adequately dressed for the weather. *Merciful Avarra,* she thought, *the Terranan are a strange people.*

As she helped them dry themselves, she could see that this particular group was going to be difficult to please, but she was confident of her ability to handle them. After all, her patron, Lord Regis Hastur himself, had personally directed her year of training with a *leronis* and had advanced her the startup funds she needed of his own revenues. As a child of the Trade City she was still astounded that the Hastur of Hasturs had not only taken the time to discuss her idea but had also given her his invaluable advice on the illusions so necessary to it, always stressing the importance of the creation of bridges between the two cultures by allowing the Terranan to glimpse the world through Darkovan eyes. It was a matter of great pride to her that she had done so well and not disappointed him.

The idea was simple enough. Daily, the huge Terranan starships landed at the spaceport in Thendara for routine maintenance and refueling, a delay for their passengers that could mean days in a utilitarian spaceport with little of any interest to do. Only a fraction of Thendara itself was open to them, and much of that offered distractions rougher than those many looked for. What Mhari gave them was an alternative that entertained while it gave an overview of the culture and history of Darkover, but the true benefit to her way of thinking was the employment of the local Thendaran artisans whose difficult way of life she understood. When her own father caught the wasting sickness, her mother, despite her important family name, had had to struggle to support them by her weaving. Mhari herself had grown up peddling bits of fancy cloth or sweet cakes to the Terranan in the Trade City market. Like many, she developed an affection for them and their peculiar ways, for the Terranan had been kind and sent her home with food and extra coins. When her *laran* came unexpectedly a few years ago, it had seemed only natural when the idea of bringing the two peoples together had taken root, it was a goal she had worked for ever since.

Mhari took the towels and directed the Terranan to where a roaring fire had been made ready, for she knew that they found even the snug inside of the building frigid; if she were not careful, one of them could develop hypothermia. She surveyed the group huddled around the fireplace and wondered as she always did what they had been thinking of when they got dressed that morning. There was a couple in identical clothing, the fabric finely knit of a brilliant color that seemed to fluoresce in the ruddy light that streamed through the narrow windows. One man wore a shirt that, as far as Mhari could piece together from the Terranan script, read something typically cryptic: "I danced on Psakren's Moon." He was accompanied by a woman who struggled to move in the tightest clothes Mhari or, to judge from their reactions, any of her workers had ever seen. The wonder of it was how she had gotten so far dressed like that. Even in the relatively open Trade City, she ran a fair risk of being stoned by the more conservative townsfolk. Surely, it looked about as comfortable as one of Zandru's lesser hells. It was all too obvious that none of them had so much as glanced at the preparatory material she had arranged for the Terra Travel Office to distribute. Later, when she had more time, she would laugh it off and try to make the brochures more colorful to catch their attention. With her assistant's help she distributed cloaks that served the dual purpose of warming her visitors while protecting the sensibilities of Thendarans. As a rule her guests enjoyed the novelty of wearing the heavy handmade woolen cloth, all part of the immersion experience that had proved successful with even the most jaded tourist. Word of mouth was so favorable that growing numbers of long-time spaceport residents had begun to come as well, and most guests left with the solid beginnings of an appreciation for Darkovan culture. It was always a satisfaction to break through the sense of superiority that so many of them had.

Still, this was a tough group. She concentrated on the *laran* she had inherited from some distant and unknown ancestor and quickly checked the placement of the small starstone chips placed around the room. They were only of a size that could be bought freely in the market, but she used them to enhance the illusions she wove for her visitors, always careful not to alarm them although the Terranan were so accustomed to the subtleties of their own technology that they naturally assumed she used some sort of sophisticated screens. She doubted she could convince them otherwise even if she tried.

While she prepared herself, her workers were busy demonstrating their skills and answering any questions. Times were so bad for small artisans that many went hungry despite their skills, so it was not difficult to recruit the normally fiercely independent Thendarans to demonstrate their skills for the tourists, all chosen in part for their proven tolerance for the bizarre behaviors of the off worlders. It was her hope that if the wealthy Terranan could be educated to appreciate the beauty of the hand-made goods, then many more would benefit besides the few she was able to employ here. The artisans were an essential part of the experience since it was a challenge for a Terranan to comprehend the complete absence of machine-made goods on her world, and the opportunity to actually handle an object in its various stages of manufacture was almost irresistible. But apparently not with this group.

The Terranan were now a little warmer and talked in front of her people as if they were not there; she had to send a warning glance to a new weaver who had already begun to bridle at their comments. Under her gaze the woman held herself to a glare. Mhari hurried her preparations while the oblivious tourists continued to talk among themselves.

"You call this dump a tourist attraction?"

"I think it's just some kind of store with atmosphere. You know, ambience."

"Those things can't possibly be hand-made. Anyone who did that would have to be crazy."

"If this is how they really live, then you could never call it living."

Mhari redoubled her efforts and concentrated. Currents of calm traveled along the starstone chips, some of it carefully diverted to soothe the other Darkovans who were well on their way to losing their tempers. She sympathized with them, it was hard enough to hold onto her own. After a little trial and error she finally found the tone that this particular collection of difficult individuals responded to and used the stones to amplify the illusions accompanying her speech. She welcomed them all as guests to her home, and with a gesture upward the ceiling seemed to disappear and the moons of Darkover did their dance across the sky. She picked up her *rryl* and played an accompaniment that furthered the sence of entering a waking dream; the group gasped as the stone walls vanished and they found themselves in the midst of one of Darkover's vast primeval forests, the first fragrant snowflowers of winter in bloom by their feet. *Now I have them,* she thought.

The street door burst open and painfully shattered the illusion she had so carefully wrought. A young, very angry red-haired man burst through the group and scowled at Mhari. "Congratulations, *mestra,*" he began, his voice sarcastic. "You have made a carnival show of Darkover for these Terranan. What a proud moment for Thendara to stoop to this."

She had seen the man before and had heard that he disapproved of her venture. Not even *Dom* Regis' patronage was enough for some. The truth was, with some notable exceptions, she heartily disliked the Comyn, particularly young and pompous ones. Especially this particular young and pompous one. It had not escaped her that he had chosen to speak in the off world tongue so that his insults could be understood by everyone, and she braced herself for trouble while she considered her limited options, resolving to hire Renunciate guards that very evening. Mhari almost laughed out loud as the two sides, Comyn and Terranan, regarded each other with identical expressions of smug cultural superiority. Obviously things were not going the way he had expected; these Terranan did not have enough sense to know that they were supposed to be mortally offended. Worse yet, some of the artisans were already beginning to snicker at his frustration. Regretfully, she had to dismiss her first inclination to throw them all out and start over again.

"Oh, good," one of the tourists stepped forward and examined the Comyn's sword with interest, "the show is really picking up now."

"You know," said another, "I think that must be one of the rulers of this frozen mudball of a planet. They all have that sort of inbred look."

The young Comyn looked at the woman who had spoken and curled his lip.

"Well, there is such a thing as overdoing it," she whispered in an offended tone to her companion. He nodded and answered, not even trying to lower his voice, "This theatrical stuff is fine, but what they really need is some kind of ride."

"You want a ride, do you?" With a sweep of his arm a whirlwind of color surrounded the bewildered Terranan. Mhari was caught completely by surprise; she had never expected more than a tirade. She shouted for him to stop and leapt into the middle of the now frightened tourists, dragging the surprised Comyn with her. It had never occurred to him that anyone would dare touch him. *Well,* she thought grimly, *we are all full of surprises.* Before he pulled away, the air seemed to fold over on itself and they vanished from the room.

The next few minutes were full unspeakable terror as Mhari and the red-haired man struggled for control of the whirlwind he had released. They careened through Darkovan time and space as around them royalty was crowned and deposed and people of different times emerged from ruins to fight for survival in a harsh land. A tornado of images too fast to comprehend spun past them as they hurtled through forests where the *chieri* still danced and were torn by the fury of a blizzard in the high passes of the Hellers. Mhari thought they would all go mad until at last the anger and distrust that blocked their cooperation burned itself out in the terror of their situation and they were able to merge and gain control. The madly tumbling images slowed and with a violent lurch they found themselves in the same spot where they had started. The artisans still sat in shocked silence which, to Mhari's great consternation, meant that almost no real time had elapsed at all. Her people rushed over, almost hysterical in their relief, and helped her look after the Terranan who had mercifully all survived, but with bewildering changes. The couple with the matching clothing were covered with snow, *kyorebni* feathers clutched in their hands, daggers strapped on their waists. One man had his clothes turned completely around, a wreath of *kireseth* flowers on his head, and many now wore kilts or knitted shawls. "That was some ride," she heard softly muttered. The others nodded their reverent agreement.

A short time later a very respectful group of tourists left with their arms laden with hand-made goods whose fine quality and rare beauty they could now recognize. In this one day her people had made enough to keep their houses warm for the winter and she would be able to start repayment of her debt to *Dom* Regis.

Mhari saw her guests out the low door to the street before getting two cups of hot *jaco* braced with the fiery Thendaran brandy. She carried them over to the still stunned Comyn lordling and sat next to him on the low bench by the fire. He took the proffered mug with thanks and spoke thoughtfully. "I believe that somehow our telepathic gifts are so perfectly matched that they meshed before we realized what was happening. But I still do not understand how we did what we did."

Mhari sat beside him and shrugged. "I do not know, but it was glorious, was it not?"

He laughed and Mhari, who now felt she had always known him, not surprising since they had just lived through so many lifetimes together, thought it was time he laughed more. "I would say," he answered, "that we gave them a ride to remember."

"Do you think it could be done again? With more control, of course."

He looked surprised and intrigued at the thought. "It would be interesting to try."

"Tell me, *vai dom,* have you ever thought about a career in education?"

He grinned at her appreciatively over his cup and they silently toasted a new idea.

Choices

by Lynn Michals

Lynn Michals is twenty-eight years old, and still working on her dissertation; when she finishes it, she'll have a Ph.D. in English Literature. This and her story, "Building," in LERONI OF DARKOVER are her only published fiction. She says she has been a student most of her life, first exploring the parochial school system in New Orleans, then running away to Cornell, and now doing her doctorate at Johns Hopkins. In between Cornell and Hopkins she took a year out and helped excavate a castle in Wales, "where I dug up bits of medieval mutton bones someone had dumped behind the kitchen six centuries ago," and "spent a summer in the graveyards of New Orleans, working for an historical society that was trying to record the names and dates on crumbling tombstones before they became completely illegible." She describes herself as a "closet writer looking for a friendly place to go public." She should come on in; we may not be all that well-educated—sometimes I feel as if I'm the only writer in these anthologies who doesn't have an advanced degree—but we're friendly, especially when you submit stories like this one.

Before the blood was dry, the ballad-sellers had turned Donal Hodge's sacrifice in the Caves of Corresanti into a fine new song. It sold well, like all his adventures. Great bards and half-penny gleemen alike belted out the catchy verses; village harpers from the Hellers to the Plains of Arilinn thrilled their audiences with the horrors Gregori Alton's paxman had endured to save him from the catmen.

But no one sang about the aftermath of Corresanti.

No one sang about a mutilated fighter lying in a dark little room, wishing himself dead; no one sang about a middle-aged nobleman sickening with grief, wishing himself in Zandru's ninth hell rather than alive at such a price.

Three months after Corresanti, Gregori Alton presided over Armida's one hundred and fifty-ninth Midwinter Festival with a face like the damned. No one said a word to stop Gregori when he stalked out of the feast; for the past three months his temper had been uncontrollable.

"Lord Alton is not himself tonight," apologized the household *leronis* to the stranger who sat next to her, a handsome young gentlemen, red-haired and green-eyed. "I think he never will be himself again, actually," she continued. "They're both still half-mad. Locked up in their private little hell—I can't reach either of them."

The stranger nodded sympathetically, and the *leronis* talked on, her usual restraint forgotten.

Gregori walked through the halls of Armida in silence, young Cedric Syrtis-Alton scurrying at his heels, in the paxman's place—in the place that had belonged to Donal Hodge for three decades.

"Wait here," Gregori ordered, when they reached the door of Donal's room.

"A vies ordonnes—" Cedric began, but Gregori was already gone. Gregori slammed the door, stalked across the dark little room, crouched over the broken body in the narrow bed, and wept.

You should have let me die, my lord, Donal said silently, refusing to pity him.

"But you're my paxman, Donal," Gregori said. "I'd be lost without you. I *am* lost without you, *bredu.*"

"I'm a blind cripple!" Donal snarled. He took a deep breath and steadied his voice. "Your paxman is standing out there in the hallway, Greg. Syrtis-Alton is young and strong, the son of a loyal family—you're a living legend to him. Be kind to the boy and he'll serve you well. He's a much more suitable paxman for you than I ever was."

There had been quite a scandal, thirty years ago, when the sixteen-year-old heir to Armida and a young spy, catamite, and assassin from the streets of Thendara swore a solemn oath that bound them together through life and death. But Donal had proved to be an exemplary paxman, and after his self-sacrificing heroism had been trumpeted across the Seven Domains for three decades, hardly anyone but the hero himself remembered that his story began in the gutters of the old city.

"The boy's an idiot," Gregori growled. "Jumps like a rabbit whenever I look at him. He's got a noisy, undisciplined mind, and he's ignorant as sin."

A shadow of Donal's old wicked grin played

across his scarred face. Despite his selfless words, he was delighted to hear that his successor still had no hope of filling his place.

On the other side of the closed door, young Cedric paced back and forth, massive shoulders thrown back, one brawny hand on his sword hilt, feeling desperately clumsy and inadequate.

In the Great Hall below, Armida's *leronis* talked on, the grief that had been pent up in her since Corresanti suddenly freed by the stranger's listening silence. "Gods above and below, just listen to me! Why am I telling you all this?" she asked at last, amazed at herself.

"What are the gods for, if not to listen to the world's sorrows?" the visitor asked in reply, with all the cold fire of nine hells dancing behind his smile.

The God of Choices, the Lord of Good and Evil, brushed the crumbs from his lap, shoved back his chair, and bowed politely.

"Please excuse me, lady," he said. "You wanted nothing from me tonight but my silence. Donal Hodge, however, may be more interested in another gift; in any case, he's ready for me now."

No longer burdened with the illusions of sight, Donal recognized Zandru as soon as the god glided through the closed door of his dark little room.

"Why'd they send you for me, sir, instead of Mother Avarra?" Donal asked, thinking his death was at hand. "Anyway, I can't go with you. I dearly wish I could, but my lord hasn't given me leave."

"Oh, I'm not here to offer you death, Donal Hodge," Zandru replied, sitting down on the edge of his bed. "Damaged as it is, this body of yours is good for another thirty years, at least. You can live on in it for a long, long time, fed and housed by Lord Alton's charity, an old blind cripple in a chair by the fire. But you have another choice. If you wish it, I'll give you Syrtis-Alton's body. He is, as you said yourself, young and strong. No cat-men have clawed out his eyes. He's taken your place. If you take his body, you could serve your lord well for the rest of his days. What's the life of one remarkably foolish boy worth, compared to that?"

"*Zandru!*" Donal whispered, dizzy with longing. He wanted to cry out his acceptance at once, before he lost his one shot at a miracle. But instead he heard a small, quiet voice at the back of his mind, the same voice he had heard for thirty years whenever he was tempted to kill a surrendered man or to strike a prisoner, to take any unfair advantage in order to serve the lord of his heart. "*Greg wouldn't like it,*" the voice said flatly. Gregori Alton was the first person Donal had ever met who did not treat people like things to be used for his own ends—and knowing Gregori had turned a murderous piece of street scum into an honorable man.

"Thank you, sir, for your kindness. But I cannot accept the gift you offer me," Donal said.

"Oh, I know nothing of kindness, child. Or of cruelty either, for that matter," Zandru replied, his green eyes amused. "I'm simply interested in choices. Do you really choose to live and die blind and lame? Think of all you'll feel, the next time raiders sweep down from Aldaran and your Lord Alton rides out to meet them alone, with only a fool of a boy to guard his back. Do you choose to bear that pain?" The god's voice was cool, but Donal felt the room blazing with a light he could not see.

"Yes, I choose to bear that—even that," Donal

answered. His throat burned with the tears he could no longer shed, but his voice was steady.

The unseen light faded.

"Your choice is made," Zandru said. "But I've taken a fancy to you, Donal Hodge. Though you refused my gift, I'll do what I can for you."

Zandru kissed Donal's forehead and was gone.

In another room in the sleeping castle, the Warden of Armida woke in a cold sweat, as the hand of the god released him. He let out a shuddering sigh of relief, looked at the boy sleeping quietly on a pallet across his door, and reached out for Donal's mind. "Bredu, *I just dreamed I murdered the Syrtis-Alton boy,"* Gregori cried silently. *"It was ghastly. I lost my fool temper and snapped his mind. And then—this is the really hideous part—then his eyes opened and you looked at me through them, you lived in his body. You knew what I had done. And I couldn't face that, so I fell on my own sword."*

"Hush, my lord; it didn't happen," Donal said, shaking with sudden gratitude for the strength that had allowed him to refuse Zandru's gift. The god had not lied, when he offered Donal the chance to serve Gregori well for the rest of his life; he simply had not mentioned that the first day of Donal's new service would have been the last day of Gregori's life.

The next morning, Donal found a fine harp lying at the foot of his bed. Such a present from any fellow human creature would have stunk of pity, but even Donal Hodge was not too proud to accept favors from a god. Donal touched the harp's strings very gently, an old skill slowly wakening in his scarred hands. He played himself all the songs he had learned and forgotten long ago about time and change and choices, and then laughed, very softly, at his own months of despair. Although it would never be celebrated by the ballad-singers, that quiet laughter marked a victory as heroic as the most famous triumph Donal had ever won against hordes of shrieking catmen, or rampaging raiders, or unlicensed sorcerers.

Donal tied a strip of black cloth around the empty place where his eyes should have been, tucked Zandru's ebony harp under his arm, and threw open the door of his dark little room. For the first time, he presented his twisted leg, uneven shoulders, and slashed ruin of a face to the merciless light of day. He hobbled slowly down the great staircase, his head held high.

Children and servants and Alton kinsmen came running to see him—to stare at the blind cripple who had once been Lord Alton's famous champion.

"Keep gaping like carp and I'll throw you all in the fishpond, y'damned ill-mannered fools!" Gregori roared, breaking through the mob to give Donal his arm, overjoyed that he had at last found the strength to get on with his life. "What're you all staring at, anyway? Can't you see it's our Donal?"

Blind, lame, and scarred beyond recognition, a harper rather than a warrior, Donal remained what he had always been to Gregori: *bredu.* For thirty more years, Donal walked with a hand on Gregori's shoulder, seeing the fields and plains of Armida through his eyes.

There are no more songs about Gregori or Donal, after the Ballad of Corresanti. In the middle of one of the most turbulent periods of Darkover's long and extremely turbulent history, while the countryside burned and feuds raged all around them, the people of Armida inexplicably enjoyed thirty golden and unpoetic years of peace. Although he knew nothing of cruelty or of kindness, Zandru had taken a fancy to Donal Hodge, and had promised to do what he could for him.

And the gods keep their word.

A Lesser Life

by Patricia Duffy Novak

One of the things I like to see in these anthologies is the return of favorite characters; readers of previous anthologies will recognize Coryn and Arielle from STORMQUEEN in this fine story by Pat Novak.

Pat says, "Unlike most of the writers you publish, I don't have a novel in the works. I am a full-time (twelve-months-a-year) faculty member in the department of Agricultural Economics and Rural Sociology at Auburn University. The job keeps me pretty busy. I also have a husband (James), a going-on-two-year-old (Sylvia), and assorted cats and dogs." Well, she has one thing in common with the rest of us. She has also had some stories in the SWORD AND SORCERESS anthologies and in Marion Zimmer Bradley's Fantasy Magazine, *all of which goes to show that a writer doesn't ever* have *time to write; she* makes *it.*

The road from Thendara to Hali was neither long nor dangerous, but Renata didn't take it. Instead, she waited for her foster son, Ari, at Hell's Blood

Pass, where the road from Thendara to Aldaran linked with the Eastern route to Hali.

Renata looked through the rear window of the coach, at the brooding sky over the trail, and prayed that the winter storms would not descend until after she and Ari had reached Aldaran in safety. She knew she should not have stayed so long in the lowlands, but she had not visited her family in years and had been loath to part from them again. But duty had forced an end to her pleasant sojourn. In little more than a tenday Renata's birth son, Brenton, would be invested as Lord of Aldaran, in the ancient ceremony, and she must be there to hand the rule of the realm to him.

She was not reluctant to end her reign; she found her duties as Warden more of a burden than a pleasure, but when she looked to the future she saw only long, empty years. Hers was to become a life of lesser importance, but still she would not be free from the demands of Aldaran. She must finalize the arrangements for Brenton's marriage and await the birth of his sons—carefully monitoring Brenton's wife to ensure that no girl child of his lived to birth. Brenton carried the deadly Rockraven *laran,* the legacy of his long-dead father; the storm gift, the dreadful *laran* of lightning and anger, the *laran* that flared so easily out of control, killing and maiming without discrimination. A *laran* that was mercifully recessive in males but tragically dominant in females.

She seemed to see for a moment, etched upon the threatening sky, the face of a young girl, lit by lightning flashes. But Renata closed her eyes against the memory, willing back the tears, refusing to relive the old pain. So much death and heartache!

"My lady, they come." The servant who attended Renata inside the coach tapped the frost-misted window. Renata followed the woman's pointing finger and saw the small band of ponies, still little more than dots on the horizon.

Renata sent forth a flicker of thought. *Ari?*

Here, foster mother! And I've brought someone with me. A surprise.

Renata let her consciousness drift across Ari's party and caught a flicker of *laran* other than his, a tantalizingly familiar pattern. She probed a little deeper, but gently, respecting the other's privacy. Then she knew.

Coryn? It must be. And yet, he was so different. Eighteen years since they had touched each other in the link. Eighteen years. But he had been her Keeper. She would never forget that touch.

He yielded slightly, letting her touch a little deeper, but not too far. She felt then the barrier upon barrier upon barrier he had constructed. Even she, with the full measure of the Alton Gift, would have difficulty piercing that resistance. But of course she did not try. *You lend us grace, Keeper,* she said through the link, stiff and uncomfortable at this unexpected meeting. *Z'vai par servu.*

She caught a sudden shiver of emotion from Coryn, remorse or sadness, perhaps; it was gone too quickly for her to say. But through the link his thought carried like a sigh. *Ah, Renata. We were friends once.*

And still are. But she was not certain that she could face Coryn without bitterness. Ari's mother, Arielle, had been dearer than a sister to Renata. In her mind, she saw the image of Arielle, dying at

Castle Aldaran, bearing Coryn's child. Renata tightened her barriers, nearly severing the link.

Foster mother? Ari's thoughts, bright and bold, tickled the edge of her awareness and Renata's spirits lifted.

Yes, my son? Renata felt Coryn drop out of contact, letting her communicate privately with Ari.

I have invited the vai tenerezu *to Brenton's coronation. Are you angered?*

Of course not. He brings honor to us. Coryn of Hali rarely consents to travel abroad. She let her thoughts caress Ari gently, like a warm hug. *I have missed you, my son.*

And I you. Their minds touched lightly, fondly, then separated.

The small band of riders, four in total, came up the last stretch of hill. Without waiting for a servant's assistance, Renata opened the door of the coach and hopped down onto the gravel road.

Ari was the first of the party to reach her. He jumped from his horse and ran the last few feet to Renata, embracing her in a rough, country hug. When he released her and went to greet his old friends among her retinue, Renata took a purposeful step toward the horses, eyes fixed on the one dark-robed figure still astride his horse. The two others of the riding party, body servants by their garb and manner, stood to one side, holding three of the horses, their own and Ari's.

As Renata approached, Coryn dismounted, swinging gracefully from the saddle. He was still whip-thin and agile, but Renata could not see his face, which was hidden in the shadow of the hooded cloak.

Renata held out her hand, and Coryn came to

meet her, brushing the cloak from his face as he walked. His flame-bright hair was barely dusted with silver, and his face still bore the stamp of the Hastur features, the arrogant tilt of chin, the angular cheeks and nose. But had they not touched minds, Renata might not have known who he was. The light had gone out of his eyes, and his mouth was set in impassive lines. Here and there across his cheeks were traces of long-healed scars, not disfiguring, but giving his face a harsher cast than Renata remembered. He had been a handsome youth. He might still be considered a handsome man, but he did not seem fully alive.

He brushed his fingers lightly against hers, the feathery touch of telepaths. "Renata," he said, still unsmiling. "It has been so many years. I should have come to see you before this."

"Better now than never, Coryn," she said. "You lend us grace." She used the familiar inflection and saw a flicker of warmth in his eyes.

For all the years of Ari's life, Renata had blamed Coryn for Arielle's death, forgetting that Coryn, too, had suffered that tragedy, that he had lost his youth and happiness when he lost Arielle. But now, reading that suffering in his face, she could not bring herself to speak a word of the bitter reproach she had held in her heart. Nothing could bring Arielle back to life, and in fairness to Coryn, he had not known until recently that he was the father of Arielle's child. That had been Arielle's decision; she had made Renata promise to send Ari to Coryn only after the boy was grown enough to work in Hali Tower. From what Renata had heard, after Coryn had found out, he had done his best for Ari. For the boy's sake alone, Renata would have made Coryn welcome at Aldaran. But as she gazed at his no longer familiar face, she remembered that Coryn, too, had been her friend. When she herself had worked at Hali, she had loved him like a brother. It was more than time to put aside her anger.

While Ari assisted Renata's retainers in setting up a wayside luncheon, Coryn took Renata lightly by the arm and led her a little away. "I was afraid you would order me gone," he said, with unnerving candor. He had always been an exquisitely sensitive telepath, and Renata did not doubt he had picked up some of her unspoken thoughts, although she had tried to hide them from him.

Renata started to mumble a polite denial, but Coryn shrugged and continued. "It doesn't matter. I would have insisted on coming, whether you wanted me or not. Ari's training is not quite finished. He should not leave the Tower, but he was adamant about attending Brenton's coronation. Ari is very fond of his foster brother."

"Yes," Renata said. "And Brenton loves Ari well. He would have been crushed if Ari had not come. But why shouldn't Ari travel? I remember no such strictures on other Keepers in training."

"Ari is Hastur. Doubly so. He has it from me in the strong form, but also from Arielle, in a weakened fashion—although Arielle herself never manifested the talent. The Di Asturien are close-kin to Hastur, and though Arielle had a little Aillard blood, she passed on to him the Hastur Gift."

Renata shook her head slightly. "And so he did not die in threshold sickness as Hastur outcrosses tend to do. He is fortunate, I would think, to have compatible *laran* gifts from his parents."

"Yes, he is fortunate, and he will make an outstanding Keeper. But perhaps you, who are of the Alton kindred, do not understand the full nature of the Hastur *laran.*"

His face warmed as he talked of the matrix work, the singular passion that had ruled his life. And under the hard lines of the man's face, Renata saw the soft features of the youth he had been. Ari's features. The two were much alike.

"We are source and sink," Coryn said, "Alton and Hastur. You Altons are battering rams, with powerful *laran* energy. We Hasturs produce little energy of our own, but we channel and augment the currents. That's why a properly trained Hastur Keeper can work with enormous matrices, with circles of twenty, even more."

Renata nodded, and Coryn went on. "To control a circle of that size, though, we Hasturs have to learn to open ourselves fully. We are vulnerable until we gain complete control, until we build enough barricades to channel the energy without risks to ourselves. Ari has learned to open himself, but his barriers are not yet fully formed. He should have remained in the Tower for another six months at least."

Renata felt a cold mountain wind tear at the edges of her cloak. She shivered. "Surely, you do not think Ari is in danger at Aldaran? We are at peace. Brenton is handfasted to the daughter of Scathfell. Our old quarrels are to be forgotten with that marriage."

Coryn spread his hands. "Mine is not a precognitive *laran.* I cannot see along that path, lady. I only know that I would have preferred that Ari remain safe with us at Hali. But he would not, so I have come with him."

Although his tone was light, she felt his fear, and she turned to him, her own heart heavy with dread. "Whatever danger you see, cousin, I beg you tell me."

He shook his head and looked at her with eyes that were empty of deceit. "Renata, I would not hide anything from you concerning Ari or the welfare of your Domain. I honestly do not know why I am afraid. Ari is at the heart of my fears; that is all I see."

"I am glad you have come, Coryn," she said, meaning it. "If anyone in the Seven Domains can keep Ari safe, it is you." Then she smiled a little as her fear ebbed. "And it is good to renew old friendships."

She took his hand, not the light touch of a telepath, but a firm clasp. At this touch, thoughts of Arielle flashed unbidden through Renata's mind: bright hair and white face, shadowed eyes, thin hand clutching Renata's, just as she herself held Coryn's now.

And Renata felt, even through Coryn's barricades, a stab of pain so intense she nearly fainted. Then he recovered himself, pulled his hand from hers, and stood white and shaking beside her.

Renata reached out with her *laran,* but Coryn was firmly barriered. Whatever demons drove him, he would keep them to himself.

"Come," said Renata gently. "Lunch is ready. They are waiting for us." He said nothing more to her as they returned.

The journey to Aldaran was uneventful; the weather held mild, and no accidents of any kind befell them. Two days only they spent on the road, arriving at the castle early in the afternoon, as the crimson sun began its slow descent behind the peaks of the Hellers.

Renata almost regretted that the journey had been so brief. Aldaran was full of guests—the families and retainers of the mountain lords, all here to kneel before Brenton and proclaim him the rightful ruler of the Domain—and she was kept busy entertaining them. She saw Ari often enough; the boy had always loved feasting and celebration, but of Coryn she saw scarcely a sign. Sometimes it seemed to Renata that he must be avoiding her, but she could not imagine why.

The morning of Brenton's investiture dawned gray and damp. All through the day, as she met with group after group of her guests, Renata heard the roll of thunder, although the storm was still not upon them by late afternoon. The weather seemed wholly natural, no work of sorcery, but she did not like it. Not since Donal's death at the hands of his own sister, Dorilys, had Renata heard thunder without fear.

Just before the ceremonies were to begin, she summoned her son to a private audience. "In a few minutes," she said, "I will step aside as regent. You know that it has been my desire to see you wed to Allira, the daughter of Scathfell, and so end our old quarrel. But I would not force you to a loveless marriage. The girl has lived here as my fosterling these last several years and seems to have found favor with you." She held up a hand as Brenton started to speak. "No, let me finish. You must tell me now if you wish to wed another. The handfasting need not be binding. We can mend our quarrel with Scathfell some other way.''

Brenton bowed his head briefly, then smiled. ''Mother, I truly wish this marriage. Allira is the bride I would have chosen for myself, regardless of her parentage.''

Renata searched her son's face; the broad brow and freckled nose were like her own, but he had his father's eyes, expressive eyes that telegraphed his thoughts more clearly than his *laran* did. She saw that he spoke the truth.

Brenton took one of Renata's hands and cupped it in both of his. ''Mother, I am glad you are staying at Aldaran. I know it is selfish of me, but I have come to rely on your advice and feel unready to do without it.''

Renata smiled. ''You will be a wise ruler, Brenton. Better than I because you were raised for the role. But I am glad that you doubt. Too much pride and confidence can bring ruin.'' As she spoke these words, she thought of Old Mikhail, her late husband, whose pride had destroyed his daughter Dorilys and cost his foster son Donal his life. Brenton knew only a little of that story; she had allowed him to grow up believing himself the son of Old Mikhail, a legal fiction allowing him to inherit. His true father, Donal Delleray, Mikhail's beloved foster son, had not a scrap of Aldaran blood. And for that reason, too, Renata was anxious for the alliance with Scathfell, to bring Aldaran blood back into the line.

''Go, then, my son,'' Renata said, ''and know that I am well pleased with you. See to your guests. I will join you shortly.''

* * *

Brenton met her at the arched entrance to the Great Hall and conducted her through the crowd. Dressed in padded brocade jacket of russet silk, he looked regal and handsome, older than his eighteen years. Pride swelled in Renata's breast at the sight of him, pride and an aching love. *This is my son, flesh of my flesh, who will be Lord of Aldaran.*

As she greeted the noble guests, she saw Coryn of Hali standing to one side, arms folded across his chest, and face set in cold lines. In that pose, he reminded her of a coiled rock viper, and she saw then why he was feared from one end of the lowlands to the other—a thing she had never understood before. All that *laran* power focused in one man was truly frightening.

She made him a bow, and he returned it, but she could see from his eyes he was in no mood to speak. So she continued through the crowd, holding the arm of her son, until at last they took their places at the long table on the dais. As she seated herself, she glimpsed Ari, taking a paxman's place behind Brenton. Ari's normally expressive face was flat and empty, and she wondered for a moment if he were ill, but there was no time to worry about that now. She would check with him once the ceremony was concluded.

A steward handed Renata the scepter of Aldaran, and as she took it and waved it thrice in the air, the assembled guests fell silent and took their own places at the tables laid out for them. Renata stood. "Today," she said, "I give up regency of Aldaran. I renounce the rule of the Domain." She handed the scepter to the steward, who bowed and knelt before Brenton. "My son," said Renata, "Brenton Aldaran, who has lived among you all his life—"

She broke off, swaying in shock as a *laran* command ripped through her. *Renata, hold Ari! Hold him now!*

It was the voice of Keeper to monitor, and she reacted without thought. "Hold!" she said in command voice, and the entire hall became deathly quiet. She sought Ari's consciousness—but encountered a stranger's mind in control of the boy's body. Reaching out with her Alton *laran,* she held Ari motionless. When she turned and saw what Ari held in his hand, a blaster aimed at the back of Brenton's head, her control almost faltered. Ari's finger twitched on the weapon, but Renata's energy surged in response and she held him firm.

Out of the corner of her eye, Renata saw Coryn dash from the otherwise motionless hall. A moment later she felt an explosion, enormous waves of energy rippling through the hall. She stared at the rock walls of the castle, amazed that they did not crumple into dust. Then she realized that the explosion was of *laran* energy only, as if a large matrix had burned itself out.

Ari fell forward and looked at her with his own eyes. "Mother?" he said. "How come I here?" He stared in horror at the blaster in his hand. "But what is this?"

Renata did not answer. As soon as she saw that Ari was himself, she turned and ran from the room, toward the source of the explosion, tracing Coryn's path down the winding halls of Aldaran.

Blue smoke drifted from the open door of a seldom used room. Renata's heart nearly stopped as she crossed the threshold. There on the cold stone floor lay five men, all of them, as far as Renata could tell, newly dead. Four of them she did not recognize by face, but their red hair and gold and black livery identified them as *laranzu'in* from Scathfell. The fifth clutched a fist-sized starstone in an unshielded hand, and Renata knew then the cause of the explosion. Coryn had extinguished the matrix with his bare hand.

She knelt on the cold stone floor, and examined the dead starstone in Coryn's lifeless fingers. On his hand, which should have been burned to ashes, she could see only the barest trace of a burn. He did not look injured, but Renata could feel no trace of life-force. Even unconscious, such a powerful *laranzu* would have a presence.

From the tableau before her, she could reconstruct what had transpired. The *laranzu'in* of Scathfell had used a matrix spell on Ari, who, as Coryn had warned, was all too open to them. And Coryn somehow had sensed it. He had broken their spell by taking the matrix into his naked hand, killing the traitors at the cost of his own life.

"Oh, Coryn, Coryn," she said aloud and hid her face in her hands as her tears began to fall.

She knelt there alone only a few moments before she heard a commotion in the corridor. She looked up to see Brenton standing in the doorway, flanked by a group of Aldaran soldiers. Then Ari pushed forward, shoving the soldiers aside, and dropped down beside Renata.

"Father!" he cried. "Oh, Lady Renata, no!" He flung himself across Coryn's chest, then hastily pushed himself up, eyes wide. "He breathes! I felt it."

Renata took Coryn's wrist and felt the blood pulsing there. But how could he live and give no hint of presence? "Coryn?" She shook his wrist gently.

Coryn's eyes flicked open and there was intelligence in them, but still Renata felt nothing through the *laran* link. "You live?"

He smiled weakly. "Apparently." The smile faded. "But perhaps I should have died with the others. I am head-blind, Renata. I suppose you already know."

Renata bowed her head, unable to speak, but Ari stared in shock and horror at Coryn, who had been the most powerful telepath in the Seven Domains. "Why, Father? Why would you take a matrix into your bare hand?"

"Those men of Scathfell meant to use you, Ari, as the instrument of your foster brother's death. It would have worked, too, had I not sensed the pulsing of a fifth-level matrix, a thing that should not be unveiled outside a Tower."

He turned to Renata. "This, then, is the plot I feared. And I am glad to have discovered it in time, even if it cost me every scrap of *laran* I possessed."

"Coryn," Renata said, "we cannot know yet that you are permanently head-blind. You have taken an enormous backlash and somehow channeled that energy so that it did not consume you in fire. Perhaps you are merely in shock. I will send for a circle from Tramontana; then we will know."

"Yes," he said, although Renata knew he had already accepted the worst. "But you must finish your ceremony and quickly! You have relinquished your claim, but Brenton has not yet accepted the rule. That is why Scathfell struck just then. Had he succeeded in killing Brenton, there would have been none to gainsay him because Aldaran had no acclaimed ruler. And has not still. Go," he said, "all of you. My body is not badly injured, and I do not need a retinue!"

Renata rose and addressed the guard. "What Lord Coryn says is true. Take Brenton back to the main hall. And you, Brenton, pick up that scepter immediately. We will skip the pretty speeches."

As the others hurried off, Renata turned back to Coryn, who was picking himself slowly off the floor. "Here," she offered, "take my arm. I will lead you to a room nearby, where you can rest. And I will send a servant to you."

"As you will." He leaned against her, and Renata held him. She was not a large woman, but Coryn was a light burden, and she had no difficulty supporting him.

As she returned to the Great Hall, the storm that had been threatening them since morning finally broke and raged against the walls of the castle.

The next days were difficult ones for Renata. First, there was the problem of Scathfell. Loren, Lord Scathfell, had confessed freely to the plot, unabashed, pointing a stout, accusing finger at Brenton. "Aldaran is mine by rights," he said. "It is no secret that Old Mikhail did not father this brat."

"Silence!" Renata ordered, using the command voice again. Then she turned to see what effect this communication would have on Brenton.

"Oh, Mother," he said, when he gained control of his own voice, for Renata's command had affected him, too. "I have known that for years! I caught it from the head of some servant when the threshold sickness first came on me. The woman was relieved that I had no Aldaran blood, which is often fatal at such times!"

"And so you knew all this time," she said, "but it does not matter. Aldaran is yours." She turned to Loren, and gazed into his haughty, defiant face. "Brenton is Mikhail's legal heir. You yourself took a vow to support his claim. Your daughter was to be married to him. Your grandchildren would have ruled Aldaran."

"And now what?" Loren sneered. "Will you unleash another war, lady? For I will not yield Scathfell without a fight."

"You should address yourself to me," Brenton said. "I rule this Domain now. And I would not fight with my future father-in-law."

Scathfell's mouth fell open and he stared at Brenton and Renata. Brenton smiled tightly. "Your daughter," he said to Scathfell, "had no part in your scheming. And she has agreed to wed me with your consent or without it. Aldaran blood will return to the line, whatever you decide to do. You may either pledge faith with me, under truthspell this time, or lose your only daughter."

In the end, Scathfell yielded. And that problem was solved, at least for a while. The treachery would go unpunished, but there would be no war in the mountains, at least not yet.

Then there was Coryn. The circle from Tramontana came, and when they had examined him, the monitor Rosaura spoke with Coryn and Renata. Rosaura had never before met Coryn face-to-face, but she had worked with him many times in the relays and was familiar with his *laran* pattern.

"You are not head-blind, Coryn," Rosaura said, "not in the usual sense. Your *laran* center is not destroyed. When you took that backlash, your barriers shifted and became fixed. Now you cannot lower them to use your *laran.*''

Coryn accepted the news without visible emotion. ''Can anything be done?''

Rosaura shrugged. ''I do not know. I could not broach those barriers, Coryn. It is not my gift.'' She glanced at Renata. ''But there is one among us who might be able to do it.''

Renata put a hand to her throat. ''I? But it has been years since I have used *laran* for anything of importance.'' And she had felt those barriers of Coryn's. ''I might kill him if I tried to force rapport.''

''I would take that risk,'' Coryn said. ''I beg you to try, Renata.''

Renata twisted in her chair. How could she refuse him this when he had saved her son and her Domain? She looked at Rosaura, but that woman kept her face averted and her mind locked tight. She would get no help from that quarter, Renata realized. She would have to make this decision alone.

''All right,'' she said slowly. ''But I do not want to kill you, Coryn. You must trust me. You must not fight the contact.''

''I will trust you, Renata,'' he said. Then he addressed himself to Rosaura. ''Meaning no disrespect, lady, and I am grateful for what hope you have offered me, but I would find it easier to be alone with Renata for this.''

Rosaura nodded. ''It is not for me to be offended, Coryn. You must do what you think is best.''

After Rosaura left, Renata gave Coryn *kirian,* the drug that lowered telepathic barriers, and he lay down, preparing to put himself in a light trance.

''Wait, Coryn,'' Renata said, and he opened his

touching and sharing until she could no longer discern the boundaries of their separate beings. She had lived so long without this type of love that she had forgotten the almost unbearable pleasure such closeness could bring. Now here was Coryn, no longer cold and austere and distant, but warm and vibrant and alive, rekindling a passion she thought had died with Donal.

When at last she and Coryn lay together, warm and content and very near sleep, he kissed her lightly on the brow and said, "You have given me back my *laran.* And something more important besides."

She sat up and touched his face, not wanting to tell him all that she had learned through the link. "You have *laran,* Coryn, but you did not escape that backlash uninjured. You are not as you were. Your barriers have changed and shifted; they will no longer be under your full control. You cannot be Keeper. You should not even work in the circles. Perhaps in a while, but not now."

"I know," he said. "Did you think I did not notice the changes? I suppose I will take myself to Carcosa. I cannot say that my brother Regnald will be overly delighted to see me, but I have no estates of my own."

Because he was still unshielded, she knew what he wanted, what he was too proud to ask. "Stay here, Coryn. For a little while, until you can return to Hali."

She felt in him both the longing and the dread. "I am not an easy man to live with. I have never been polite. I have a terrible temper."

He spoke sincerely, but Renata laughed. "I know

all that. And you sing off-key, too, unless your voice has improved with age."

He touched his heart in mocked surprise. "My voice? How you wound me, Renata! I had hoped to spend my retirement here singing tenor in Aldaran's opera."

She smiled at his jest and then sobered. "I wonder, can you be content to stay here? You are used to the power and excitement of the Tower. Will you be happy with a lesser life?"

He took her hand. "Not a lesser life, *chiya.* A different one, perhaps. I will stay as long as you will have me. I have no desire to return to my old life. That is the one truth I have finally learned, Renata. When I thought I was permanently head-blind, I did not care so much as long as you and Ari were safe. Do you know that Ari had never called me 'father' until he thought me dead? 'Keeper' and '*Vai Tenerezu*' and 'Lord Coryn' but never 'father.' There are more important things than *laran.* And I praise all the gods for finally letting me know that."

Then he closed his eyes, drifting into a gentle, untroubled sleep, and Renata lay beside him, not sleeping, remembering love and loss, and the rage of lightnings across these unquiet mountains. She did not know what the future would bring for her and Coryn, and she was glad of her ignorance, grateful she did not have the precognitive gift.

Coryn's breath was warm against the bare flesh of her arm, and his proud Hastur features were softened in repose. He had laid aside his role as Keeper, and for a little while at least, he was no longer Coryn of Hali, but merely Coryn Hastur of Carcosa, a landless younger son. But Renata was still

Lady of Aldaran, and a thousand niggling concerns demanded her attention. Reluctantly she rose and dressed, but she paused in the doorway to look back at the sleeping man. And she knew that whatever the future brought, she would have this memory of shared joy. That would be enough; she would ask no more.

Summer Storms

by Glenn Sixbury

Glenn says he was "tricked into being a science fiction writer. Well on my way to discovering great literature through my creative writing courses . . ." (ah, that's what did it; I always tell young writers to stay out of those creative writing classes) ". . . (and being bored silly), I discovered an electronic fanzine called FSF/NET. I enjoyed sf but had always been told it wasn't real *literature. Still, I opted to put my literary career in jeopardy by trying my hand at writing it." (Surely you jest; most of the great literature of the ages from* The Iliad *on down was fantasy. What is now called contemporary literature was invented as penny dreadfuls for servant girls who lacked a classical education, and were considered incapable of understanding the great classics—which were fantasy.)*

Currently he is waiting for "the ink to dry on my first novel MISTHAVEN." By the time this anthology comes out it will at least have tried its wings on some editorial desks. (That's a nicely mixed metaphor; I can just see a new novel trying its wings on a crowded editorial desk. Flap, flap!)

Glenn has a wife, Brenda, a five-year-old daughter, Amanda, and a two-year-old son, Brian. His father, Robert Sixbury, suffered a heart attack two weeks before this story was accepted, and Glenn would like to dedicate this story to him. "This one's for you, Dad."

When Mergo saw Mikhael, her face flushed and she pulled herself to her feet, her hands clenched in tight fists. "That was the most disrespectful, uncaring thing I have ever seen you do. Poor, sweet Judith—who *you know* I took care of these past few months and did my best to help—she lay there, waiting to go to her final rest until her uncaring brother, the *Lord* of Aldaran, showed up late to his own sister's funeral. You have shamed yourself."

Mikhael massaged his temples with shaking fingers. A sharp pain had started behind his eyes and was spreading across his forehead. He almost said that Judith no longer cared what he did, but he had retreated to his bedchamber to relax—not to argue with Aunt Mergo. Keeping his voice level, he said, "I did not mean to be late, and I *am* ashamed—"

"Yes, I am *sure* you are." Sarcasm clung to her words like sap to a resin-tree. "I suppose there was some *urgent* matter which needed your attention, some pressing issue that could not wait."

He almost told the old woman the truth: that he had desperately needed to be alone, to regain his inner peace by watching the storm tumble in off the mountain—but if he did, the woman would never let the matter lie! *Perhaps if I just keep quiet,* he thought, *she will leave.*

Mergo was a younger sister of Mikhael's grandfather, the first Lord of Aldaran. She had come to live at Castle Aldaran only within the last year, five years after her brother had passed away. As a young man, Mikhael's grandfather had forged the domain from the Hellers, one of the more fierce wildernesses on Darkover. It had not been easy and none of his family had volunteered to help; but now that the wilderness was almost conquered and the domain was established, what was left of the old family of Aldaran had been eager to set up closer family ties. Mikhael had resented their actions, but he had never cared much for his great aunt.

Mergo pushed her way by him, but instead of heading for the door, she lumbered to the fireplace. Unlike women raised in the Hellers, she was lumpish, marked by sagging rolls of flesh and a puffy face. She had worn her finest red outfit for the funeral and she reminded Mikhael of Darkover's bloody sun, low in the sky, but close as a midsummer sunset.

Mikhael thought of his own appearance: a dark blue tunic under a decorative leather jerkin, velvet breeches, a jeweled belt about his waist, his black curls combed neatly around the hawkish face that he had inherited from his grandfather. *Why do people dress in their best finery for a funeral?*

Digging through a small pouch, Mergo snatched something between her fleshy fingers and held it near the flames. When she turned to face Mikhael, she had a lit cigarette in her hand.

They both knew that Mikhael hated her smoking; he considered asking her to put it out, but she was carrying the cigarette with her hand held wide, as if she wanted to make sure he saw it. *She is just trying to irritate me!*

Mergo stepped close and the foul smoke burned in his nostrils. "If only your grandfather were alive, he would teach you how to be respectful." Pausing, she sucked on the cigarette, and pursing her lips, exhaled a haze of blue-gray that hovered around his head like clouds around a snow-capped mountain. Watching him cough, she smiled. "How you can call yourself Lord Aldaran, I will never know. Sometimes I think my brother's first wife had a fancy for the guards."

"Enough!" Mikhael bellowed. *Aldaran! Always Aldaran!* Since before he had learned to walk, he had been taught his responsibilities to the domain. And it had been for Aldaran that he had married Judith to Donalt.

From the day of the wedding, she had been unhappy, moping about the castle like a little girl, mourning the loss of a favorite doll. He had assumed she only needed time and had persuaded Donalt to stay at Castle Aldaran, feigning the need for help with the domain. He had wanted to explain to his sister that there had been no choice—that her wedding vows sealed two domains, strengthening both. It was political, necessary, something they would bear together—but he had not been available when she had needed him most.

There were always fire-lines to be checked, work on the castle to be supervised, crops to be overseen; he had been gone more in the last two months than he had been home. When he was told that she had taken her own life, it had been easy to convince himself that things would have been different—if only he had been around for her to talk to. But he did not need Mergo to remind him of it. Waving the old woman's smoke away from his face, he said, "I did not ask for my destiny!" Shaking a fist, he added, "Sometimes I wish I was Lord Aldaran no longer!"

Mergo leered at him with her lopsided smile. "Be careful what you pray for," she reminded him, "you may get it!" Then she crushed her cigarette against his bedpost and, swinging in a wide arc, lugged her bloated body from the room and shut the door behind her.

As her footsteps shuffled away, Mikhael scowled out his bedchamber window and watched swirling snowflakes dance in minuets across the frosted glass. *All I want is to be left alone!* But he knew it was not to be. Every available room in Castle Aldaran was packed with guests, and with the mountain snowbound, no one would be able to leave for days.

A knock at the door turned him from the window, but he refused to answer. Mergo could be mistress to Zandru himself. *Hasn't she tormented me enough for today?*

But it was Rafe D'Austerien who cautiously entered the room. Rafe was Mikhael's paxman, his best friend, his *bredu.* Rafe did not have *laran,* but he had seen Mergo retreating down the hallway, and he knew Mikhael well enough to recognize the pain in his eyes. "I should not have come," he said. "I will tell the people waiting there will be no audiences given today. They are unfair even to expect—"

"No, no," Mikhael said, shaking a finger. He had not surrendered his title yet. "Show them to the Great Hall. I will see them."

Rafe hesitated, wanting to argue—to convince Mikhael to relax, if only for today. But he decided the work might distract his *bredu,* and sighing, he followed his Lord's orders.

For the rest of the day, Mikhael welcomed people to his audience hall. Most of the guests came only to express their sympathy, but some used the opportunity to ask a favor or suggest a business agreement. Finally, when the stream of people thinned to a trickle, Rafe stepped into the room. Mikhael assumed he would announce there was no one left to see, but instead, he apologized. "I am sorry. I tried to persuade him that this would be better settled at another time, but—"

"But I would not listen!" a voice boomed from the doorway. Donalt's father, Samels Delleray, swept into the room.

Samels was barrel-chested, his rugged face hugged by a gray-streaked mane of russet hair and supported by a fading auburn beard. In younger days, he had fought the Ya-men alongside Mikhael's grandfather. In recent years, he had become Lord of the domain to the west of Aldaran.

Straightening, Mikhael tried to forget that he had locked his sister into a marriage she did not want at Samels' insistence. "Greetings Lord Delleray. Please give my condolences to your son. I'm sure that he mourns the loss of my sister almost as much as I."

Samels waved the comment aside and answered in monotone, "It is indeed sad, to have such a fine woman for childbearing take her own life before the birth of a single boy."

Mikhael gasped; then muttered, "I don't see what bearing a child has to do with my sister's death."

"But that is the very reason I have come to speak with you, young Mikhael. Less than a year has passed since we agreed to unite our domains in marriage. I rejoiced at the alliance, but it has not come to pass. My son has no bride, I have no grandchildren, and the year is passing quickly."

Mikhael swallowed the bile burning in his throat and wiped the sweat from his forehead with the back of his hand. "I do not understand," he stammered. "Judith is dead. You have come to me on the day of her funeral—to say what? Why are you telling me this?"

Samels looked surprised. "I thought it was obvious," he said. "I am no longer a young man. My son still needs a bride and you have another sister."

"No!" Mikhael leapt from his chair and charged toward Samels. He did not notice the older man stumbling backward, reaching for his blade; he did not see Rafe running toward him from across the room. He saw only Samels' eyes, wide with shocked wonder; and his mouth, gaping open to reveal yellowed teeth. He stretched out his hands, wanting to grab, to squeeze, to hurt. He ignored the sword tip at his chest, but before the weapon had penetrated his tunic, he was pulled away, strong arms around his shoulders, a soothing voice at his ear.

"It's all right, Mikhael," Rafe was saying. "It's just a misunderstanding."

Mikhael heard the words but did not heed them. He struggled against the hold, but Rafe refused to let go, squeezing his arms white against his body. "Leave!" Mikhael snarled. "Go. Get out of this castle. Get out of Aldaran!"

Samels closed his mouth, his shock turning to anger. Rafe tried again, his tone calm, controlled. "The storm, *bredu.* He cannot leave. He is our guest."

The storm. Mikhael latched onto the thought. He saw the hard-driven snowflakes and felt the biting cold of Hellers winds. "The storm," he mumbled, and stopped struggling. Sensing the change, Rafe released him. Smoothing his clothes, he said, "Of course I did not mean it, *Dom* Samels. No one could survive outside the castle walls this night."

"No, son of Aldaran, you are wrong." Samels eyes gleamed with fixed determination and his mouth was tight and tense when he spoke. "I have seen your hospitality, and I do not care for it. You are young. I have lived in these mountains at mid-winter with only a cave for shelter. I will be fine. It is *your* safety that should concern you now."

His boot squeaked against the marble floor as he spun and strode quickly from the room. "No," Rafe said and started to follow, but Mikhael grabbed his arm.

"Let him go. He is a stubborn old man. If he wants to die in the storm . . . it does not sadden me."

Rafe shook his head. "He will not die, Mik-hael—not that one. He will be back." Turning to stare at his Lord, he added, "*Bredu,* do you understand what you have done?"

Mikhael considered it, tempted for a moment to pursue Samels and apologize. Then he nodded. "I know what I have done, Rafe, but I cannot be sorry for it. To him, Judith was nothing more than breeding stock. Worse, he had come back to complain and ask for a replacement—like a rider leading a newly purchased horse, lame from abuse.

"My only regret is that I did not kill him," he added, "or that he did not kill me."

* * *

The storm's intensity had decreased in the two days since Lord Delleray had left, but heavy drifts continued to gather inside the battlements and wind still rattled the shutters.

Mikhael had no way to know if Lord Delleray was as good at surviving in the Hellers as he had claimed or if he had died before reaching the bottom of the Castle Road.

But Mikhael was certain: *If he lives, he will be back.*

Once again, Aldaran must be defended: The responsibility weighed on Mikhael like snow on a mountain cliff waiting for an avalanche. From his first moments as Lord Aldaran, he had been fighting to retain the title and keep the domain intact. His stamina had worn as thin as an old man's hair.

A daydream, a sweet imagination, filled his mind. He saw himself as a farmer, living in a little cottage, working the land, a good healthy woman and a tangle of children at his side—with no politics and no responsibilities except to crops and family.

Suddenly a noise interrupted the vision, a soft creaking of wood and metal. Mikhael turned and found Elholyn in his room, a bashful smile on her lips.

She had come through the wall, through a secret door similar to the ones installed in most rooms of the castle. Turning away, she pushed on the left side of the massive door, and it spun on the great metal axle that ran through its middle; her end twisted back into the wall while the other end came forward from inside the tunnel. When both ends met the walls, the lines of the door blended perfectly with the room's decorations and the door disappeared.

Except for a handful of well-trusted architects and

builders, Mikhael and Elholyn were the only ones that knew the doors existed. "At first I didn't like these," she said, "but on nights like this, they are convenient."

"*Convenient* is hardly the word I would use," Mikhael said, thinking back five years to when the old Keep of Aldaran had fallen and the bandit Beltran had locked Mikhael and his sisters in a bedchamber. Their father had died in that battle. Less than a year later, their youngest sister, Lori, had died giving birth to Beltran's child as their mother had died giving birth to her. With Judith gone, the only member left of the original family besides Mikhael was Elholyn, Judith's twin. "With the tunnels and doors in place," he stated flatly, "no one will ever be able to lock us in again."

Elholyn shook her head and her long blonde hair splayed across her shoulders. She wore only her long, heavy night shift and a woolen pair of bed socks, and when she walked to Mikhael's bed, she lay down, curling her body around a pillow. "It's sad, isn't it?"

Mikhael walked to the bed and sat down beside his sister. "What's that?"

Blue eyes turned to stare at him. They were cold and empty, lacking the fire they usually carried. "It's sad that we're all that's left. I miss everyone."

Mikhael wanted to say something comforting, but the words stuck in his throat as he remembered a midwinter evening long past when the family was whole; they ate spice cakes around the fire and sang happy songs.

"Now you are gone, too," Elholyn continued. "Oh, you are still here, but the life is gone from your heart. So often now, I feel like I am all alone."

Mikhael jumped up from the bed and moved several paces away, suddenly uncomfortable. "I cannot help it," he said. Thoughts of Judith tormented him; visions of the night he had come home and had been greeted at the gate with tears and hushed voices. "I did not mean to do it, Elholyn. I would give anything, *anything* to bring her back."

"And you think *I* would not? Do you believe you are in this alone?"

"Why not? It was *my* responsibility. I am Lord Aldaran. I forced her to marry someone she did not wish to marry; I am the one who made her miserable."

"You did what you had to do."

Mikhael started to protest, but Elholyn hushed him with her hand. "Mikhael, you are *Lord Aldaran.* I know, I know; of late women are told they do not understand politics or the hardships of responsibility, but when I was little, times were different. Grandfather used to tell me of the times when women chose their own husbands *and* their own lovers. And he spun tales about how he had come to the Hellers and why he had wanted to create a new domain. He said that the people of this world were growing, but where he came from, they were growing in the wrong direction. There are always the bad ones, he said, the ones that want to lead people down the easy road, the wrong road. He just wanted to lead a few down the right one."

Mikhael wanted to argue with Elholyn, but her soft tone of her voice caressed his ears, and he no longer felt like Lord Aldaran. It was as if he were a young child again, a little brother listening to his older sister. "What do you think Grandfather would have done?"

Elholyn smiled gently and stood up. "He would have said you did what all the Lords of Aldaran do: what they think is best for the Domain." She raised up on her toes, gave Mikhael a soft hug, and kissed him on the cheek. Pushing the wall in, she swung the secret door open.

"Elholyn," Mikhael said, watching her turn gracefully at his voice. "I do not remember Grandfather saying any of those things."

Elholyn smiled faintly and let her gaze wander slowly around the room. "It is what he tried to say, when you listened closely."

Even after Elholyn disappeared, a warm glow lingered in the room, and Mikhael slept peacefully for the first time in days.

After pausing at the rear corner of the battlements, Mikhael headed toward the front of the castle. A penetrating north wind whipped around his shoulders, and he pulled his night cloak tight against his body. For three weeks, he had been taking similar nightly walks. Except the time Elholyn had come to his room, he had not slept well since Judith's death; the walks helped him to relax.

When he came to the front of the castle, he stopped. Looking out over the moonlit countryside, he wished once more that his grandfather were alive, or his father. They would know better what to do. To Mikhael, they were still the real lords of Aldaran.

In the distance, he could see the first hint of sunlight as an eerie glow at the horizon. Fascinated, he watched the start of another sunrise, awed by the crimson beauty of Darkover's dawning sun. But when the first blood-red light of daybreak drifted into the valley, he tensed, his eyes straining against the brilliant morning light.

An army was trudging slowly up the castle road. Samels Delleray had returned.

Mikhael, his starstone in hand, waited for the others to arrive. When he had seen Samels' forces, he had immediately called a meeting of the Aldaran circle. He recalled too well how the old Keep of Aldaran had fallen to Beltran, five years before. The bandit had marched toward the main gate, his offensive hopeless, the castle's defenses at the ready. Then the red-haired leader had retrieved the starstone from beneath his cloak and within moments, had done what no army could; he had killed all but a few of the men defending the Keep and had destroyed the outer wall, allowing his band to storm through without resistance.

The Aldaran circle had always met in the Sun Room because of its cheerfulness. Plants dotted the window sill, intricate tapestries decorated the walls, and a circular, delicately crafted crystal crowned the mantlepiece. Judith had loved this room and had come here often when she was troubled.

Aunt Mergo had overseen the room's decoration, like the crystal above the fireplace. Exquisite and fragile, Aunt Mergo had brought it back herself on her last visit to the southern flatlands to see the other, older branch of the Aldaran family. Mikhael still did not understand how someone so cruel could create an atmosphere so pleasant.

Elholyn arrived first, then six-fingered Stephen—one of his grandfather's original servants—and young Petran, a stable boy whose *laran* talents had been discovered last spring. Judith's absence was a gaping hole noticed by everyone.

When everyone was seated and ready, Mikhael tugged on a leather thong around his neck and pulled his *laran* stone from beneath his tunic. Removing its protective silk wrappings, he looked deep into the fires that danced within. A visiting *laranzu* had once named the blue gems starstones and had explained how crystals could be used to amplify power. Mikhael knew only that the starstones were a necessity—a way to protect the domain and his family.

Mikhael relaxed, allowing his thoughts to tap the energy of the crystal. His awareness increased, and he sensed Elholyn's presence in the room; but it was weak, as if she were far away. Concentrating harder, he tried to imagine walking toward Elholyn, but a sticky cloud of blue-gray smoke blocked his way.

Mikhael imagined a storm to blow the smoke aside, and an image of Elholyn reached out to him, taking his hand in hers. *I am struggling, Mikhael.* Elholyn's thoughts were still weak, like a flag wavering in a stiff breeze. *I do not know if we can do this.*

We must, Mikhael thought, knowing Elholyn would hear the words in her mind as he had heard hers. *Remember Beltran. We cannot let it happen again.* He lent his power to Elholyn's, trying to strengthen the bond; but the harder he pushed, the stronger the resistance became.

For a moment, Elholyn reached the others: he felt the strong, cool presence of old Stephen and Petran's lighter, shaky tangle of thoughts. Then Stephen and Petran dropped out of contact, and he heard Elholyn's mental cry of anguish: *It is too hard!* Her *laran* was the strongest, so she had always acted as the central point, the Keeper; but even she could not hold everyone together.

Mikhael felt as if his mind might shatter at any moment; but he forced the last of his energy into the bond, and slowly, the resistance eroded. The power started to flow, but it was wrong—terribly wrong.

Mikhael! It hurts! Elholyn's thoughts were shards of glass, cutting him, and he tried to stop, to break the forced contact, but he could not, and suddenly they were on a gray, featureless plain, a storm rumbling toward them, sending jagged bolts of lightning across the endless sky, and then twisting into great blue streaks of energy that whipped into a wild tornado, trapping them, frosting their hands and faces even as it burned across their minds like a Hellers fire at midsummer. Mikhael heard the terror of Elholyn's soul screaming out to him, but he could do nothing; in seconds their minds would evaporate, flashing up like a wick without a candle.

Then an image of Elholyn's face, pained and desperate, wavered close to his. Her mental cries of anguish had stopped, and she was concentrating, reaching out for the blue lightning. He understood then what she intended to do and tried to move toward her, to stop her; but he was too weak—drained and exhausted.

Elholyn's fingers closed around the lightning and she pulled it to her, drawing all of it into her body until cyan flames danced about her head and shoulders and her eyes glowed like starstones. She screamed as the power flowed through her, but fighting it, she bent it to her will, channeling it out again, directing it into the heart of the storm. It erupted in a powerful explosion, and blinding blue light struck Mikhael, its percussion slamming into his consciousness.

As the gray plain faded away, the blue light darkened to black.

Mikhael awoke, his head pounding like the drums of the forge-folk. Dazed, he opened his eyes and sat up, shaking. He was no longer in the Sun Room—someone must have carried him to his bedchamber—and the shadows stretched wide across the room from the west: The sun was setting.

Rafe entered and forced a smile. "I thought I heard you rousting about in here." He had tried to make his voice sound cheery, but it cracked, the same way it had done the night he'd greeted Mikhael at the gate with the news about Judith.

"Elholyn is dead, isn't she?"

"No, no," Rafe said, shaking his head, "but she is not yet out of danger. If you are able, you should come to see her."

"I am able," Mikhael said, but when he stood, he grabbed his head and collapsed back onto the bed. "Perhaps I do need help, though. I feel horrible."

Wrapping one of Mikhael's arms around his neck, Rafe half-carried, half-walked him to Elholyn's room. As they went, he tried to answer Mikhael's unspoken questions.

Rafe spoke of Samels first. His army had camped just out of bowshot. They seemed content to wait until dawn to attack, but Rafe admitted that shortly after they had set up camp, some of the men guarding the walls had been assailed by demons that appeared out of midair and taunted them. Mikhael's fear that this battle would be fought with *laran* had been vindicated.

The news of Elholyn was worse. No one knew what had happened, but she had not regained consciousness and several parts of her body were burned. Her hands looked the worst, but the healers were worried more about burns inside her body. No one was certain yet, but because of the location of the injuries, the castle midwife had been summoned, and she had agreed with the healers. All of Elholyn's reproductive organs were damaged beyond healing.

Rafe led Mikhael into Elholyn's room. Several people were standing around Elholyn's bed, but the one that Mikhael noticed first was Mergo. The old woman turned to glare at him. Ignoring her, he moved toward Elholyn unsteadily, one hand still on Rafe's shoulder.

But as he reached the bed, Mergo wedged her wide body between Mikhael and his sister. "Haven't you done enough?" she snapped.

Mikhael tried to move around her, but Mergo stayed in front of him easily. "I have always known you did not have the strength to defend this place, but did you have to bring your sister down with you? Wasn't Judith enough?"

"Listen, you old banshee," Rafe said, stepping in front of Mikhael, "he has come to see his sister. You will leave him alone, or I will personally throw you over the castle's front wall."

Mergo's eyes flared, but when Rafe reached for her, she backed away. Squeezing Rafe's elbow, Mikhael pulled him back. "No," he croaked. "She's right. I pushed Elholyn too far. She knew something was wrong, but *I* forced it, and we created some kind of an uncontrollable back flow. I could do nothing, but Elholyn managed to throw us clear. If she hadn't, we both would have died.''

Peering around Mergo, Mikhael saw his sister, her hands bandaged, her body covered by a light sheet. She was asleep and lying so still she might have been dead. Mikhael's stomach tightened into knots and he struggled to breathe. Aunt Mergo was right: First he had killed Judith—now he had almost killed Elholyn. Tears started at the corners of his eyes, and spinning away on unsteady legs, he fled the room, batting away Rafe's attempts to help him.

When Mikhael's head finally cleared, he found himself at the castle's front wall. The sun had set, and thick storm clouds covered the evening sky. Samels' camp was still visible, humped beside the road like a tick swollen on a horse's flank.

Mikhael saw now that this was what he had often hoped for: If he gave Samels the castle and the Domain, he would be Lord Aldaran no longer.

He shuddered.

The thoughts he'd had once—about being a poor farmer with just a wife and children to worry over—seemed as silly now as a night's pleasant dream seemed at mid-morning.

Clouds rolled in from the north, and the breeze bit at Mikhael's face. A storm was surely coming; the battle might be fought in snow—that is, if Samels' *laranzu* allowed a normal battle to be fought at all.

Using a trick he had learned as a child, Mikhael pulled out his starstone to check on the approaching storm. Looking deep into the crystal, he projected his thoughts out beyond the castle walls, out toward the approaching storm.

The realization dawned on him slowly, a long lost memory, a childhood recollection not remembered for years: He was using his *laran*. There was no thick, sticky smoke, no resistance. *We could form a circle!* Forgetting the storm, Mikhael ran toward the main building. He needed to find Stephen and Petran immediately!

This time, they did not meet in the Sun Room. Mikhael ordered Stephen and Petran to come by stealth to the stables, and then sneaked there himself. There was no way to know what had went wrong before, but he refused to risk letting it happening again.

While he waited for Stephen and Petran to slip away, Mikhael watched the approaching storm and realized there was power in the rolling clouds and the biting wind. Slowly, an idea took shape, and by the time Stephen and Petran joined him on the straw-covered floor, he knew what they must do.

This time, nothing kept them from bonding together, and Mikhael found that he could control the circle's power almost as well as Elholyn. He sent their awareness out into the night, and by reenforcing the storm that already existed, he increased its natural potential, turning a small spring snowfall into a full blizzard, with high winds and driving snow that would rival any storm at midwinter.

The work was strenuous, and shortly before morning, Mikhael could no longer hold the circle together. Letting it dissolve, he led the way back into the castle. Food and hot drinks were summoned from the kitchens, and after they had eaten, Rafe arrived with good news: When the storm worsened in the night, most of Samels' men—realizing they could not survive in the open—had surrendered, and only minutes ago, men from the castle had captured Samels without a struggle!

The battle was over and Aldaran had won.

Mikhael cleared four steps at a time on his way up the stairs, and he slipped on the slick stones at every corner. He had just come from Elholyn's room. She was still alive, but they had said she had almost died shortly before dawn. A healer had heard her choking as he approached her chamber, and had found Mergo standing over Elholyn, trying to *save* her. With the healer's help, they had managed to get her breathing normally again.

The news had confirmed what Samels Delleray had said at his surrender. After he had been given food and a change of clothes, Mikhael had greeted him in the audience chamber. The old man had feared he would be put to death, but Mikhael had accepted his apology and had told him he was free. At that point, the astonished old warrior had broken down, shouting, "I should have never trusted the old witch!" Then he explained that after Mikhael had thrown him out of Aldaran, he had realized how callous his actions had been. "Then the message arrived," he went on, "warning me about you." His face wrinkled up in anger and he paced, furious. "It said that you were going to attack me, take away my domain, make it a part of Aldaran; and gods help me, I believed it. It was foolish, but the old witch said that she had warned me because I had been one of her brother's closest allies. And she had claimed that if I attacked immediately, she could insure a painless victory—something about a *laran* crystal she had."

Now as Mikhael ran toward the Sun Room, he unraveled the threads of events since Judith's death. Everything that had gone wrong was traceable to one person: *Mergo!* Mikhael no longer believed that Judith's death was a suicide. She had been upset for weeks and when they had found her in the Sun Room, a scribbled note clutched in her palm, everyone had assumed—

As he ran down the hallway, images danced through his mind: Judith, lying white in death; Mergo, smoke rising past a sneer on her pudgy, wrinkled face; Elholyn, blue-gray clouds and lightning around her. Turning, he came to a stop in the Sun Room, his gaze searching the mantlepiece—the crystal was gone! Spinning, he ran for Mergo's room, fear clutching at his stomach with a bony hand. If the old woman had already retrieved the crystal, she might have fled the castle; but when he burst into her room, Mergo was calmly standing by her bed, carefully placing clothing into a traveling bag.

Mikhael stopped in the doorway, hands on his knees; panting hard, he scanned the room. "Looking for this?" Mergo asked and pulled the Sun Room crystal from her bag.

Mikhael noticed now that the crystal seemed strange; it hurt his eyes to look at it. Then Mergo twisted a piece on it and a low hum started between Mikhael's ears, slowly moving up behind his eyes and giving him a headache. Mikhael started toward his aunt, rubbing his forehead. "Put down the crystal, Mergo. I understand everything now; you are only making things worse for yourself."

"Actually," Mergo said, the crystal held before her, "you have that quite backward." Reaching down between her breasts, she touched something, and a blinding pain shot through Mikhael's head, hitting him so hard he went to his knees. Too late, he realized he should not have come alone. The pain worsened, and Mikhael fell forward, sprawling uncontrollably on the floor. Gritting his teeth, he groaned and rolled over to his back. Mergo lumbered across the room to loom above him, the slightest hint of a smile on her fleshy face.

"You never have been very bright, you know. Even now, you do not understand." Mikhael's vision had blurred from the pain, but when she bent closer, he saw the blue fires of a starstone between her fingers. She continued, "I had wanted to make it look like an accident. After all, the loyal knights and servants of the castle would not have taken kindly to my killing the three of you. Now, I suppose it doesn't matter. With the last of my brother's descendants gone, the real Aldaran family—not some bastard branch of it—will take the domain by force, if necessary."

As Mergo talked, her concentration lessened and the throbbing in Mikhael's brain subsided slightly. Able to move now, he tried to crawl away from Mergo, wanting only to get away from the crystal and the pain.

"It is quite fortunate, really," Mergo said, staying a step behind him, "that you have never been trained to use your *laran*. It's a science now—although they still make mistakes. This crystal should have killed the whole lot of you yesterday. I admit it came close, but not close enough. Still, I had the threshold set quite high; the crystal acted only as a damper up to a point. Until you pushed it, it was harmless. That's the funny part.''

Mikhael touched a wall with his fingers, but he was unsure which one. His vision was still blurred and he trembled uncontrollably. He had never believed anything could cause so much pain.

''This crystal has other properties. For example, it is tuned to me. When you use *laran*, it distorts and amplifies the mental energy and feeds it back, and you send it again, and it feeds it back, until you overload and break the link. If I use mine, the patterns match exactly; it stills amplifies the energy, but I can control it, directing it as I wish. Of course, getting and keeping a crystal like this in balance is a very delicate operation; it takes a great deal of effort, but you would be surprised what some *laranzu'in* will do for a piece of a domain.''

Mergo turned away and set the crystal on a chair by the wall. Immediately, Mikhael's pain lessened a little, and he pulled himself into a sitting position.

Mergo had pulled out her tobacco pouch, and was making a cigarette. ''You know,'' she said, ''I just had an idea. Perhaps I should not kill you; I could simply burn away your intelligence. You would still be alive, and I, as your loving aunt, could care for you.'' Mergo lit her cigarette, and blew a puff of smoke toward the ceiling. ''Of course, I would need to bring up one of my nephews to run the domain, but with your brain turned to spice cake, I don't think any of the castle staff would complain. What do you think?''

Mikhael's head had partially cleared, and he found that his back was resting against the room's secret door. Trying to figure out how he could use it to escape, he noticed that if he pushed his end of the door in, the other end would come out and just might catch a piece of the chair the crystal was sitting on.

After blowing a puff of smoke in Mikhael's face, Mergo set her cigarette on the chair beside the crystal. "Since you don't seem to have an opinion, I have decided for myself." She reached for the crystal, adding, "And I think you are better *almost* alive than you are dead."

Mikhael had no time to wonder if his plan would work. He heaved all of his weight into the door, and it twisted open. His head hit the stone floor of the tunnel, and Mergo squealed as the crystal tumbled from the chair. He smiled, hearing the tinkle of glass; then groaned as the crystal rolled across the wooden floor.

The crystal had not broken!

Mikhael's head still throbbed, but he half-stumbled, half-crawled into the secret passageway. He pushed at the door with his legs, but missed. Then Mergo was beside him, violently kicking his ribs with her thick traveling boots. "That was stupid," she sputtered, her huge chest heaving in great gulps of air. She held the crystal over him and promised, "I will make this as painful as possible."

Mikhael rolled over to his back. Mergo caressed her starstone. Her face was relaxed and expressionless. She concentrated on the crystal, and he instinctively held up his arms—as if he could ward off the force of the blow.

But it never came.

When Mergo activated the crystal, her face contorted in agony. Stumbling, she fell against the wall, blue sparks dancing around her head. Her eyelids fluttered and her mouth opened in a silent scream.

She crumpled, her heavy body thudding as it sprawled across the floor. The crystal fell from her limp hand and rolled to a stop by Mikhael's feet.

Elholyn's hands had almost healed; there would always be scars, but at least she would be able to use them. Mikhael had delayed the burning until she was well enough to come to the stables. She—most of all—had the right to do it, and when everyone had gathered around the smelting pit, Mikhael gave her the signal. Her face, sober, she pitched the crystal into the hot coals and stepped back beside Mikhael. "Are you sure it will be harmless after this?"

"Yes," he said, putting an arm around her shoulders. "The *laranzu* assured me the structure inside the crystal was artificial. When it is melted, it will simply be glass again—as harmless as any window pane."

Rafe stepped next to them. "Why would anyone invent such a device?"

"It was created originally as a damper," Mikhael answered. "It simply dissipated *laran*. When Mergo had the structure modified to amplify and distort all *laran* except her own, she created the danger. It's too bad, really. Some of the internal structure was destroyed when I knocked it onto the floor, or I might have had the *laranzu* change it back into a damper."

Elholyn elbowed his ribs—hard. "No, you wouldn't have."

"I suppose not, but I still think such a device

could be useful for creating a place free from *laran.*''

''I already have one,'' Rafe said. Grinning broadly, he tapped a finger to his forehead.

Conscience

by Alexandra Sarris

Alexandra Sarris is a California-licensed psychotherapist who lived in Berkeley and Oakland for over 22 years, then moved to Santa Fe a year ago. She was thinking she might like to move back, when the Oakland firestorm caused her to reconsider. She likes "to run workshops and classes on the Inner Child, the emotional causes of weight and finding the Goddess inside us, but I also seem to be finding myself in demand as an exorcist and helping people deal with cults." She agrees with me that most of the most exciting work in the fantasy field is being done by women. I don't think there's much argument that it's been that way since Mary Shelley created Frankenstein; and look at who's been writing most of the pulps since the 50s. These statements can be documented, in spite of the trendy "Women's Lib" types who try to tell us that women in science fiction and fantasy all started in the 60s with Joanna Russ and Ursula LeGuin. 'Taint so and I can prove it. . . . Besides, I was there—'writin' pulps with the best/worst of 'em.

"But he must have some!" Lady Armina protested, her voice clearly reflecting confusion about her young son, Vardin.

Dorian Aillard looked at her, a puzzled frown wrinkling his thin, delicately sculpted face. Her reaction was quite unexpected. After all, he was a trained *laranzu* and knew what to look for when testing Vardin for *laran.* The boy had shown a small gift, but nothing that could be useful in the Towers.

"I'm sorry, Lady Armina," Dorian said gently. "I know we hope that our children will have received our gifts (especially since we have been so assiduous in our breeding programs, he thought.)

"No, no," Armina objected, her voice taking on a sharp edge. "I can't believe you've tested him right." Dorian suppressed a sigh. Another hysterical mother, he thought briefly; but she must have caught the essence of his thoughts because she tightened her lips and glared at him. "Then please explain to me what is going on when he goes into a trance. And I know what a trance is, thank you," she snapped before he could say anything. "Often when he's lying down alone, he goes away, and it takes much to rouse him."

"Maybe he's sleeping heavily," Dorian offered, admitting to himself that he was trying to appease the woman.

"I know the difference between heavy sleep and a trance," she retorted. "That's why I wanted him tested. He's been monitored for any kind of brain illness, and there is nothing wrong. It's as though he were out of his body."

A icy thread of danger coiled in his abdomen. Could the boy be going into the overworld, untrained as he was? "But I tested him," he argued, half to himself and half to the boy's mother. He couldn't be wrong, could he—although he knew of a number of instances when *laranzu'in* had missed deep-hidden *laran.* "Did Vardin ever experience any threshold sickness?"

She shook her head. "Not so you'd really notice. Not like Armand." Armand was her first son, now at Neskaya. He was one of their strongest *laranzu'in,* powerful and deadly. Dorian had a great respect and wariness for Armand Leynier. His skill was protean—and so was his temper. But Vardin was an entirely different story.

"Sometimes *laran* skips a child," he ventured, but she shook her head.

"I know something's going on with him," she said firmly, "even though he tries to hide it from me." She paused and leaned toward him. "Four out of my five children have *laran,* so having one without it does not concern me," she added with hint of asperity. "But there's something odd with Vardin. Please test him again. Trust in my own mother's sense."

Dorian bowed his acquiescence and departed for his room. He needed some time to himself to prepare. The symptoms sounded like VArdin was going into the overworld, but the boy didn't seem to use his starstone to focus with. He had been tested for *laran* but showed little more than minimal telepathic ability. And yet. . . . Dorian resolved to keep his thoughts more hooded. If Vardin did have *laran,* the less the boy knew of his intent, the better.

In his room, he took out his matrix and focused on its crystalline blue facets. Lady Armina believed her son was doing something in trance. He felt the familiar feeling of well-being as it drew him into its core. He let his mind expand throughout the whole house and gradually the whole estate, searching for he knew not what. Perhaps just an irregularity in the pattern, a disjunction of some sort, something that might indicate the presence of an unsuspected talent. He could spot instantly those people who had power. Armina and her husband Curran radiated *laran.* He noted a few nodes of greater intensity than normal—probably *nedestro* children or servants with some degree of *laran.*

A sudden unease tingled through his frame. Something *was* there, but as he tried to pinpoint its location, it vanished; and everything remained as quiescent as before. He slipped back into waking consciousness and covered his matrix. Dorian intended to find out what was going on with Vardin. No longer would it be a simple test; he would probe into the boy's very cells if he had to.

He summoned a servant to request Vardin's presence in his room. As a *laranzu,* he felt the awesome challenge of that position and he reached for the strength to focus his will on this task. He centered himself, breathing steadily and slowly, as calmness radiated through him.

There was a tentative knock.

"Come in," he said loudly, and the door opened. A sharp-featured boy of about sixteen years slid into the room. The dark auburn hair falling into his narrow, pale face gave him an air of furtive distrust. Dorian motioned him to a chair across from him, and the boy sidled up to it and sat down tentatively on the edge, as if ready to bolt. The last interview, he reflected, had been quite different. Then Vardin had been nonchalant, even indifferent. This time he seemed concerned. Perhaps he suspected something of what Dorian intended to do.

"*Vai laranzu,*" greeted the boy hesitantly with a thin, tentative smile. His gaze slid away from Dorian's toward the floor. Dorian took a deep breath and let his inner calm radiate out of him and fill the room. As he did so, he noticed Vardin's nervousness gradually drain away so that the boy sat back in the chair and gave a heaving sigh. He seemed to palpably relax.

"Vardin, I'd like you to tell me about your trance," Dorian said in a low but penetrating voice, the voice that he used to coax unwilling admissions from reluctant people he often questioned when they were brought to Hali. Sometimes the results were not pleasant for them.

The boy gasped and then muttered, as though under a spell, "I go away into my mind."

"What do you mean," urged Dorian, giving Vardin a mental nudge.

"I—I dream of far places where I'd like to go." In his mind Dorian caught the image of the boy's imagined Dry Towns and the possibility of riding there under a hot sun; then a fragment of what his concept of being beside the ocean was like. Aha, Dorian decided, Vardin's *laran* is not much more than a strong ability to daydream, to get deeply lost in his own mind. After a few more moments, he released the boy from his mental control, and Vardin sagged in the chair.

"What happened?" he asked in bewilderment.

"You went away," Dorian said gently. "Do you like to do that?"

Vardin's face lit up. "Oh, yes!" he agreed fervently. "I'd like to travel far away," and he shrugged, "but I don't know that I ever will. I'm not really strong enough for hard riding and work."

Ah, yes, thought Dorian. He recognized this type—the weakling son, overpampered until he could barely survive outside the estate, much less the domain. "Well, I'm sure there will be a way," he said soothingly. He spent some time talking with the boy about bringing his vivid daydreams to life before reporting to Lady Armina.

A boy caught in his own vivid daydreams: it was a simple explanation which she could accept. Dorian recommended that the boy take some arms practice so that he could begin building up the strength that would allow him to make his dreams come true. Although outwardly agreeable, he could see her flinch at the thought of helping her weakling son get free of her. She had done her duty well with the other children. They were successfully placed in the Towers or well married. All she had left now was her next-to-last child.

He left her solar and went into his own room. His work was definitely done here, and he'd leave for Hali in the morning—if the storms held off. He yearned to be back at the Tower with its womblike closeness and the intensity of his fellow matrix workers. There was something exhilarating and powerful about taking the threads of their energy into his hands and welding them into a force that he could guide and lead. His hands itched for the familiar pressure of his circle.

When he woke, he discovered that a storm had indeed sprung up overnight, howling and slashing outside his windows, blowing hard pellets of snow across the rolling hills. In a way, he appreciated the delay because he had been on the road for many weeks, traveling across the war-torn lands, searching for likely candidates for the Towers and, of course, assessing the strengths and weaknesses of the battling domains. This journey had taken its toll, and he needed some relaxation. So whether he wanted to leave or not, he would be spending a few days at least with the Leyniers. It might be a good opportunity to help Vardin work on realizing his daydreams, perhaps even teach him a few tricks that would help direct his feeble *laran.*

First, though, he wanted to check in with Hali Tower, to let them know where he was. He took out his starstone and concentrated on its blue crystal depths, projecting an image of the matrix circle at the tower. Suddenly, a sharp clear image sprang forth. His friend, technician Rakhal Storn, greeted him with a grave face. Dorian could feel the tremors of fear radiating from him.

"What?" he demanded. "What has happened?"

"It was Erlanna this time." Dorian inhaled sharply. One of their best new *leroni.* "Just two days ago."

"How many does that make?"

"Fifteen." Dorian shuddered with horror. Somehow, matrix workers were dying, and no one knew why. Hali had been hit once before, while Neskaya had had the worst—seven losses in as many weeks. Only Tramontana had been spared. Now it had happened again.

"How did she die?" he asked, knowing full well the answer.

"She convulsed and then died," Rakhal said bitterly.

Dorian sighed heavily. The same symptoms as the others. She had been killed in the overworld. After the first incident, Tower had nearly come to war with Tower, each one accusing the others of using their *laran* as a tool for one of the domains to destroy the other towers. Only truthspell had put that suspicion to rest. Now they all believed that some *laranzu* or *leronis* attached to a great house had chosen to do the bidding of some ambitious warlord to destroy the Towers. Such a tactic, if it continued, might indeed succeed, wiping out the laran breeding lines so carefully cultivated and leaving the Towers vulnerable and weak.

"We have got to stop this renegade," Rakhal gritted.

"Then we must find him," Dorian said firmly. "He's a human being, he exists. Therefore, we must walk the overworld and find him; then we will trace him back to his body and stop him. Let us call all the Towers to send search parties into the overworld."

"I will contact them," Rakhal said with relief and broke off the connection. Only minutes later it seemed, Dorian felt that familiar tug in his mind, and uncovering his starstone, found Rakhal waiting to talk to him.

"We have agreed to start tonight—all of the Towers. We must wipe out this assassin, and with all of us looking, we will eventually find him."

Although he was not in the Tower and therefore more vulnerable, Dorian decided that he, too, would meet with the Hali circle in the overworld. Perhaps from his vantage point on the outside he might see something different.

"Be careful," Rakhal cautioned.

As Dorian lay on his bed preparing himself for the coming work, he felt a premonitory shudder along with the thought that he might not survive tonight, though he did not have the Aldaran Gift of precognition. But he resolutely emptied his mind of all thoughts and worries, calming and centering himself so that he could be totally focused on his task—to find this renegade who killed *leroni* in the most effective way possible—in the overworld—where thoughts could indeed kill.

He could feel that familiar release as he slid out of his body and moved into the grayness of the overworld. Scanning the landscape, he could see nothing out of the ordinary. He unerringly began walking over the land toward Hali's Tower. The reassuring tingle of the silver cord reminded him of the connection to his body. With his thoughts he crafted a kind of energy shield around him to protect himself from an all too real harm.

Gradually, he discerned other forms walking along the horizon and recognized the familiar energies of his circle at Hali. All of a sudden, he heard a strange whirring sound coming from behind him, and he instinctively ducked. He felt a sharp blow to his back, almost stunning him, that propelled him to the ground. Immediately, he sent a mental thought to stiffen his shield. He realized the pain wasn't bad; the impact of whatever had hit him had knocked him down. Dorian rolled over to see who had attacked him from behind. As he did so, a silver flanged projectile, like a bloated, stubby arrow, fell off his back. He looked at it in horror. Such a device would have killed him instantly if he hadn't been protected.

Coming toward him was a smiling young man, holding a weapon that held a similar projectile aimed at his chest. "I know you," he gasped. "You're Vardin Leynier." His mother was right, he thought inanely; he has been up to something—killing *leroni!*

Vardin scowled as he noticed the arrow lying on the ground. "You should have been dead," he muttered, glaring at Dorian. His voice was like venom.

Dorian felt a chill, listening to the boy. "Why are you doing this? Who are you fighting for?"

"For myself," Vardin said. "I love to come into the overworld and watch you all fighting each other with your *laran* weapons. First one and then another—destroying each other, getting this little advantage and then that one. So I thought, what great fun it would be to throw confusion at all of you." His presence radiated hate.

"By killing us," Dorian said quietly.

"Yes," Vardin agreed, and he smiled. "And you never knew. That was much of the fun—watching you all running around blaming each other."

Dorian had no illusions now about this boy. This was a game to Vardin, a deadly but delightful game. But Dorian was obviously the first one who had survived—so far. He had no illusions that Vardin would not try to kill him. He needed just a few seconds, to focus his attention on the Hali circle. With them, he would have no problem subduing this child. But without them, he wondered how difficult it might be. After all, Vardin was obviously far more powerful than anyone suspected—and he had concealed it all too well.

"Warfare is not fun," Dorian said.

"Then why are you all so intent on finding better and deadlier weapons?" Vardin retorted. "If you didn't enjoy it, you wouldn't be fighting each other all the time, devising new and horrible ways to destroy.'' He stared at the *laranzu,* his face smoothing out into a flat glassiness.

''Whatever the causes, people do not kill each other for the joy of it; we are not animals hunting other animals like ourselves just for the fun of the kill.'' But Vardin laughed loudly at that. He thought, if our children are enjoying this so much, there is something truly wrong with this warfare. ''We do not use our *laran* in this way,'' he added.

''Perhaps not you,'' the boy said haughtily, ''but I'm my own power. I am strong here, no one tells me what to do. No one!'' Dorian felt the lash of hostility and hate underlying the cocky words. ''I want to see you all die!''

Whatever had happened to twist this boy? He needed to know. ''Why do you want to kill us? You must have some reason. I can't believe it's simply because you enjoy it'' Vardin smiled at him.

''Who's hurt you?'' Dorian demanded—and suddenly knew. Vardin, the weakest of five children, the others having very strong *laran,* especially Armand, the oldest, smartest, most arrogant. ''It must have been difficult living with your family, particularly Armand,'' he said quietly. Vardin's arm spasmed and the weapon shook. He steadied it with a snarl and raised it toward Dorian's chest.

''Just one more thing,'' Dorian said quickly. ''How did you fool me when I tested you?''

''I went away,'' Vardin said. I submerged myself and left you with the most witless part of me. I learned that a long time ago. That's how I survived in my family. I wasn't as *laran* gifted as they were, but I swore I'd get them.'' He sneered. ''I fooled you all.'' He squeezed the trigger, and the projectile exploded harmlessly between them.

A kind of force shield radiated around the surprised boy. He beat helplessly at it. Dorian released his breath as the members of the Hali circle crowded in around him—Rakhal, Jorana, Aliana, Gervis, Kaylin. He felt weak and shaken. Perhaps he could have deflected the weapon, but he was glad he didn't have to try. Rakhal Storn embraced him in a warmth-giving bear hug.

"We were so afraid we wouldn't get to you before he attacked again," he said.

"How did you know?" Dorian asked.

"We saw you coming toward us, and then suddenly we all felt this enormous pain—and we knew you were under attack," Jorana said.

Dorian took a deep breath. "We must stop him from ever doing this again," he said fervently, "but I do not feel it is right to kill him."

"I have an idea," Aliana said. They listened quietly as she outlined her suggestion and nodded their acceptance.

"What a fitting punishment," Dorian said. "This will let him to think about what he's done." As a group they focused their wills and within minutes it was prepared. As one, they moved toward the trapped Vardin.

"What do you want?" he demanded; his voice sounded thin inside the shield. "How can you keep me like this?"

"Do you think you can withstand the power of a *laran* circle?" Rakhal asked. "You have killed for the last time, Vardin Leynier."

Iron hands picked him up and carried his twisting, resisting body ungently over to a room-sized dark gray cube. The boy wrestled helplessly trying to free himself. Aliana pushed open a narrow door, and stood aside as the others threw Vardin inside.

"This room has been woven by the combined *laran* of our circle," Dorian said. "You cannot get out. Although it would be easy for us to kill you, we feel it would be a far better punishment for you to suffer for the agony you have given to others."

"No!" shrieked Vardin, flinging himself at the door. Gervis carelessly tossed him back against the far wall where he bounced, slightly dazed.

"Perhaps at some far later date others might be more inclined to set you free, if they believe you have suffered enough." Dorian's face hardened. "But not us."

Vardin glared back at him. "I'll hate you forever!" he spat.

"Perhaps," the other acknowledged. "By the way, your body cannot wake up because your consciousness is here. Good-bye." His companions shut the door, and he locked it with an intricate copper key. Then he held it up. "Let this remain in Hali Tower along with its story so that at some later time if some *laranzu* is more forgiving, he may let this creature go."

Dorian gave one last look at the cube. There was silence. "Let's go home," he said.

They turned and vanished from the overworld, leaving Vardin screaming into nothingness, while in the waking world, his lifeless body remained, unchanging and unmoving, a vessel emptied of its consciousness.

Shame

by Charley Pearson

Charley Pearson says that this is his first professional fiction sale. Actually, most of what he writes is classified; and he lists, in addition, one "small press" credit. He has been an engineer for the Naval Nuclear Propulsion Program for many years, and that, presumably, is what all the classified writing is about.

"Four years ago," he says, "in a burst of questionable ego, I decided I could write fiction as well as 'technical stuff,' on the feeble grounds that I had been reading science fiction and fantasy for some twenty-five years." (I wish half of my writers were one-tenth so well prepared!)

He guesses that he doesn't fit my normal mold of would-be writer. Why not? Writers come in all sizes and shapes. Many are academics; some of the best are scientists—or didn't you ever read anything by Hal Clement? Some are housewives, some librarians; a good few are teachers, and one of the very best of mystery writers (Dick Francis) is an ex-jockey. Changing jobs frequently and keeping cats is not absolutely required for a writing career.

He says he has two daughters but "keeps forcing in time to write." I think most of us would agree that's really all it takes; that and a typewriter. Of course one can *write with a pencil and notebook—but who, except your seventh grade classmates, will read it?*

"Father, I cannot go to a Tower."

Garrett stood by the window of his chamber, the glow of sunset casting a bloody flush over his face. A jingling of harness drew his attention from his father's glare. The *leronis* and her guards. The representative of Neskaya Tower, come to escort him to his alleged new home.

Except he would not go.

"You will at least come and meet her. I know the power of your *laran* when you are not too lazy to use it. The Tower needs you, and you cannot stay here forever. I will not have the household torn apart by jealous younger sons. Already you are fifteen, past time to make a commitment with your life. Go to Nevarsin if you don't like the Tower."

"Never!" He was no *cristoforo.* Besides, they would expose his sick, corrupt mind as quickly as could the technicians at the Tower. His violent, brutal visions. Holy Bearer of Burdens, why was he ever born? If his father only knew. . . .

But that was the whole problem, wasn't it? This man he named *father* had not sired him. This man had killed the one who properly owned that title. Tracked him down and butchered him.

Thank Avarra for that. For his real sire had been a brigand, who had ambushed Garrett's mother during a trip to visit her relatives—murdered her escort, stolen her jewels, raped her, and left her for dead. Garrett's next oldest brother had taken especial delight in telling him this in the midst of a furious argument many years before. The fact his brother had been beaten had destroyed Garrett's feeble hope the tale had been a lie.

Yet somehow, all his life *Dom* Esteban had found it in him to treat Garrett just like his own sons. Garrett shuddered; he could never be so forgiving. Not when he knew so well what thoughts the son of such a horror could have. And the evil such a son might do, if ever he lost control, as when he saw that dark-haired maid smile at him in the hall, or that girlfriend of his sister's, or . . . or damn near any other woman, and he wanted to. . . .

He slammed down his shields when his father frowned. Had he seen? Did he have any idea what a warped, demented "stepson" he had accepted into his house? Garrett repressed his trembling and waited, but his father only seemed upset at his never-ending intransigence, so the secret must still be safe. His father was right, though—he must leave. Even here, in his own home, he was getting careless; and now there was some old *leronis* downstairs, able to see the most deeply hidden thoughts even from a distant chamber. He would disgrace his whole family if anyone ever penetrated his mind, if anyone ever sensed what nasty dreams ripped through his brain when he looked at their sister, their daughter, their wife. Holy Avarra, why did you have to make all women so desirable? And why can't I look at one without wanting to take her and . . . and grab her, and. . . .

Someone screamed. Gods, he'd let his shields slip! Pay attention, you fool! He raced after his father, down the stairs, clamping ever tighter on his shields, tighter than he'd ever tried before. Nothing must get out. Not his thoughts, not his plans—nothing. He clutched the bag dangling about his neck, the bag holding his starstone. Strength, Goddess; for the sake of your own daughters, give me strength.

His father knelt by the *leronis*. Garrett could see the flush of her cheek as he came up beside her.

"I am sorry, *Dom* Esteban," said the woman, accepting a cup of warm wine from Garrett's Father. "I don't know what I sensed, it seemed so . . . offensive. But it was nebulous, and quickly gone. I suppose I am merely tired from my journey." She threw back the cowl of her deep green wool cloak to drink, and a mass of burnished bronze hair tumbled down her back, caught loosely in a copper clasp in the shape of a *kireseth* blossom. One delicate hand brushed at a stray lock, and Garrett froze, watching her regain her composure, relieved she didn't understand the source of the repugnant assault. She was so sensitive! He'd never come so close to inflicting his disgusting mind on a woman.

Abruptly she turned and stared at Garrett, then rose and took a step toward him.

He couldn't move. She wasn't old at all. She was hardly older than he. Her eyes were as green as her cloak. No, not that dark, but her eyebrows were thick and dark, and her lashes, and her mouth. . . . He couldn't concentrate. His mind slid off the details, and he took a step forward. She was beautiful. Stunning. So calm, confident, self-possessed; and she worked in a Tower, so she had to be intelligent. How could such a woman exist?

"Garrett, where are your manners?" said his father.

He flushed and bowed. "I apologize, lady. I am Garrett, fourth son to *Dom* Esteban Ardais. I, uh, that is, my father says I am to, I think, go with you." He wasn't going with her. He had already decided that. Why didn't he say so? What was wrong with his mouth, anyway? He never stuttered!

His father started to introduce the woman, but she cut him short and spoke for herself. "I am Alicia, of Neskaya Tower. I am your escort. My coworker Donal told me of your terrible threshold sickness, and your strength upon subsequent testing." She frowned, as if unsure of something.

As well she might, thought Garrett. He had his shields pulled down so tightly he'd be surprised if she didn't think him head-blind. Well, what if she did? That was better than letting her see his filth. Maybe she would refuse to take him.

Now there was a thought. So why did it leave him such an aching, yearning void?

No. He could not afford to like her. There had to be some reason he might wish to avoid her. Her scar. Yes, perhaps some men would find that burn on the side of her face undesirable. How did she get it? An accident with *laran?* Fighting a forest fire? It didn't matter. The underlying beauty shone through, and she held herself so proudly, she was . . . just perfect. That's all.

"Garrett!"

He tore away his eyes and looked at his father, wondering what was wrong.

"Don't stare," hissed *Dom* Esteban, glancing once more at the woman, then away. "Let us adjourn to dinner. You can finish packing tonight."

So, he was to leave immediately. Then he blinked as Alicia turned away. Surely his father didn't think he had been staring at her scar, like the cruelest urchin in the gutter? Did he have such a reputation for incivility, for lack of common decency? He followed them slowly to the dining hall. Yes, he probably did. He had taken to avoiding gatherings of people his age. He had fled in terror from the girl who had danced with him, then led him eagerly into an alcove, last Midsummer Festival. What rumors had that sparked, or fanned into raging flames? That he was a sandal wearer? Or had the girl been too embarrassed to admit his "lack of interest?"

He snorted. He lacked interest the way a *cralmac* lacked teeth. Too blasted much of it, and not even remotely under control. Best if he was indeed known as one to avoid, for whatever reason. Avarra help whatever girl or woman he was with when he lost the final rein on his raging fantasies. At least his mother, may Evanda grant her peace, would be spared the knowledge of her youngest son's failure.

All through dinner the *leronis* Alicia tried to engage him in conversation, while politely answering his father and others eager to ask about the Towers. Garrett avoided her eyes, admiring her grace, her wit, her laughter, whenever she and his father were not watching him. There was so much more power here than in any other woman he knew, so much that other women paled to triviality. He was smitten. He knew the signs. Who cared about the willing surrender of a silly, brainless girl who wanted nothing more than did the crassest boy in the streets? How much more valuable the adoring surrender of a woman who had no need to submit, a woman who gave her all only because she wanted to give it to *him* . . . as if any woman, given the choice, could even conceive of looking at him twice.

As if any woman should even need to surrender, just to please some repulsive man's desires.

Yet all he could think of doing, if he had the chance, was taking that woman and . . . and forcing. . . .

He ground his teeth and tried to think of something else. Anything else. He was a foul, foolish, obnoxious boy, grown to manhood without the common sense of Durraman's donkey, and single-mindedly bent on destroying his whole family if he didn't get away from here before he lost his last feeble shreds of decency.

"*—laran,*" he heard. Oh. His father and *Domna* Alicia were discussing him.

"There's something there, I think, but it's so tumultuous," said the lady. "Are you sure he hasn't suppressed it entirely?"

"No," his father said, leaning close to her, but Garrett heard anyway. His shields were as thick as ever, but he had concentrated on blocking his own mental trash; he could still hear others. "No, he heals things now and then—a horse, a falcon—and though I have not yet questioned him, my ulcer has not bothered me since I complained of it a month ago."

Garrett blinked and looked down at his plate. Zandru's Pits! So much for subtlety. There were spies all over this damned estate. Or he'd just been careless. If they had thought he no longer possessed *laran,* maybe they would not have summoned the *leronis.* That's what he should have been doing all along—hiding it better. Damn and blast.

"Anyway," his father was saying, "he does have other interests. He seems passable at his letters and numbers, and he nearly burned down the barn last year with some foolish lightning experiment, so maybe he's trying to imitate those *Terranan* scientists.'' *Dom* Esteban chuckled, and the woman smiled and looked over at him.

Garrett didn't look away in time. Alicia caught his eyes, paused, then slowly lost her smile. He jumped to his feet and fled the room, brushing past his Father's paxman and ignoring the shouts behind. She had seen, or almost. No, she had to have seen. He'd just be whipping his tongue to claim innocence with her. He ran outside, slammed the heavy wooden door to keep out the swirling white eddies of snow settling over the ground, and fought the wind all the way to the barn. A thin cry of rage in the distance, from the direction of Scaravel, heralded the beginning of banshee season; they never came this low in summer. He glanced at the main gate, but it was shut and guards were posted, so all was well.

He entered the barn and stamped down the center to where his saddle and harness rested against the wall; he had a spare cloak in his saddlebags, and he needed it right now. Check the horses, he told himself. Anything to get his mind on something else, something other than that *leronis*. He walked down the line, adding feed and chipping ice off the tops of the water troughs. The Tower's mounts were good quality, as good as their own. He talked to each and gave them some dried fruit, so they'd know his voice and scent, then walked to the back aisle and began shoveling out the rear of the stalls. He smiled as he finished the last one, wondering what his father would say if he knew a son of Ardais were indulging in such plebeian pursuits. But the dark and snow prevented high speed chases through the woods on the fastest horse he could borrow, his preferred method for clearing his mind.

He put the shovel away and glanced up at the blackened patch in the roof where the lightning had struck. No, his father would never let him forget that, but it really was rather amusing. It shouldn't have embarrassed him so much for the Tower woman to be told.

Damn, he was thinking of her again.

The door across the barn creaked open, paused, then clicked shut, dulling once more the howl of the rising wind. Garrett pulled back into a shadow and snuck back to where he could see the central aisle.

"Garrett?" A tentative voice. Alicia's. What was she doing out here? "Garrett, something is troubling you. Where are you? Will you not speak with me?"

He peeked around the edge of the stall. She was alone, but at least she'd had the sense to get her warm cloak before coming out here. The torchlight flickered off the reddish highlights in her hair like so many falling stars flashing through the night. And she was worried about him. What a wonderful, foolish woman.

She turned and looked straight where he hid, and he jerked back. How could she sense him? He was shielding, blast it! The best he knew how, and her Tower friend Donal had taught him when he'd visited a few years ago.

Her Tower friend. Gods, he didn't even know her, and he was jealous, even though he liked Donal, admired him as much as he did his oldest brother. Was there no end to his stupidity? He scrambled back as her steps approached. She couldn't know he was out here. She couldn't really sense him. She was just guessing. She had to be.

His hand brushed a ladder against the wall and his eyes darted upward. Yes, the loft; he could hide there. He lifted the ladder off its pegs, leaned it against the edge of the loft, and scurried up. Silently, he told himself, working his way back and behind a bale of hay. She would give up soon, or go look for him elsewhere. The wind moaned louder, as if daring either of them to leave the barn and return to the house.

"Garrett, I know you are out here. There were tracks the wind had not yet hidden."

Oh, Bearer, he thought. He was so busy thinking about *laran* he'd completely forgotten more mundane clues. But he might have left by a different door. She couldn't know he was still out here, could she? The soft brushing of her cloak along the straw-covered floor reached the end of the line of stalls, and then he saw the ladder quiver. She wouldn't try climbing, would she?

She climbed. He looked behind him, but the loft was small and went nowhere. He was treed. Brilliant. He was absolutely brilliant.

Her head poked above the ledge, and her gaze swept the loft. She didn't seem to see him, but she stopped, concentrated a moment, then looked straight at his bale of hay. She didn't look happy.

"Look," she said, "you are here. Stop playing. I have to evaluate you, even if you don't want to go with me. The sooner we get this over with, the sooner I'll be gone, and you can go back to arguing with your father over what you should do next!"

Garrett didn't reply. He crouched down behind the bale and tried to figure out what he was doing wrong. He thought his shields were perfect. What was she seeing? And why was she out here all alone, anyway? Where were her guards, or her lady traveling companion?

The ladder creaked. Suddenly there came the sound of ripping cloth, a muffled oath, a scraping of wood on wood, a scream, a splintering crash and abrupt, horrifying silence.

Garrett leapt from behind the hay and dove to the edge of the loft. Below, Alicia lay twisted amidst the remains of the ladder, not moving, one foot thrust between two rungs, the hem of her cloak ripped and caught about her ankle.

He didn't say anything. Her curse had covered it all. He slithered over the edge, held on a second, and dropped, grabbing out his matrix and bending to monitor her. Her head seemed not too bad, considering she had been knocked out; the bone sticking out of her calf was the worst injury. He lifted her body enough to pull away pieces of ladder and stuff a handful of straw under her head, then went to work on the leg, slowly straightening it, disinfecting the bone as it slid beneath the skin, then concentrating on mending the break. She was lucky, in an unlucky sort of way—no punctured arteries.

When the bone was set and grown together, he mended the layers of torn muscle, fascia, and skin, knitting together numerous capillaries in the process. He had no idea how long he had been working when, finally, he sat back and shuddered, reaching absently in his pocket for some leftover dried fruit. Her leg looked different, now it was healed. No longer was it merely a project, a task. It needed washing, what with the dried blood and all, but now it seemed such a shapely, lovely leg, and it connected with such a beautiful, tempting. . . . Thank Avarra she was unconscious; with this kind of intimate touching he could never have hidden his mind, his horrid thoughts of how he wanted to take this woman and—

Her eyes were open. Zandru's Shade, she was lying there watching him, reading him, he was wide open, he had to be to heal, she—

She smiled? Gods, what was she planning, what was she going to. . . ?

She shook her head. "I am going to do nothing," she said softly.

Garrett stared. He started to pull back and raise his barriers, but she simply lay there and looked at him. He stopped, and let them fall again. It was hopeless, she'd seen everything, she knew what he was. What a terrible threat he was.

Then he blinked. "Nothing?" he said. "Nothing?"

Her smile grew larger. "Well, maybe not nothing." Slowly she sat up. He began to back away, but she reached out and firmly clasped her hands behind his head. And gently, ever so gently, she pulled him forward, as he gazed into her shining, glowing eyes. Closer she pulled, and then she kissed him—a long, lingering kiss, full of more delight than all his dreams of terror. The stiffness gradually fell from his body as he relaxed and let himself savor her gift.

They separated when a torch on the wall sputtered and died. Alicia laughed, and Garrett flicked a smile in response, shivering and helping her rise.

"It's . . . uh . . . time to get back," he mumbled, looking away at last. He couldn't for the life of him think of anything intelligent to say. "Why did your escort let you come alone?" He began picking up pieces of ladder and tossing them in the corner.

"No one knows I am here; I was taken to my room, and came after they left me. And you, it appears, are known for running off."

"Yes, well, all the more reason you should have an—"

"Garrett?"

"Yes, *domna?*"

"Shut up."

"Yes, *domna.*"

"And it is *mestra.*"

"Oh, sorry—"

"Or *vai leronis.*"

"Oh, of course. I—"

"But call me Alicia."

"I . . . I mean. . . ."

"And we do need sleep. We leave early in the morning."

He stopped cleaning up the floor where she had fallen. Without saying a word, he kicked the last piece of ladder to the side and turned away.

Alicia took two steps, grabbed his shoulders, and spun him around. "Do you think you are the first adolescent with a head full of fantasies? That you are unique in your dreams of women?"

"No," he said bitterly. "The world is full of rapists and worse. I am *trying* not to join them, nor inflict myself on—"

She yanked him forward and kissed him again. It didn't last as long, but he relaxed more quickly this time.

"Do you not understand?" she asked after a while. "I see your fears. But these dreams are not what is *you.* You are not a copy of the man who attacked your mother. What haunts you is nothing more than an overdose of youthful lust. We can help you control your thoughts, hide them if you wish while not blocking off the rest of your mind, channel them into more satisfying fantasies if you will let us. Give us a chance! Please?"

Garrett stared at her. She wasn't rejecting him. She'd seen everything he was, all the filth he'd ever conjured, and she still wanted him to go to the Tower with her. He couldn't believe it. It was another fantasy. It had to be.

"No," she said, smiling with the radiance of spring. "No more than it's a fantasy that you think me pretty, me with the ugliest scar in the Hellers."

"It is not—"

"Hush. Enough. Or do I again have to break my leg and force you to open up before you will be convinced?"

"You didn't . . . you are not going to claim you broke that leg on purpose?!"

"Well, of course I—"

"You did not! You were out cold! I saw you—"

"I can shield anything I—"

"Not like that, you can't. I know—"

"Oh, so now you know—"

They argued all the way back to the house. In the morning they resumed, when Alicia discovered her scar had been removed in the middle of the night with nary a by-your-leave. Garrett bid his father farewell, ignoring the diatribe from Alicia, and *Dom* Esteban merely stood there shaking his head as the two rode off with their escort, bickering like an ancient married couple.

The old man sighed. He still didn't understand his youngest son. And now it looked like he never would.

The Frontier

by Diana L. Paxson

Diana L. Paxson is one of the shining lights in my crown of young writers—though, like me, she is no longer so very *young.*

She recently came over to my house and borrowed a whole slew of books about the odd corner of psychology inhabited by multiple personalities. She says she borrowed them for another reason, but a few days later she appeared on my doorstep bearing this story. So much of Diana's historical fiction is so sad and unreservedly grim that it was a delight to read this much lighter story. Actually, I wrote a short story ("Elbow Room") from the viewpoint of a multiple personality who had to go insane to retain her sanity; Diana, after pointing that out to me, said "now I've done the therapist." And on Darkover, too. . . .

Diana also updated her biography, speaking of the final volume JEWEL OF FIRE in her wildly fantastic "Westria" series, the historical novel she's working on with Adrienne Martine-Barnes about Fionn MacComhail (Pronounced Finn MacCool in case you can't speak Gaelic), and a new trilogy about the Siegfried legend, WODEN'S CHILDREN. She also composes and plays music for the Celtic harp; like most of us, she combines children, mar-

riage, and work. She's contributed to most of these anthologies.

"Well, Lieutenant Berenstein, are you ready for the realities of the frontier?" said a deep, amused voice at my elbow.

I set my pocket reader on the scratched duralloy table of the transport's lounge with a sigh, resigned to leaving the article on personality integration in second-stage Xerasian metamorphs in the *Annals of the Imperial Institute of Psychology* unread.

Security Sergeant Randall, returning from leave on Prima, had been favoring me with his advice throughout the journey. He seemed to feel that any young woman traveling alone needed shepherding, even if she was his superior officer. He meant well, but perhaps I was more anxious about landing than I had realized, because the broad smile above the sergeant's grizzled beard irritated me into a reply.

"Sergeant, I don't know what you think I'm expecting. Dar—Cottman IV may be unusual, but human beings are depressingly consistent from world to world. I trust that my training has prepared me to function in a professional manner whatever I may encounter there."

I knew just how pompous that sounded, though I would never admit it. Spaceforce had paid my way through medical school, and I had earned high marks in officer training, but I was only too familiar with the limits of simulation conditioning. There was a slight jerk and a vibration that rolled through the metal floor plates and I realized that the transport had docked.

"Cottman IV, or *Darkover?*" the sergeant laughed. "I heard you! I'll wager I know just the kind of vids you used to watch—full of dashing red-headed swordsmen and sorceresses in crimson veils!"

I glared at him. Popular culture had spread Darkover's fame in the Empire all out of proportion to its importance, considering that it was still a Class D Closed World. Its people were human enough for the average Imperial citizen to identify with, exotic enough to titillate the most romantic taste.

"Or don't you head-shrinkers believe in romance? They've no love for Terrans in Thendara, anyway," said the sergeant. "And since the Sharra incident, there's no welcome for us in the countryside," he grimaced. "Not that military police are ever exactly welcome. But they don't seem to like each other much better—" We both looked up as the warning buzzer rang. Fellow passengers set down their drinks and began to collect luggage, chattering loudly.

"I must go." I got to my feet, tugging at the black fabric of my uniform with the discreet red and blue caduceus of the Medical Service: Psychiatric Division on the collar while he eyed me appreciatively. I snapped shut my reader and jammed it into my shoulder pack. That was all I had to carry, but I wanted to get a good place in line.

He nodded. "Journey's end. Well, good-bye to you, Lieutenant Doctor C. Berenstein. By the way, what does the 'C' stand for? It can't be that bad, girl," he said encouragingly. "And to have a name to go with that curly black hair will sweeten my memories."

If I had not outranked him, he might have been

more than avuncular, but his conversation had enlivened a boring trip. He deserved an answer, but he was not going to get it from me.

"Goodby, Sergeant Randall," I said repressively, and pushed through the crowd toward the passageway.

I had been determined to treat Cottman IV like any other assignment, and at least for the first few months, that's all it seemed likely to be. The spaceport was the transfer hub for this sector of the Empire, and administration, maintenance and security all required personnel. The Terran Zone that had sprung up around it contained numerous institutes trying to study Darkover's culture before it disappeared, as well as more ordinary services like Empire Medical to which I was assigned. The only link between them and the rest of the planet was the Comyn Council, and the Comyn seemed to live in a world of their own.

Sergeant Randall had been right. Darkover was not romantic. It was impoverished, frigid, and socially fragmented. Except for the crimson sun and the four moons that chased each other like pastel jewels across the night sky, I could have been living in an urban center anywhere in the Empire.

Not that I had much time to admire them. Empire Medical was chronically understaffed, and glad to make use of whatever personnel Spaceforce assigned. I soon had a full caseload of sleep disorders and sexual dysfunctions, a borderline schizophrenic, and several phototropic depressions. There were patients who complained of never being warm, and others who had manic outbreaks whenever there was a conjunction of the planet's four moons. I was able to truthfully report to my mother that except for a glimpse of Regis Hastur on his way to a dinner party at the Terran Legate's, I had seen nothing of the romantic Darkover of tri-vid fame.

The long winter was giving way to what the locals laughingly referred to as spring when the Emp. Med. computer assigned me the young man whom I will call Stevie Eisler, and though I did not know it at the time, my life began to change.

"I probably shouldn't be here at all. . . ." Stevie sat on the edge of the easy chair as if he were afraid it would swallow him, a slight young man with mousy hair whose records said he was a data entry clerk in Transport and Supply. He looked up at me in appeal, and I was glad that when I was working I could exchange my Spaceforce blacks for a white smock like the rest of the medical personnel.

"It's just that the headaches are getting worse, and the docs don't seem to be able to find anything wrong. And sometimes . . . sometimes when they go away, time has passed and I don't know where I've been!"

"Hmm—" I said noncommittally, but my heartbeat quickened. The standard battery of tests had indicated a rigid and rather limited personality, and I had been prepared for repressions, but not amnesia.

"Why don't you lean back in the chair?" I asked him. "It's very comfortable. . . ." It also had its own heating and could provide a soothing vibration, subliminal music or a maternal heartbeat, and restraints, in the event they should be required.

The chair did its work, and I listened with increasing interest to the litany of symptoms. Stevie had a variety of psychosomatic disorders. He was on drugs for his nightmares about the Trade City orphanage in which he had been raised, and such settings were notorious for physical and sexual abuse, no matter how well they were run. He had lived in a succession of apartments, and did not seem to keep friends for long.

"It says here that the Spaceforce MPs picked you up at the Goldenflower Inn after you had knocked out several crew members from the *Star Whore,* destroyed most of the chairs, and broken a chervine-drover's arm in a brawl—" I looked up from the screen, finding it hard to believe.

Stevie shook his head as if he were having the same problem.

"They say I did that, but I only remember waking up in the hospital. It doesn't make sense. I don't even like to drink. I would never go to a bar in that part of town."

"Hmm. It sounds as if you might have had another episode of amnesia. Would you be willing to let me use hypnosis to see if we can find out what when on?" I touched a spot on the desk, and the lights began to dim. The photosensors were already recording the session; I touched the controls to compensate and increase the pickup of sound.

"Will it hurt?" He looked tense, even in the embrace of the chair.

"Not at all. If there's something you're not ready to deal with, you won't even remember it. But in order to help you, I need to know."

"I guess so. . . ." He leaned back, and I keyed the subliminal drumbeat to begin. The relaxation induction went smoothly, and in a few minutes I could see that the tension had left his body.

"Stevie, can you hear me? Raise your little finger if you can—that's very good. Now, Stevie, I want you to go even deeper into trance. I want to speak to the part of you that can tell me what happened at the Goldenflower Inn. . . ."

Stevie twitched, but there was only silence. I sighed, brought him back to the relaxed state, then took him down again. This resistance was annoying, but clearly at some level he wanted help, or he would not have come.

"I know there's a part of you that would like to talk to me. Will that part of you tell me how I can help you now?"

For a long moment I thought this was not going to work either. Then he stiffened. I could see his eyelids quivering, he took a few deep, controlled breaths, and opened his eyes.

Stevie's eyes had seemed as colorless as the rest of him, but even in that dim light I could have sworn that now they were a pellucid pale blue. Slowly he straightened in the chair, slender fingers brushing at his head for all the world as if he were putting back a veil.

"Dealing with this would all be much simpler in the Tower, but I suppose you will have to do." The tone was brisk, composed.

"Who are you?" I spoke more sharply than I had intended, because it was a woman's voice that had answered me, and despite the form, it was impossible not to see a woman sitting there.

"I am Allirinda Aillard, Keeper of Neskaya Tower."

Dissociative states . . . multiple personality . . . a paper for the Annals . . . I had read enough to recognize the rare condition I was seeing now. This case could make my career.

"But *you* didn't start the fight at the Goldenflower Inn—" I found my voice at last.

"No—" Allirinda frowned fastidiously, "That . . . was *Dom* Esteban-Gabriel Alton, and if we do not learn how to control him, he is going to do it again!"

"Dr. Berenstein, do you have a moment? You've been treating a multiple personality, I hear."

I stopped in the white glare of the passageway, trying to place the man who had greeted me. Long and lean, with wiry dark hair, he had the slightly harried look of an administrator though he wore a doctor's smock like my own.

"I'm Dr. Jason Allison from the Department of Alien Anthropology over in Section Eight," he said pleasantly. I was astonished he knew my name. But I had been working with Stevie for over a month now. Obviously, the word had gotten around.

"Yes, sir, I have." I strove to sound professional.

"A Terran?"

"Stevie was raised in the Spacemen's Orphanage. I gather things were somewhat unsettled at the time he was taken, so we don't really know. Consciously, at least, he is as Terran as they come. But . . . all of his alternative personalities are from Darkover."

A technician maneuvered a slider laden with specimens around us, eyeing us curiously.

"Multiple personalities are a coping mechanism in which the ego splits off other selves to deal with situations beyond the capacity of the primary identity," I went on. "Once you understand the problems which the alternates were created to solve, you can begin to treat them."

"Yes . . . I know." He seemed privately amused, and I wondered why, since his specialty was parasitology. "What progress have you made?"

"Not much, since I can't even guess what traumas could have caused the dissociations. So far they include a Keeper, a Comyn swordsman, a *cristoforo* monk and a Free Amazon."

I waited, wondering how long it would take the doctor to ask whether Stevie was an actor, as several of my colleagues had already done. But my patient hadn't found those personalities in popular literature. He never checked out a tri-vid. He didn't even read fiction.

"Interesting," Dr. Allison said finally, still with that odd smile. He looked as if he might have said more, but unless I asked his help, professional courtesy would not let him interfere. "I wonder if any of the other identities have *laran.*"

The days lengthened and brightened, and green buds began to appear on the trees. Not that I had much leisure to enjoy them, for though my caseload grew lighter, Stevie's therapy was taking up more and more of my time. Giving the various personalities an opportunity to communicate during our sessions allowed Stevie to maintain a precarious stability. He was even able to go back to work, but I was under no illusion that we had achieved anything but time in which to look for a cure. I began to wonder whether I would have to involve Dr. Allison after all.

In the meantime, the Science Division was ecstatic at the prospect of testing him. Persuading

Stevie's other selves to cooperate was another matter. Brother Timeo the *cristoforo* never did agree, but since the matrix technician they brought in to observe him sensed no trace of the talent, it probably did not matter. Ellie the Renunciate had no *laran* either, but Allirinda and Esteban both showed the same unusual neural patterns and energy flows.

"Dr. Berenstein, they want to send me to one of the Towers," Stevie told me one day shortly before the Festival of the Four Moons.

I looked at him sharply. For a moment I had thought it was Brother Timeo talking. The *cristoforo* disapproved of the old Darkovan matrix magic and Terran science equally. But Timeo tended to look down his nose at the rest of the world. Only Stevie sat huddled into the therapy chair like a mouse peeping out of its hole.

"How do you feel about that?" I asked.

"I don't want to," he mumbled. "I don't believe in that stuff, and I don't trust them. I'll bet it was Allirinda's idea—I'll never get rid of her if I go to a Tower!"

Stevie had resisted belief in his other personalities almost as stoutly as some of my colleagues on the staff. He had now progressed to the point of accepting their presence in his body, but he persisted in viewing them as enemies.

"What do you think the others want to do?"

"Who cares!" he answered sullenly, but even that trace of spirit was more than he had shown before. "I'd like to kill them all!"

I refrained from pointing out that this would involve killing himself as well. Stevie had tried suicide once already, when he first started hearing his alter egos arguing inside his skull.

"Well, you know they won't give you any peace if we don't ask them. Why don't you relax now and rest—that's right—" I watched as the chair received him into its cushioned embrace and the tension in his body drained away. It was an interesting problem in ethics. Legally, Stevie was the one who must decide. But morally, was I obligated to get the agreement of all four personalities, or did the majority rule?

"*Mestra* Ellie," I called when he was still. "Can you hear me?"

"Hear you!" He, or rather she, sat up suddenly, surveying the room with a wry smile. "I've been waiting for that ____ ! to get out of the way." She used a word which the tapes had not taught me, but its sense was clear. "And I've heard the great debate about the Tower. I don't want to go either, though I hate to agree with him. Do us all a lot more good to spend a year in the Guild House, learning to get along! You, too!" Ellie gave me a companionable grin. "You're not bad for a Terran, but you'll turn into as dry a Terranan stick as Stevie if you stay here!"

"I doubt that he, Esteban, or Brother Timeo would be very welcome there," I said dryly. "You know, I can almost understand why Stevie needs them, but where did you come from, Ellie? What's the earliest memory you have?"

She closed her eyes, and for a moment I thought the question might have scared her away, but it was still Ellie sitting there.

"I remember my older sister was crying. Stevie was crying, too. We were in the Trade City in front of an awful building made out of white stone. Then people in strange clothes took Stevie away."

"And what did you do, Ellie? Where did you go?" I asked.

"Back to the Thendara Guild House with my sister, of course," she replied. I wondered if Stevie really had a sister. Usually in these cases one had an early history with which to compare these stories, but Stevie's origins were unknown. Was that what Ellie was remembering? Were we reaching a point in the therapy when the other personalities would be willing to remember as well?

"We haven't heard from *Dom* Esteban for awhile," I said then. "Is he there, Ellie, and would he like to talk to me?"

"He won't talk," she said finally, "but he doesn't have much use for either the Council or the Towers. I don't like it, Doctor. I think he's planning something. . . ." She fell silent, frowning, and I watched her, doing a little brooding of my own.

According to the literature, I was supposed to persuade each of them to face the trauma which had required his or her creation and fuse with the others or disappear, leaving the original person whole and free. But Stevie's warring personalities tolerated him only for the sake of their own survival, and each other not at all.

"Perhaps at our next session we'll be able to find out what it is. But it's time for you to go back in, Ellie. I'll see you soon."

"What if I don't want to wait?" she said anxiously. "What if something happens?"

"In an emergency you can always call me. You know that, and Stevie does, too. Watch out for him, will you?"

"I suppose I am the most responsible." Ellie

smiled ruefully. Then her eyes closed, and she was gone.

Perhaps Ellie's comment had stung me more than I realized, because three nights later I found myself putting on my black dress uniform and taking the walkway to the Trade City's concert hall. A touring opera company was performing *Un Ballo in Maschera,* a new production set during the Colonial Period on Theia IV. Attending would give me something to report to my mother, and perhaps the distraction would give me a new insight into Stevie's problems.

Aside from a nagging disbelief in the inability of the characters to penetrate each other's disguises, I found the opera enjoyable. But I never got to see the end of it. The hero was just having his future read by the sorceress when an electronic prickling from my ID bracelet forced me to leave my seat, squeeze past a row of glaring music lovers and run for the nearest visiphone.

"Berenstein here—"

"Sorry to bother you at the theater," said the face on the screen. "Got an audio message from someone called Ellie. Says she's your patient, though the records don't show you treating anyone of that name. Thought we better let you know just the same."

"Where was she?" I broke in.

"The point of origin was the public phone in the Old City," the voice said dubiously. "She said she would try again."

"I'll stay at this number. Route the call directly to me."

Echoes of the drama on stage reverberated faintly

through the lobby walls, but it was the story that had been played out in my office that concerned me. The first act ended, the audience spilled out of the hall in search of refreshment, and returned. And still there was no call. Perhaps the problem Ellie feared had not developed. Perhaps she had given up on me. Or perhaps—and this was what made me suddenly cold—Ellie was no longer in charge.

The audience was just emerging for the second act intermission when I keyed the visiphone once more.

"This is Lieutenant Berenstein. I want to bring my patient in. No, you can't just have someone pick him—her—up," I stumbled over the pronouns, "it will have to be someone she knows! I'll need two MPs for escort and outdoor gear. Can fix? Good—at the West Gate. I'm leaving now."

"Lieutenant, this is where the call was made," said Private Kung, the younger of the two MPs who had been assigned to me. He nodded toward the phone, an incongruous glimmer of artificial lighting peeping from beneath the shingled overhand with which they had attempted to disguise it.

"So, where do you figure your girl might be?" asked Sergeant Randall, who had, I suspected, volunteered out of a misplaced feeling of responsibility. In his sheepskin jacket he looked even bulkier than before.

"My patient may appear to be male," I said carefully. "In this weather, I would guess she, or he, has taken refuge in one of those inns."

The city might be gearing up for the Spring Festival, but the shingles over the visiphone bore a frosting of snow, and even through my heavy cloak

I could feel the icy wind. Any Terran would have headed for shelter. I wondered if Stevie's Darkovan personalities felt the cold.

"Let's go take a look, then, but keep your cloaks on. Spaceforce leathers are not too popular around here."

Darkovan inns were hot and noisy, overwhelming me with a bewildering mixture of unfamiliar words and smells.

"No Terrans so far," said Kung when we emerged from the cheerful chaos of the second.

"My patient might be wearing Darkovan clothes." I took a grateful breath of crisp air.

Sergeant Randall swung me around to face him. "Doctor Berenstein . . . Sir! Would you like to tell us just what the hell we *are* looking for?"

"Stevie Eisler is a Terran clerk who suffers from a dissociative personality disorder . . . he has multiple personalities. The one who called me is Ellie n'ha Lenora . . . a Free Amazon." I hoped that the light of the inn's lantern would not show how red my face had become. "She's the one I'm looking for."

"And which is the one you don't want to find?" he asked in the same controlled tone.

"A Comyn swordsman—" I said defiantly, "who calls himself Esteban-Gabriel Alton."

On the sergeant's face I could see the struggle to suppress some powerful emotion. But in the end he simply nodded and led us toward the inn at the far side of the square.

The volume of sound from this place made the others sound civilized. To me it was all just noise, but as we neared I saw Private Kung hesitate, trading glances with Randall.

"Maybe the doctor had better wait here while we check inside," said Kung.

"I'll stay out of your way, gentlemen, but I'm not going to stay out and freeze." I told them, but by now even I could recognize the ugly undertones in the shouting, and I tensed as I followed them beneath the heavy beams of the door.

But nobody noticed us. All eyes were on the man who stood on a table at the other end of the room, following the white flicker of his sword.

"Cowards! You've about as much spirit among you as a *cristoforo* mule!" The blade jabbed and a man in drover's leathers recoiled. Instantly the swordsman was back on guard, laughing.

"That's tellin' em, Estebano!" shouted someone from the crowd.

I gasped, and Randall looked at me questioningly. Under his fur vest the swordsman was wearing a Terran jersey and trousers. But his cloak swung from his shoulders with an air that no Terran could command.

"What have the Comyn done to deserve your loyalty?" Esteban cried. "They walk clad in spider silk while we wear rags, and dine on chervine steaks while we starve. They sell our secrets to the Terrans and refuse the medicines that could save our lives!"

"Fine talk from you, *Dom* Esteban!" came a growl from behind him. "Conspiring against your own kin and kind!"

"Kin, but hardly kind." Esteban laughed bitterly. In the torchlight, I seemed to see red glints in his hair. "They let my mother be dragged from the Tower. I saw her bloody body lying in the snow! And then they tossed her *nedestro* brat out to starve. Comyn Council claims no loyalty from me!"

Was this the trauma that had shattered Stevie's psyche? I held my breath, waiting for him to go on.

"What'cha goin' t' do, then?" came the drunken cry.

"A single sword can do little—except to frighten she-males." He whirled, and the men fell back again. Esteban might reject the Comyn, but it was their glamour that he had laid upon the folk who listened here. He moved with the vital grace of some wild thing.

"But if you were men . . ." he drew out the word insultingly, "we could get rid of the Comyn and the Terrans as well. Together, we could burn their Council Chamber about their ears!"

I winced as Sergeant Randall's fingers dug into my arm. "If this madman is your patient, Doctor, I recommend that you get him out of here now! Do you think the Comyn will believe this tale of multiple personalities when they learn a Terran clerk is trying to start a civil war?"

I blinked. I had been so close to *knowing* . . . then the sense of what the sergeant had said sank in. Even behind the walls of the Terran Zone I had heard how delicate the relationship between Darkover and the Empire was now. I shook off Randall's hand and pushed forward.

"Esteban!" My higher voice was barely audible above the shouts of the men, but he turned. "Esteban, do you remember me?" I looked into those blazing eyes, and realized that the man I had seen in my office had been but a sketch of this personality. Mad he might be, but I could not deny his power.

"I know you . . ." his eyes narrowed, "but do

you know *me?* You must not make me angry, healer. You do not want to find out what I might do.''

I could guess, though. I had seen literature on the psi abilities of the Comyn caste. If this story of a mother who had been in a Tower were not all fantasy, we might have on our hands an untrained telepath of unknown powers.

''Would you like to tell me about it?'' I said softly, wishing I had him in my chair. Around us men were growing restive, aware of something they could not understand.

Esteban looked at me and laughed. ''Still after me to play your games? Talk is the only weapon you have, and if it does not work, what will you do?''

I stared at him. What he had said was all too true. Drugs were useful only as a stopgap. We knew how to dissociate suppressed personalities, but it was harder to put them back together again. In the end the only tools Terran medical science could give me were talk, and time. I heard Randall and Kung move and Esteban stilled, his eyes glittering dangerously. I held up a hand in warning. That part of him that was still Stevie had recognized them, and even I could feel danger building in the room.

I could think of only one person who might stop him now.

''That was a terrible story, about the Tower,'' I said gently. ''You must have been very young then, very much alone. But you can relax now. You are safe here. You can remember. Who was the Keeper of the Tower? Was her name Allirinda?'' His hand was trembling; light shimmered along the sword. His gaze flicked down to it and I moved closer.

''Allirinda Aillard of Neskaya . . . Allirinda, are you there?''

He jerked, and his face seemed to crumple. He straightened, grimacing, he was fighting it, fighting, but his hand went to his eyes as if the light gave him pain.

''Allirinda . . .'' I murmured, ''come out now. I need to talk to you.''

''No. . . .'' the denial became a moan, and the sword slipped from a suddenly nerveless hand. He swayed, and Kung and Randall got ready to catch him. But he did not fall.

Gradually the tremors ceased. And when the eyes opened, the warrior's defiance had become a queenly dignity, the hot glare cleared to a pellucid blue.

''Well, children, have you nothing better to do than stare at me?'' Allirinda's scornful gaze moved around the room, and one by one the men flushed and looked away.

''Kung, give me your cloak, now!'' I muttered, then passed it up to Allirinda, who wrapped it around herself gratefully, and at that moment, men in the green and black of the Thendara City Guard began to pour into the room.

Allirinda looked around her and shuddered distastefully, gave me a colleague's nod, and deliberately let her eyes close. Once more I saw the eyelids flutter, and when they opened once more it was Stevie Eisler's terrified gaze that fluttered about the room.

''Stevie,'' I called. ''It's all right, I am here—''

''I accept that I may not comprehend the explanation, but you will admit that I have the right to ask? The incident occurred in the Old City, and the man may be one of my people, after all."

I winced at the steel beneath the velvet voice and forced myself to meet the speaker's gaze, aware that Sergeant Randall had stiffened to even more rigid attention behind me. This was not the way I would have chosen to meet Regis Hastur.

But at least my story was well-polished. I had told it often enough in the past few days, and if the Darkovan leader did not understand it, well, I was used to that, too.

"Yes, sir." I watched the play of expression in a fine-boned face that in other circumstances would have been distracting as I summarized Stevie Eisler's therapy. "And with those clues and the cooperation of your people," I finished, "we have been able to put together some facts that may account for his memories.

"There was a woman called Lenora at Neskaya thirty years ago, when the Keeper was an Aillard," I began. "Lenora was some kind of Alton cross-cousin, with moderate *laran.* She had had a daughter by her husband, but after he died she went back to work in the Tower. A Terran research group was prospecting in the area. One of them fell in love with Lenora, and fathered a son. Things went well enough for a time, then feeling against the Terrans began to grow. The man was killed, and Lenora and her child took refuge in the Tower. It wasn't enough. While the Keeper was away, the mob demanded Lenora and she went out to them to save the others. And they killed her." I drew breath, seeing pain flicker in Hastur's clear eyes and wondering what griefs this man could reveal if I got him into my chair.

"They were afraid to keep the boy. A wandering *cristoforo* cared for him until they could find his sister, who had become a Renunciate in Thendara. But they could not keep a male child in the Guild House, so in the end she took him to the Spacemen's Orphanage. She did not know his father's name, only that he was a Terran's child. And by then, Stevie could not, or dared not, remember anything of his past."

"Amazing," said the stocky young man with the watchful eyes who leaned against the wall between us and Hastur's chair.

"But it could well be true, Danilo," his lord said slowly, pushing back that startling silver hair. "This kind of thing has happened before. And it was from these experiences," he turned back to me, "that Steven Eisler fashioned the other personalities?"

"With each trauma—with each thing that was beyond bearing—a part was split off for whom it had not happened. Part of the child stayed in the Tower and became a Keeper, another part followed the *cristoforo,* and a third went back to the Guild House with the girl."

"And *Dom* Esteban?"

I sighed, remembering the sheer beauty with which he had handled that sword. "I think that Esteban comes closest to the man that Stevie might have been, if all the other parts of him had not been at war."

Regis Hastur looked at me, and I did not need telepathy to understand that there were times when only his own strength of spirit kept him whole.

I remembered then how Steven Eisler had sobbed in my arms, knowing himself once more, but this time with all the memories of the Keeper and the swordsman, the *cristoforo* and the Free Amazon. Romantic stereotypes, Sergeant Randall would have called them, but it seemed to me that this little Terran clerk had contained within him the psyche of Darkover.

"Will he become one person, now that you know his history?" asked the man called Danilo.

"Perhaps," I answered, "with acceptance and stability . . . if he really wants to. We'll do the best we can."

"So may we all!" said Regis Hastur.

"Lieutenant, I may have misjudged you," said Sergeant Randall as we walked back through the town.

"You don't think I came to Darkover in search of the romance of the frontier?" I lifted one eyebrow.

"I think you have found it," he said slowly, "in your office chair."

For a moment I stared at him, but the gate to the Terran Zone loomed ahead, and I escaped having to reply.

"By the way," the sergeant said plaintively when we had been passed through, "after all this, don't you think you might tell me your first name?"

He was in Security. He could find it out if he really wanted to. And he had just given me a gift, though he might not know.

"Cassilda . . ." I muttered finally. "It's not my fault, so don't laugh. My mother dyes her hair red and memorizes every tri-vid about Darkover that appears. If junior officers were allowed any say in their postings, do you think I would be here?"

He *was* laughing, damn him, great guffaws that shook his broad frame. But as the walkway carried me toward Medical, I realized that I was glad that I had come.

The Aillard Anomaly

by Diann Partridge

Diann Partridge is another of the real oldtimers in writing about Darkover; she wrote her first amateur Darkover stories for the fanzine Starstone, *long before these anthologies were ever thought of—a good bit more than a decade now.*

She says this story is almost a sequel to her former story "Childish Pranks" in LERONI OF DARKOVER.

Diann lives in Wyoming. She is 38, has three kids (two of whom are teenagers—which, say I, might as well be eight), the same husband, two cats, and a little apricot-colored mouse. She has a job in a pizza parlor which she says "proved (without a doubt) that what Marion has always said is true—writers take the strangest jobs to make ends meet."

Well, of course it's true or I wouldn't have said it. How could I, a fantasy writer and storyteller, stretch the truth even a little bit?

Alizia Aillard slowly unrolled the diagram and watched in amazement as the material flattened itself on the table. No need to weight the corners. She rubbed the smooth translucent stuff with one finger. Definitely not natural. It wasn't the parchment that the MacArans were currently producing nor the finer resin bond stuff from the Leynier estate. The lettering was precise block letters, again not something produced by human hands. And totally incomprehensible.

"Fascinating, isn't it?" stated Brother Ian, moving a lamp so that the light fell directly on the diagram. "This was made by a technology that we are no longer capable of. Watch this."

He touched one of the blue squares in the upper right hand corner and before her startled eyes the lines on the diagram began to shift.

His craggy face crinkled up in a grin at her shocked expression.

"It has a memory of sorts, cousin, that allows us to call up eight different sections of the original floor plans of Thendara Castle. It is believed that during the Ages of Chaos, when this was obviously produced, there were maps of this type for all the Towers and Castles. I am sorry to say, though, that this one and the one for Caer Donn are the only two that survived that awful time."

Exhaustion made Idriel Hastur speak more sharply than she should have. "Can you read this—writing?" Her heavy marl-lined cloak was pinned closed with the jeweled crown and silver fir tree of the Hasturs, and when she pulled it tighter around her, a curious double-headed raptor spread wide embroidered wings to enfold her shoulders. She was the current reigning Hastur of Hasturs.

"I can, *domna.* It isn't so much that the spelling has changed over the centuries, but these letters were made by a machine and they differ somewhat from those written by a human hand. The script is much simpler in form."

"This first plan," he touched the bottom square and the lines changed to form eight squares, "shows the original rooms of Thendara Castle. Then it was merely the fortress of the Di Asturiens. This second one shows what was built on at the end of the third generation. And it continues on until the Castle was four stories high and contained more than two hundred rooms. As you can see when all the plans are placed together," and here he touched a red circle set beneath the blue squares, "what a rabbit-horn warren this place becomes. The first two levels are underground now and parts of this place," he gestured vaguely at the ceiling, "are twelve stories high. I doubt if anyone could give you an accurate count on the number of rooms now."

"So what you are saying, Brother Ian, is this is not going to be an easy search." Alizia voiced the unspoken thoughts of everyone in the room.

"That's right, cousin. You said that Luz's room was in the oldest part of the castle, a second-floor room. That would put it on the fourth level of this map. As you can see, the fourth level branches out in all directions. Fortunately, her room faces east, with a window. So it should be along this outside wall someplace. This room would be my suggestion." He touched a square with a broad finger. "These other rooms all run along together in a line. This one is on the end and should open onto this tunnel."

"Where does the tunnel lead?" asked Alaynna Di Asturien, the Keeper of Thendara Castle. Dark blue smudges under her eyes drained the beauty from her face. A number of heavy winter garments under the red robe made even her slender figure look bulky.

Ever since the young trainee, Luz Valeron, had disappeared on Midsummer's Eve, fires would not remain lit. It started first in the Tower and had spread throughout all of Thendara Castle. Ice covered the walls in many rooms. No sign had been found of the child. Her matrix stone showed up on the screens, so they knew she was still alive. And after much consideration and debate, the Tower circle decided she was someplace *inside* the Castle. An exhaustive physical search was made, from the attics to the cellars, but no one found her. Two attempts were made to search the overworld. Both ended with disastrous, nearly fatal results.

Finally, someone suggested asking the record keepers at Nevarsin. It galled Idriel Hastur to have to ask for help from those sandal-wearers, but at least they had sent someone who looked like a real man and not the effeminate brown-robes one sometimes saw in the City.

And help they did need.

At first it had been ghostly pranks that bothered the Tower circle. Sand in someone's shoes, clothing with the seams ripped, beds short-sheeted, irritating little pranks that annoyed. In the past two tendays the pranks had become much more personal and, in several cases, almost deadly. Isak Ardais, the Tower monitor, lay in the infirmary with two broken legs and a cracked skull, the victim of an invisible hand that pushed him down a flight of steps. Caleb Elhalyn dared not stir from his room anymore. Icy buckets of water appeared over his head, drenching him without warning. Any attempt to use the matrix screen in the Tower resulted in a backlash of power that was almost deadly in its unexpected breakage of mental rapport. And then there was the cold. Everyone who possibly could had left Thendara Castle by now.

But worse than the cold and all the personal attacks combined were the heartbreaking sobs that permeated everyone's sleep at night. Anyone with the barest scrap of *laran* heard them. A small child, lost and alone, crying for help and begging for someone to find her. No one dared close their eyes for fear of the haunting dreams of being lost themselves.

"I don't know what's beyond the tunnel, Lady Alaynna. This diagram shows a wall but nothing beyond it. There isn't even anything that shows a way into the tunnel. If the child got into the tunnel, she would be dead by now. If she were merely hiding, surely someone would have seen her by now."

"We have had a guard posted at the door to her room for the past four tendays. There is no way she could get in or out without being seen. But this problem is to the point now where we dare not use the matrix screens for fear of being attacked through them. We can't even sleep. It is definitely Luz Valeron, but somehow she is *inside* the matrices."

Brother Ian turned and motioned to a man who had been standing quietly by the fireplace.

"This is my cousin, Luis Valeron, the child's father. I asked him to join us here because I felt he might be able to shed some light on her mother."

"I thought Luz's mother was dead?" Alizia's breath puffed out in little clouds.

"Dead she might be by this time," Luis answered in a bitter voice. "I told Luz that her mother died. I didna know what else to do. Brigie ran off one fall an' took the whole year's profits with her. Luz wasn't much morn' four years old at the time. She adored her mother. How could I tell a babbie like that that her mother had deserted her? A year after that I married Lorra Alton. She tried to mother Luz, but the child had built such an image of her mother in her mind that she wouldna accept Lorra. Brigie's *laran* was always strong, but verra unstable. Neskeya Tower kept her long enough to see her through threshold sickness an' then they sent her home. When I sent Luz here, I prayed she'd find an easier road in life than the one her mother took.''

Ian slipped a long arm around Luis' shoulders. Alizia watched with the double vision of her extended *laran* and saw Ian's own special talent enfold the bitter man with warmth and understanding like a blanket. Cousin he called her and cousin he probably was. She was the only one in the room who knew exactly who he was. The Aillard Anomaly. The one true born Aillard male in every other generation of the female-dominated line. With his wife dead, the last of his children grown and a grandson appropriately born, he had removed the *di catenas* bracelet from his wrist, applied for admission at Nevarsin, and had lived there ever since.

''Do you know who Brigie's father was, *bredu?*'' Ian asked gently.

''She was festival-got. Her mother never told Brigie any morn' that. But she always said it as though it were somethin' to be proud of, so I naturally thought her father was Comyn. Brigid's hair was red enough to warrant it. The same shade as Luz's an Alizia's here.''

''And you married her for that, no doubt, thinking to make some kind of *nedestro* claim on her father's estate if you could find out who he was,'' snapped Idriel irritably, rubbing her cold hands. The light from the lamp was the only heat in the room and it was slowly fading.

''I married her because I loved her!'' barked Luis in return. ''I asked no more of her than to be my wife and mother to my children. I didna ask to be betrayed with any man who came along who could offer her morn' I could! She gave me the one lone child an' made sure there were never no more after her. She ran off, stealing the profits from the North Field sheep, leavin' me and her own child to make it as best we could through—''

''Luis,'' said Brother Ian quietly, laying a hand on the man's arm. Luis stopped shouting and drew himself up straight. He drew the plain woolen cape tighter and turned his back on the group, staring into the cold fireplace.

Idriel Hastur had the grace to drop her eyes.

''This kind of argument is getting us nowhere,'' stated the Keeper in a soft, tired voice. ''And we know that these kinds of violent emotions seem to make an opening for these mysterious accidents that have been happening. I beg you, all of you,'' she looked directly at Idriel, ''to shield your minds as strongly as possible.''

The man from Nevarsin nodded in agreement. ''I think wherever the child is, she's alive. And crying out for help. There must be some Hastur blood in this child if she is able to merge with the matrices. No other Family has that Gift. Now that we have that bit of the puzzle, let's go and look at her room.''

They warmed up a bit tramping down the long halls in the wake of Brother Ian. The cold didn't seem to bother him in the least. At the door of Luz's room, the guard saluted smartly and stood aside to let them enter.

Something made a soft *pop!* A bilious green fog billowed forth and the vile smell sent them all coughing and hacking, eyes streaming tears, stumbling back out of the room. Affected worse than the others, Idriel Hastur dropped to her knees and threw up.

"Well," said Brother Ian a few minutes later, wiping his face on a corner of his cloak, "It would seem that whatever this is doesn't want a Hastur involved."

"What makes you think that?" asked Alizia, breathing deeply of the cold clean air in the hallway. She assisted Idriel in wiping her face and mouth and directed the guard to get a servant to clean up the mess.

"The Lady Idriel was affected much more strongly than the rest of us. It was directed more at her than us. I think we are on the right track. Will you go on with us, lady?"

The tall slender woman straightened and squared her shoulders. "I have never run away from anything in my life!" she snapped, her face scarlet. "I intend to see that this problem is solved, monk, as quickly as possible."

Ian threw back his head and laughed, then threw a comradely arm around the Hastur of Hasturs and bundled her back into the room. Idriel would have shrunk from such a gesture from the most intimate of her lovers, but Alizia could see the mental shield that Ian had constructed to protect them both. She shot a quick explanation with her *laran* to Idriel. Ian's *laran* was like a warm brick at the foot of your bed on a cold night, radiating comfort and security. The others moved closer to him.

Nothing in the room greeted them this time except the cold. The smell was gone as mysteriously as it had appeared. Luis picked up a round stone from a table by the narrow bed.

"I gave her this when she left home. I told her that way she would always have a bit of home along with her." He handed it to Ian.

"That was found here by the fireplace," explained Idriel.

The lamp was fading again. Ian placed it on the table and with a flick of his hand called up a bright bluish glow to hover overhead. It gave off no warmth but provided ample illumination.

"I am often chastised for my witchery by my monkish brothers," he said in an amused tone. "I tell them I can only be as I am, nothing more." He weighed the stone in his hand. "By the fireplace, did you say?"

Idriel nodded. Her stomach hurt. Even thinking of that smell made her want to gag. And this *man* irritated her. He made her feel like a rebellious child instead of the most powerful woman in all of the Seven Domains. She knew it was only the cold and being so tired that made her short tempered, but she wished she dared order him out of her sight.

Brother Ian was kneeling in front of the fireplace. He glanced at Idriel Hastur and grinned. Alizia caught the silent exchange and hid a smile.

"Look at these carvings," he mused softly to himself. He traced a finger over the stonework that marched up and over and back down the fireplace. "Such fanciful work. None of these creatures ever existed on Darkover. Look at this." He pointed to what was obviously a horse, but with giant eagle wings sprouting from its back. "This one looks a little like a kitten thing, only with wings and very big teeth. And this little creature. He carries his wagon upside down on his back."

Bang!

His finger touched the carving and he was thrown across the room, crashing into the bed. A burnt smell filled the room. Ian lay in a crumpled heap for a second, then struggled to get up.

"Another piece of the puzzle," he muttered, smoothing down the thick homespun robe. "Cousin, you try."

"Try what?" asked Alizia skeptically.

"Touch the same carving. You are her cousin, alike enough to be her sister. And come to think of it, none of these accidents have happened to you. She may be protecting you."

"I don't know about that. The last time I saw her I gave her a good switching for arranging a nasty prank. She may be saving the worst for me."

Ian stuck his burnt finger in his mouth. Alizia finally shrugged and moved hesitantly toward the fireplace.

Nothing happened when she touched it. She used her *laran* to search for Luz's presence. Only a faint trace remained. Ian knelt beside her on the floor.

"Try pushing on it," he whispered.

She did and the rounded shell of the animal slid in. There was a grating sound that followed and one wall of the fireplace slid aside.

"A secret door. Leading where?" He gestured at the witch ball and sent it inside the opening. The rest crowded close to look. The tunnel curved downward into the dark.

Brother Ian stood up. "Well, we have found where the child went. Now we have to see where the tunnel leads. I would suggest that Luis and I go ahead alone, but, but . . ." and he raised his large hands to ward off the protest that Idriel boiled over with. "From what I have seen it is quite apparent that we will need all the power that you three women possess. I would not dare walk down that tunnel without the rest of you at my back."

I think he enjoys irritating people, thought Alizia as she followed the rest, ducking through the opening. *I can be only what I am, cousin,* echoed softly inside her mind. She choked back a laugh.

There was room inside the tunnel to stand upright. They wound down and around, following the blue sphere. It was cold. Alizia found herself wishing for a blazing fire and a large cup of spiced wine. But she just pulled her cloak tighter and bumped into Ian as he stopped in front of her. A wide blank wall barred their way.

The monk ran his hands cautiously over the wall. He stopped at a spot below his waist on his right side. His shoulders tensed under his robe but nothing happened.

"A mind lock. How fascinating. It will take more than my *laran* to open this. Lady," he motioned the Keeper forward. Alaynna stepped close, her head barely reaching his shoulder. She placed a small frail hand on the spot that Ian indicated.

"It's very complicated," she murmured softly, but a few seconds later the wall slid upward with a hiss. She stepped forward automatically.

Everyone else followed her. The first thing Alizia noticed was the warmth. It was dry and hot in the room. With a snap of his fingers, the witch ball went out and everyone jumped as a bell chimed three times, then watched in amazement as strips along the walls lit up.

"You know what this is, don't you?" he asked to no one in particular. The room was round, dominated by a circular desk. Inside the desk was a huge lattice screen. It was empty. Alizia could not conceive of the matrix stone that would be large enough to fill it. Metal chairs were scattered all over. "This is a Tower work room, built by the ancients. This technology must have come from the original crew."

"What are you talking about?" asked Idriel sharply.

But the monk wasn't listening to her. He moved around the room, not quite touching everything. The force of his curiosity almost glowed. Alizia stood with the Keeper and Luis Valeron by the door. Brother Ian shoved back the hood on his robe and wiped sweat from his bald head.

"It's hot in here," he said abstractedly. He picked up something from the floor and shook it out. It was a child's sweater, embroidered along the edges with *kireseth* flowers.

"That's Luz's," stated her father.

"And here is her name." Idriel Hastur had moved opposite the monk and pointed to a flat gray panel embedded into the desk.

Luz Valeron. Printed in a childish scrawl.

"She was here, but where is she now?" asked Ian. He picked up a pen that was attached by a fine chain to the desk and hunkered down until he could rest his arm on the desk and before anyone could stop him, proceded to spell out his own name.

The lights flickered and a mechanical voice

boomed out: *"INTRUDER ALERT! NO SUCH TOWER WORKER AT THIS STATION! INTRUDER ALERT! AFFIRMATIVE ACTION REQUIRED IMMEDIATELY. LEVEL FOUR HAS BEEN REACHED!"*

The opening behind then slid closed. Alizia and the others huddled together, hands over their ears. Cold descended and they watched in horror as a matrix stone began to form inside the lattice screen. It was enormous. Light pulsated and sparks snapped. Brother Ian watched, fascinated, as a malicious face appeared in the ghostly stone. Then they heard a childish voice cry out, "Father!"

"Idriel, I'm going to need your help on this," Ian said quickly. The Hastur of Hasturs nodded and stepped in front of him, throwing her arms wide as though she would pick up the pulsating matrix from the lattice screen.

The face grinned wider and incorporate hands reached out. Idriel Hastur was a living matrix. Of all those born with *laran* she alone wore no blue starstone. Automatically, Alaynna threw up a mind link between them. Ian stepped behind Idriel and joined his mind to hers, too.

The eerie hands enveloped Ian and Idriel and a second later they disappeared. A heartbeat after that, the ghostly matrix was gone. Warmth and light seeped back into the room. A bell rang and the voice boomed out again: *"AFFIRMATIVE ACTION COMPLETE. RETURN TO LEVEL ONE."*

"Where did they go?" Alizia screamed out, looking around at the empty room.

Alaynna's face was completely blank as she spoke. "They are still alive, but there is a strong barrier between them and us. Whatever plane they are on, it is not one that I have ever breached before. I can still sense them.'' She staggered a little. Alizia caught her before Luis could touch her, then helped her into one of the rolling chairs. She shared a frightened look with Luis and they both wondered what they would do next.

Brother Ian knew he was alive. His mind was working, but his body seemed to have disappeared. Curiously enough, his mind shared whatever space this was with the furious mind of Idriel Hastur.

Where are we?!! she demanded.

I have no idea, but with a guess I would say we are inside the matrix.

You are here, where intruders are kept, boomed a hungry voice. Someone else joined with them. It was the child, Luz Valeron. She was frightened and crying and her mind clung pathetically to Ian's and Idriel's.

I saw my father, she cried. *Where is he? I want to go to him.*

Ian automatically shushed her, offering what comfort he could in this astral form. The child continued to cry.

What do you want from us? Idriel thought angrily. *Who are you that you would treat the Hastur of Hasturs in such a manner? Have you no idea who I am?*

Laughter echoed around them. *You are held here, Hastur of Hasturs. This plane was created to trap those who had no business in a secured area. You will be detained here until given the proper clearance.*

And what if we do not receive this ''proper clearance?'' asked Ian.

Then here you will remain, the voice announced.

So what do we do now? Idriel snapped at Ian.

You are the educated monk from Nevarsin, you think of something.

Nevarsin? There is no proper clearance for this Nevarsin. There is no Tower there, the voice answered Idriel. Ian could sense how brittle her mind had become. The little girl cried harder.

Luz, Ian asked suddenly, *why did you play all those nasty tricks on everyone in the Tower at first, but recently all you have done is cry?*

At first it was fun, Luz answered. *Like hide and seek. I could see them, but they couldn't see me.* She snuffled and he imagined her wiping her nose. *Then it wouldn't help me anymore unless I told it stuff. But I didn't understand what it wanted and I just wanted to go home. I'm sorry I pushed Isak down the steps. I just want to go home!* She began crying again.

Idriel, take the child and go back, Ian said. *I will keep whatever this is occupied.*

And how do you propose I do that, monk? I have no idea how to get back.

Avarra's eyes, woman, you're the Hastur of Hasturs! Or so you keep telling anyone who will listen. You have the power inside you to get out. Find it! Use it! And stop sniveling and do what you were born and bred to do! You wouldn't want to be grateful to some sandal-wearing monk from Nevarsin for saving you, would you? So get on with it! Ian could sense the blaze of rage that his words lit in Idriel.

Nevarsin? Nevarsin? What is this place? The child was interesting, but her mind is full of simple things. Is this Nevarsin a new group headquarters?

No, Nevarsin is a place of learning. Release this woman and the child and I will tell you about it. She knows nothing of interest to you and you know the child is harmless . . . Idriel, take the child and go . . . I know many interesting things to tell you, but we can't be disturbed by the whining of women and children.

You are right, boomed the voice. *Women know nothing of strategy or plans. They will be sent elsewhere.*

The rage in Idriel Hastur built and reached a bursting point. She felt her mind merge with the matrix, the two become one. She wanted out! Taking control of herself and the child she walked away, tearing asunder the astral boundries that kept her penned here. As she and Luz dropped out of the restraining net, the last thing she heard was the admiration in Brother Ian's mind as he shouted, *You are indeed Hastur of Hasturs!*

And as she hit the hard floor of the strange Tower room, his voice came once again across the boundary, *And now, my friend, we shall see what we can learn from each other.*

Idriel awoke to the comfort of her own bed. Blazing in the hearth was a roaring fire and on her bedside table was a pitcher of mulled wine. Alizia Aillard sat in a chair beside the bed.

"We thought you would never wake up," she chided softly, helping Idriel to sit up and handing her a cup of the wine. "You've been asleep for two days."

"I feel like I've been run over by a herd of chervines," Idriel answered between sips of wine. She felt bruised from head to toe and each movement was agony. "What happened?"

"You brought Luz out of the matrix. You reappeared just like you disappeared, only this time you had her in your arms. Alaynna opened the door and we carried you out. Since then the icy pall that has frozen this Castle has disappeared and things have returned to normal.''

Idriel groaned and pushed herself up. Alizia arranged several pillows behind her and she collapsed against them.

''Brother Ian. Did he get out, too?''

From the look on Alizia's face Idriel knew what the answer was.

''He made me deliberately mad, Alizia. He knew I couldn't open that plane unless I was furious. And he distracted whatever that guardian was long enough for me to do it. I should have brought him back out with me, but all I could think of was getting myself out.''

''You did bring Luz back with you.''

''Only with Ian's help. I can't believe the risk he took. Now I have to owe that man.

''I think he was counting on that, Idriel. I think he knew that somehow, someway you will go back and get him out.''

Idriel slid down flat in the bed and pulled the covers up under her chin.

''And how does he expect me to do that?''

''I don't know,'' answered Alizia. ''You are the Hastur of Hasturs. It's up to you to think of something.''

Destined for the Tower

by Deborah Wheeler and Elisabeth Waters

Elisabeth Waters has had a story in each of the Darkover anthologies to date; Deborah Wheeler is in all but three of them.

What, then, can I say about either of them that hasn't been said? Well, each of them has written a novel, and DAW Books has bought both novels! Elisabeth's won the Gryphon Award offered by Andre Norton, and I have no doubt whatever that Deborah's book will be equally readable.

I'm glad to claim these two gifted young women—along with Diana, though like Diana, they are not really that *young except by contrast with me—as my literary daughters.*

Deborah and Elisabeth were both too tasteful to say so, but I can tell you that the point of this story is that Diotima Ridenow (whom you may remember from SHARRA's EXILE) chose the most obvious method of making herself unsuitable for a Keeper. And of course you remember the main distinction of a Keeper. . . .

Diotima Ridenow wandered through a blue fog, searching for someone, someone important, she couldn't think who. There was something subtly, horribly wrong about the blue. Surely the overworld should be gray. She remembered she was looking for her mother, and her mother was dead. Did the dead feel so cold, as if they were encased in ice?

With every step now, it was harder to go on, as if her body were freezing solid. She could no longer move, could no longer feel her arms and legs. It was becoming harder and harder to breathe. She wasn't breathing. Was she dead, too?

Before her lay a coffin. Expecting to see her mother, she peered into it. Inside, Ashara opened her ice colored eyes and reached long thin arms toward her. Dio recoiled with a terrified scream. . . .

She jerked awake and found herself sitting upright in her bed, shivering violently. Her blonde hair tumbled about her face. Around her, the Tower walls were hard and gray, still ringing with the echoes of her scream.

The door opened smoothly and her aunt Jerana glided in, a faded shadow of a woman in the crimson draperies of an under-Keeper. Her brows creased slightly in disapproval.

"Dio, you know better than to leave your body without a monitor there to watch it. Surely by this stage of your training you know how dangerous that can be." She sat down on the foot of the bed, ignoring both the rumpled bedcovers and Dio's obvious distress.

Dio swallowed, trying to speak.

"We all know how disturbed you are by your mother's death," Jerana went on calmly. "It is particularly unfortunate that it should occur at this stage of your training. Later on, you would have been able to deal with it better."

Dio looked into her aunt's eyes and noticed they were pale gray. Surely they'd been green when she was a girl. She shivered again, remembering the dream. "I saw . . . in the coffin . . . I saw Mother Ashara. . . ."

"Of course you did. She's a mother to all of us. But I assure you, she is still very much with us. You need not worry, child; Mother Ashara will never leave you." Jerana tucked the covers around her niece with a firm hand. "Go to sleep now. You have a long journey ahead of you tomorrow, but you will be back among us and safe soon enough.

The next morning, Dio went to take her formal leave of Ashara, Keeper of Comyn Tower. Ashara's chamber was at the very top of the Tower, reached by some mysterious ancient machinery, a relic from the Ages of Chaos, which carried Dio up a smooth tunnel as if she were floating on a calm wind. As she entered Ashara's presence, Dio was struck by the immense, almost inhuman stillness that emanated from the room. It seemed unusually quiet today, almost as if she were the only living creature in this portion of the Tower.

Dio straightened her shoulders and composed her face into the proper neutrality for an under-Keeper-in-training. This room always made her feel claustrophobic, which was odd because it appeared to be infinite. Daylight filtered through the translucent walls, making the figure of Ashara, sitting on her great carven glass throne and wearing a loose blue-gray robe, virtually invisible. Dio had the fanciful thought that the entire room was part of Ashara, that Ashara encompassed the room, rather than the other way around. She told herself uneasily that this notion was just a residue from her nightmare, and she stood quietly, waiting for Ashara to speak.

"My daughter." Ashara's voice flowed out across the room, seeming to come at Dio from all angles. As always, she felt surrounded, inundated by Ashara's presence.

"I am sorry for the death of your mother."

"Thank you," Dio murmured mechanically.

"It is particularly unfortunate that it should occur at this time. It is unusual for a Keeper to leave the Tower at this point in her training, but I have no choice. Since you are not yet formally sworn to me, your duty to your family takes precedence."

"Yes, Mother Ashara," Dio said numbly.

"But it need not be too long a delay. You will return directly after Midsummer, and then you will take your Keeper's Oath."

Ashara's words, her very presence, clung to Dio as she was carried downward in the strange vertical shaft. She found herself remembering her aunt Jerana's words, "Mother Ashara will never leave you," but they filled her with uneasiness instead of comfort.

Nonsense, she told herself, *I'm just upset, that's all. Going home to Serrais for the funeral is a duty like any other, easily borne and soon passed. Then I'll be back and take my place as Ashara's under-Keeper, as is my right as a Comynara. It's what I've worked so hard all these years for. . . .*

The day was bright and windy, and the roads muddy from last night's rain. Only a few miles out of Thendara, one of the guards spotted a party on the road ahead. Dio saw a flash of red-gold hair in the center of the group. Instantly she recognized

Lerrys, her favorite of her five older brothers. He, too, would have been summoned to Serrais for the funeral, probably from a round of partying in Thendara.

She sent out a mental call. Lerrys spun his horse around and gave the order to halt. In a few minutes her party had drawn even with his.

"Little sister, how you've grown!" As usual, Lerrys was elegantly dressed, even in his most somber clothing. A smile crossed his fair, angular features. "You left for the Tower a child, and return to us a woman!"

"I am hardly returning to you," Dio replied with spirit. "Only a few days' visit to see our mother decently buried."

"And for Midsummer Festival, as much as Father will allow us," Lerrys said. He'd never lied to Dio as a child, and now he made no pretense of disguising his disappointment at missing the Festival in Thendara with his friends to pretend mourning for a woman he'd scarcely known. Lady Serrais had taken little interest in him as a child and none at all from the time she realized he had no intention of giving her grandsons. And she had been ill even before Dio had left for the Tower several years earlier, so her death now had come as no particular surprise.

Dio shook her head, her travel veils rippling in the wind. "You may be able to dance away most of the night and end it in any bed you wish, but Father will doubtless pack me off to my room after the first few dances. I'll be going back to the Tower the next morning to take my final Oath."

Lerrys gave her a quick, discerning glance, and she felt his mind brush briefly against hers. For a moment he was silent, thoughtful. "Are you sure that's what you really want, little sister?"

She opened her mouth to answer, but he'd already spurred his horse forward, mud splashing behind him. Dio, an enthusiastic rider, booted her horse into a gallop after him. Her chaperone, a young Tower technician, followed with a patient sigh.

They pushed on as far as possible that day, until the last rays of the red sun vanished behind the hills and they were forced to make camp. Dio climbed stiffly out of her saddle and handed the reins to one of the guards. She shocked her sedate, proper chaperone by helping to set up the tents and picket lines. After dinner, she sat with Lerrys around the dying fire, her face shadowed by Kyrrdis' blue light. She stretched and groaned.

"Sore muscles?" he asked, raising one eyebrow.

"Yes, but they're worth it. I'd forgotten how much I love riding."

"You always were a tomboy."

"A what?"

He grinned wickedly. "It's a Terranan term. Invented to describe you."

Dio made a face at him, feeling oddly childlike and free. It was good to be able to laugh and joke, to be with someone who was not trying to mold her into the image of a perfect Comyn Keeper. "At least we can be sure of one thing," she pointed out. "After today's ride, we'll all sleep well tonight."

In her dreams, Dio was once again a small child, watching the Festival Ball dancers with a mixture of delight and anticipation. This was the first year she had been allowed to attend at all, and she was so excited she could hardly stand still. Aunt Jerana danced past, her hair shining to match the gold trim of her elegant gown. Her eyes sparkled the same brilliant green as the full skirt that billowed about her as she spun in the intricate figures of the pattern dance. Dio watched, rapt in admiration; surely her aunt was the most beautiful lady in the room.

As the music came to an end, Jerana saw Dio watching from the corner and danced lightly over to her. "Are you enjoying this, little one?" she asked in a light, musical voice.

"Oh, yes," Dio replied enthusiastically. "It's wonderful! I wish I could dance like you." Jerana laughed and scooped Dio up into her arms as the music started again.

"So you shall, *chiya.*" She whirled back into the pattern, still holding the child, and Dio laughed in delight.

But suddenly the room turned cold; she was so cold. Blue fog swirled around them, shrouding the other dancers and muffling the sound of the music, which gradually faded into silence. The blue light grew stronger, and Jerana's eyes no longer brimmed with vivacious laughter and joy of being alive. Her face had gone inhumanly serene, without even the memory of a smile, and the color faded from her cheeks and eyes.

Now the blue fog was turning solid, like ice freezing from the outside in. Jerana danced on, unheeding, still holding Dio, but seemingly no longer aware of her. Dio looked around in wild desperation, searching for a way out. The blueness was faceted at the edges, smooth regular planes closing in on them. Horrified, Dio realized that they were in the center of a matrix.

She tried to call out for help, but her voice bounced back from the sides of the matrix, nearly deafening her with reverberations. Her words were trapped within the crystal, trapped as securely as her body in her aunt's arms.

She awoke, gasping, her face covered with cold sweat. Kyrrdis, now near descent, bathed her pallet in blue-green light through an opening in the tent. Her blankets lay heaped to one side. She must have tossed them off in her sleep. That was why she felt so cold, she told herself, the reason for her nightmare. Yet it was a long time before she could sleep again.

Throughout the next day's journey, the arrival at Serrais, and her mother's funeral, Lerrys' words echoed through Dio's mind. "Are you sure that's what you really want, little sister?"

Am I sure. . . ? She had never asked herself this question before. No one had ever asked it. It had been planned from the time she was born that she would go to the Tower to serve Mother Ashara and the Comyn, even as her aunt Jerana had done. She thought of her aunt, who had been gay and laughing when she played with her as a small child. When Dio first came to Comyn Tower, she had been surprised to find her aunt a stranger, pale and quiet in her red draperies, a faint shadow of her former self.

No, Dio realized with a shock. *Not of her former self. A faint shadow of Ashara. Is that what will happen to me?*

Suddenly she wanted very much *not* to return to the Tower in two days' time. Squaring her shoulders, she went in search of her father, who had retired to his study after the funeral and had been there all afternoon. She'd have just enough to time to speak to him before dinner.

The heat from the roaring fire struck her full in the face. Her father slumped in a chair nearby, an empty brandy glass in his hand. She went to him but did not reach out, the Keeper's habit of isolation already ingrained in her. He looked up, his eyes red-rimmed, whether with weeping or brandy she could not tell. If he had been anyone else, she would have sensed what he was feeling, but her father had always kept himself tightly barriered against his children. In fact, all members of her family had strong shields against their empathic gifts, although Lerrys sometimes allowed his to drop around her so they could talk mind to mind.

There was no graceful way to begin. ''Father,'' she blurted out, ''I don't want to go straight back to the Tower. I want to stay home for awhile.''

He blinked at her in surprise. ''What? Whatever for?'' He indicated a letter lying on his small secretary desk. ''My sister writes that you are doing well, a credit to our family. She says you'll be taking your Oath as soon as you return.''

Dio hesitated. ''I'm not sure I'm ready for that.''

''Surely Ashara and Jerana are better judges of that then you are,'' he said gruffly.

''But it's my life,'' Dio said slowly, ''and I'm not sure I want to end up like Aunt Jerana. I remember what she was like before she went to the Tower—and you must remember even better than I. You saw her again when you took me there. She's not the same person, you must know that.''

''Of course not,'' he replied impatiently. ''She's a Keeper.''

"But she's not Jerana any more! Even her eyes are a different color!"

He scowled. "What are you talking about?"

"They used to be green, and now they're pale, blue-gray, like ice."

"Don't be silly, child." He got up and poured himself another glass of brandy from the decanter on the sideboard, turning his back on her. "Everyone's eyes fade as they get older."

Dio walked around him and locked her eyes with his. "Your eyes are still green, and you're older than she is."

"What difference does it make what color her eyes are? A Keeper's work is more important than her physical appearance. Jerana is a credit to her family and her caste, as you will be as soon as you get over this foolishness. It is a great honor to be chosen by Ashara. Do you know how few girls she finds suitable?"

"And have you ever wondered why that is?" Dio shot back. "And why do many of them fail the training? The other Towers don't even require a Keeper to remain a virgin all her life, and Ashara's training only starts there!"

Her father scowled fiercely at her. "Mind your tongue, girl. That is not a proper subject for discussion between father and daughter." Dio flushed and lowered her eyes. "Ashara trains Keepers in the old ways," he continued, "the ways that have kept the Towers strong for centuries. My sister was trained in that way, and my aunt before her; the daughters of our family have been Keepers, good Keepers, for generations. I'll not have you whining and asking impertinent questions about things that are none of your affair!"

Dio felt the blood burn within her veins. She lifted her chin and looked straight into her father's eyes. "You are saying that my life and my body are not my business. You know what happened to Aunt Jerana—whether you admit it or not—and what will happen to me, and you don't care!"

"Don't you dare talk to me like that!" her father thundered. "Go to your room and stay there until you remember your manners! And you *are* going back to the Tower, first thing in the morning after the Festival. I'd send you back this instant if I could!"

But then my escort would miss their Festival celebration in the village, Dio thought angrily, *and you care more for them than for me!* She whirled and ran from the room, slamming the door behind her.

Dio's anger spilled over into her dreams, for when she found herself once more trapped in the blue matrix, she punched through the nearest faceted wall with her bare fist. It shattered with a satisfying crack, followed by a tinkling sound as the fragments tumbled to the floor. Heedless of her bare feet, she pushed her way through the opening, only to discover that there was no floor on the other side. She floated slowly downward, the shattered crystal receding above her head. Only then did she realize she was still in her nightgown, surrounded by the nearly featureless gray of the overworld.

In the distance she could see Comyn Tower, a steady blue light surrounded by the small firefly lights of the Thendaran matrix mechanics, but not all the imps in Zandru's forge could induce her to return there. She could see the flicker of other towers—Arilinn, Dalereuth, Neskaya, Corandolis—but she knew there was no help for her from any of them. Yet she could not remain here, in the overworld, for any length of time without discovery.

The next moment she found herself standing beside her mother's grave in the family burial ground at Serrais. "I wish you were still here, Mother," she whispered. "Father would listen to you." Cold tears began to trickle down her cheeks. "But then, you might simply tell me to obey my father."

She sighed, her anger draining away and leaving an almost paralyzing weariness in its wake. "Maybe I should obey him. It's what I've worked toward; it's all I know. And I would be a Keeper of Comyn Tower; they might even let me have Arilinn or Neskaya. Maybe it wouldn't be so bad—and it's not as if I have anywhere else to go." She stared down at the unresponsive mound of earth at her feet for several minutes before returning to the house. She walked through the door of her bedroom, where her body waited on the bed, but suddenly stopped, confronted by the mirror which stood directly opposite the door.

The reflection in the mirror was Ashara's.

Dio gasped in horror, her hand flying to her mouth, and for an instant the reflection flickered and she saw herself, green eyes wide and staring and blonde hair hanging lank and loose about her shoulders. But as she watched, her expression grew calm, her hair changed to silver, her eyes faded from green through gray to ice-blue, and once again the image was Ashara's.

Dio woke once again sitting bolt upright in bed with her heart hammering. It took her several long minutes to get up the nerve to leave her bed and look in the mirror. The image in the mirror was her own, with no hint of Ashara visible. Still, Dio spent the remainder of the night pacing the floor and checking the mirror at frequent intervals.

With trembling hands, Dio pulled off the dress of soft blue wool embroidered with flaxen lilies which had been her only formal gown when she still lived at Serrais. The years in Thendara had added inches as well as curves to her body and there was no way she could appear in public wearing it. And if she had to remain in her room tonight, she would have no chance to speak to Lerrys, the one person who might conceivably help her, and she would be shipped back to Thendara in the morning just as surely as if she were a sheep for the slaughter. Close to tears, she rumpled the dress and threw it down in a heap.

Dio wrapped herself in an oversized dressing gown and stormed down the hallway. Perhaps some visiting lady had left a gown, out of style no doubt, but still wearable. In one of the guest bedrooms, she spied a huge old chest. She lifted the lid and reached in, pushing aside the heavy layers of cedar-scented fabric. She laid aside a heavy cloak in black wool trimmed with tatty fur, more suitable for a grandmother than . . . whatever she was. The dress beneath it was faded and carefully patched but clean. Evanda alone knew how it got there; it was the sort of cast-off a village girl might wear to Festival.

At the bottom of the chest, Dio spied something in bright green and gold, the Ridenow colors. Hardly daring to breathe, she drew out the gown and held it up. The folds of rich fabric gleamed in the candlelight. The bodice tapered to a point, the skirt flared out, full and graceful. It was a dress fit for a Comynara, and, yes, she thought it might fit.

Dio scooped up the gown, folded the village girl's dress in it, and hurried back to her room. She hid the dress under her travel cloak and rang for a maid to help lace her into the gown. When that was done and the maid off on another errand, she studied herself in the mirror. The gown fit perfectly, as if it had been made for her. She smiled at her image, and then frowned. There was something oddly familiar about the gown, but she had never worn one like it before. She pirouetted, watching the skirt billow around her, and suddenly it came to her where she had seen this dress before.

Jerana had worn it that Festival Night so long ago, Dio's first and Jerana's last. Jerana had worn it in her dream.

Dio's chin lifted in a gesture of defiance. She hoped her father would remember the dress, too. Tonight might be the last time he would permit her to wear the Ridenow green and gold. If so, she would wear them proudly.

The Great Hall at Serrais was full but slightly subdued in deference to the recent death. Some of the guests wore somber colors, but many had donned their usual Midsummer finery. After all, Lady Serrais had been decently buried, with all due solemnity and honor, and the Festival Ball came only once a year. Down in the village, the tenants and craftsmen held their own much less formal celebrations. There would be a new crop of village babies in seven months.

"I give it about two hours," Lerrys murmured to Dio as the pattern of the first dance carried them briefly together. "After that, Father will go to bed and everyone else will liven up."

Dio tossed her head and smiled absently at her partner, a portly, middle-aged man of impeccable propriety, a distant cousin. She waited until she was again close enough to Lerrys to whisper. "The first couples dance—with me!"

Lerrys raised one eyebrow speculatively but did not have an opportunity to reply.

Shortly afterward, Lord Serrais retired to his ornately carved chair on the dais, signaling the end of the first round of formal set dances. The orchestra began a sedate tune, suitable for the older couples to dance together while they still had the energy. Moving with elegant grace, Lerrys returned his last partner to her female relatives and crossed the floor to Dio. His mouth curled in a sardonic smile as he bowed to her.

"The honor, dear sister?"

Dio took his proffered hand with a sweeping curtsy. His hand around her waist was light but comforting. She leaned closer so that they could talk without being overheard.

"What is it, *chiya?*"

"Lerrys, I need your help!" she blurted out. "Father's going to send me back to the Tower and I'll never get away again. Ashara will take me over, just the way she did Aunt Jerana."

"Ahhh . . ." He glanced across the room, turbulent now with swirling plaids and skirts. "I was right, then." Dio could hear the pain behind his bantering words. Her brother's only value to Lord Serrais was as a father of sons, just as hers was as a Keeper.

Lerrys . . . She cried out with her mind. He flinched as if she had struck him.

"I'll stick by you, little sister. Do you want to run away, or are you going to just dig in your heels and refuse to go?"

She shrugged. "I don't have much choice. If I don't go to the Tower, Father won't want me here, either, will he?"

"We can always run away to Vainwal together and become professional dancers," Lerrys said lightly. "Unless you're desperate enough to become a Free Amazon."

Dio shuddered and grimaced. "I hope it won't come to that."

"It will be hard to hide you from Ashara."

"Unless Ashara doesn't want me any more. But after that, nobody else might, either."

Lerrys looked sharply at her. "Whatever happens, you'll always be my sister."

The dance ended. As their hands parted, Dio sent Lerrys a mental message of gratitude. Lord Serrais had risen at the end of the dance and now he approached them. "Come, Diotima, it is time for us both to retire."

"Yes, Father," she murmured, dropping her eyes. She went quietly to her room, the perfect picture of a modest Comyn Keeper-in-training.

Dio sat on the stone windowsill of her room, wearing the village girl's Festival dress. The night was unseasonably warm, even for Midsummer, and she'd opened the shutters. The great house lay about her, dark and still, but music and laughter from the village below floated up to her.

Above her, pearly Mormallor had risen to join its three companions. Dio recalled the old proverb,

"Nobody remembers next day what was done under the four moons." In her case, she thought somberly, nobody would ever forget it.

She thought of the life she could never return to. Her father would be furious. He might even disown her. But then again, he might not, as long as she didn't get with child from this night, and she had training enough to prevent that. But Ashara would never take her back as a Keeper.

She was throwing away all the dreams she'd had, all the plans she had ever made, all the long years of work in the Tower. She might have been Lady of Thendara. Now she would be . . . what?

Dio. Dio and nobody else.

She would have no more nightmares.

She smiled faintly and picked up her shawl. Quietly she slipped out of the house and down to the village.

The Madwoman of the Kilghard Hills

by Joan Marie Verba

Joan Marie Verba has had stories printed in many of these anthologies as well as in SCIENCE FICTION REVIEW. Her first book, VOYAGER: EXPLORING THE OUTER PLANETS, was published in 1991; it is, of course, nonfiction. Like many of the writers in these anthologies, she is also working on a novel.

One of the more notable things about this story is that it features Kennard Alton, one of the main characters in the middle period Darkover stories. He appears first in STAR OF DANGER, makes further appearances in HERITAGE OF HASTUR and THE BLOODY SUN, then dies in SHARRA'S EXILE. Just what I like—a story about a favorite character, at least of mine.

Young Kennard Lanart sat on the grassy hillside to catch his breath. His brother, Lewis-Valentine, and his foster sister, Dorilys, had run too far ahead for him to catch up. He could no longer see them through the woods and the thick underbrush. But above the trees, he could see the tops of the walls surrounding his Armida home. They were probably in the house by now, snatching pieces of fresh-baked sweets from the kitchen folk.

A pair of antlers stuck up among the grasses, rocking back and forth as they moved across Kennard's path. Cautiously, Kennard crept forward. Two paces away from the antlers, he stopped. A rabbit-horn mother was leading her brood through the woods. The young ones only had bumps where horns would later grow. Kennard counted five babies.

A tiny rustling made him turn. Another rabbit-thorn was tangled in thorns, unable to extract itself. Kennard took his gloves from his belt—his father had given him the gloves last winter on his seventh birthday—and walked over to the thornbush.

"So your brothers and sisters left you behind, too?" Kennard said softly. Gently, without touching the entangled creature, he parted the thorns with his hands. The rabbit-thorn, only slightly scratched, quickly hopped after its siblings.

Something larger rustled the branches uphill from Kennard. A chervine? They were about as big as a horse, and had antlers like a rabbit-horn, only larger. Kennard shifted his weight back and forth, straining to see, but there was too much brush and too many trees between him and what was making the noise. Or maybe Lewis and Dorilys had doubled back, to sneak up from behind and scare him?

The noise continued, but no one appeared. Kennard put his hands on his hips. "All right! I know you're there! Just come out. I'm not walking up there." The rustling stopped. Kennard took a step toward where he last heard the noise. "I said I'm not coming up there."

A large red shape leapt out at him. Kennard got

the swift impression of a melon head covered with scraggly hair before he turned and ran, screaming, to the gates of Armida.

One of the guards at the gate, Edric, caught Kennard about the waist, swung him off his feet, and set him back down. "Here, now, what is it, young Ken? Bandits?"

"I don't know," said Kennard. "This *thing* came at me." He had had such a brief glimpse that even the impression he had was fading, and he found he could not describe it.

Edric motioned to two other men. "We'll have a look," he told Kennard. "Let me take you in to your father and tell him, in case there are bandits outside."

The family had settled in the Great Hall by the time Edric returned. Kennard's father Valdir sat in a soft chair, reading a book; Elorie, Kennard's mother, embroidered a shirt nearby. Lewis and Dorilys worked on puzzle pieces spread on the floor. Kennard did not feel like putting a puzzle together, and he found reading hard since he had to hold books at arm's length just to make out the letters. Instead, he arranged his toy guardsmen on the table in various fighting positions.

"We've searched the woods all around Armida, Lord Alton," said Edric to Valdir, "but we've seen nothing. It's possible that your son saw a chervine or a *cralmac* out of its territory. There are no signs of bandits, and no word of any in the nearby villages. We'll keep a close watch for the next day or two just in case, though."

Valdir nodded. "Thank you."

"Maybe Kennard saw that wood hag that Mirella told us about," volunteered Dorilys.

Elorie looked up from her needlework and smiled. "Don't tell me you believe old Mirella's tale about that woman with the spindly fingers who snatches disobedient children and eats them for supper," she said. "She was scaring your Uncle Valdir with those stories when he was a child."

Valdir turned to Lewis and Dorilys. "Now you see why I told you children not to separate, even in sight of these walls? What if there *had* been bandits in the hills? We might never have seen Kennard again."

Lewis looked down at the floor as he answered, "We didn't *mean* to lose him. He just didn't keep up."

Elorie and Valdir exchanged knowing glances. Valdir said, "It will be a while before I let you out of these walls without an escort. And Kennard can go ask the kitchen folk for an extra plate of sweets, while you two go without. Maybe you'll think again before leaving your brother to fend for himself."

The kitchen folk let Kennard sit on the counter with a jar of baked sweets at his side. He listened to their talk as he ate.

Janna, the head cook, patted Kennard's leg with a thick hand. "Don't feel too hard about Lewis leaving you out in the woods. He loves you none the less, he's just showing off for your cousin Dorilys. After she's been here a while, he'll go rock-hunting or butterfly-chasing with you as he always did."

Kennard shrugged. He was annoyed at Lewis for leaving him behind, but it had not been the first time, Dorilys or no, and besides, Kennard felt much better now that he could eat his fill.

"What do you think he saw?" asked Liriel, as she washed up the pots and plates from the midday meal.

"Oh, not Mirella's witch-hag, to be sure," said Janna, taking her cleaning cloth to a flour-dusty counter. "That tale was old in my granddam's time."

"When I was at my mother's a tenday ago," said Fiona, who rinsed and dried the dishes and gave them to Tani to put away, "she told me a woman came to her village not long ago, begging for rags, and asking to trade dolls for thread and a bit of food. She was a bit addled, my mother said, but the dolls were beautifully sewn. Some of the little girls in the village pestered their mothers for the dolls, and the woman got what she wanted and went away."

"Why," said Tani, reaching to put the clean plates on a high shelf, "that sounds a bit like the story my sister told me of a woman come to her town, only she told fortunes for food."

"Ah, that's it, then," said Janna, putting a hand on her back and straightening up, "young Kennard here saw nought but a peddler woman."

"It didn't *look* like a peddler woman," Kennard mumbled.

Janna patted Kennard's shoulder. "Well, you were startled, *chiyu.* A brief glance in an unguarded moment would make a stout tree look like a giant with a battle ax."

Several *leroni* had stopped at Armida on their way from visiting kin in the Ridenow lands to their home at Arilinn Tower. After joining in the formal greetings, the three children left Valdir and Elorie talking to the guests. Kennard was aware that the adults hoped that each child would grow up with *laran,* but to Kennard, this business about reading minds was mostly boring grownup stuff. He was glad when the adults let them go.

Lewis and Dorilys quickly ran out of sight, down a long corridor and around a corner. Kennard did not even try to follow. He walked to the barn to see his pony. As he stroked the animal's sides, Bard, the horsemaster, walked up.

"Deserted again, young Kennard?"

The boy shrugged.

"Well, if it makes you feel any better, lots of boys Lewis' age show off when there are girls around. When you're a year or two older, you may find yourself doing the same thing."

Kennard went on stroking the horse.

"Why not saddle up and get some exercise? Whatever startled you hasn't come back, and since the worst of winter's so close now, there shouldn't be any bandits around. I'm sure the guardsmen at the gate will let you go just up the road and back."

As Kennard trotted out, Edric simply called to him not to ride too far and to come back soon. The day was sunny and the horse seemed glad for the air. Beyond the first bend of the road a woman wearing a dirty red-plaid skirt sat on the grassy bank, sewing. Kennard reined in the horse and turned. He saw Edric at the gate, but the guard could not see the woman because the hill's foot, which had caused the road to take a turn, blocked his view. Kennard decided it was safe enough to approach her. He was within shouting distance of

Edric, and besides, he had his horse and his knife, plus his short sword that his father was teaching him to use. He dismounted and led the horse to where the woman sat.

The woman did not look up. Her oily hair, which could have been light brown or light red, fell forward over her face. Kennard wondered how she could see. He leaned back a little to get a clearer view. Her fine stitches outlined a beautiful eye on the rag head, a head stuffed with fresh-smelling wild grass.

The woman rocked back and forth as she stitched. "Want me to tell your fortune?" she asked. The voice was soft and clear, not old and cracked, as Kennard half-expected.

Kennard glanced back the way he came to reassure himself that he could get away quickly if he wished. "I . . . I don't have any money with me."

"Din't ask for none." She took the needle and rag doll in one hand. "Saw you before, but you ran off 'fore I could tell you nothing." Still rocking, she patted the ground beside her with the other hand.

Kennard sat about a pace away from her, holding tightly to the reins. There was enough slack for the horse to graze.

The woman edged closer. "Tell your future?"

He shrugged.

She reached inside her blouse. He could not see what she took out, but a blue glow came from her cupped hands. She concentrated for what Kennard thought was a long time. "See a wife and two boys for you," she said at last.

"But that's my mother and father and Lewis and I."

She shook her head. Her hair, long and in disarray, still covered her face. She reached back in her blouse.

Kennard heard horses' hooves on the road and turned. The *leroni* and their escort were leaving Armida. He pulled his horse to the side of the road and watched as they passed by. When they had gone, he looked back at the hill behind him. The woman had disappeared. He opened his mouth to call, but realized he did not know her name. Looking down, he saw the doll with the half-finished face. The one eye stared up at him. The woman might come back for it, but he hated to leave it on the ground. Resolving to give it back to the woman later, he picked it up and stuffed it deep inside his jacket.

"Father, what's it like to have *laran?*"

Valdir put down his book. "You can tell what people are thinking, or feeling, for one."

The boy shifted his weight uncomfortably. He knew only too well that his father often sensed what he thought or felt.

Valdir smiled. "I suppose you meant something more, such as what the *leroni* do?"

Kennard nodded.

Valdir reached into his shirt. The gesture was nearly the same one the woman on the road had used. Kennard watched, stunned. But his father did not seem to notice. He brought out a silk bag at the end of the necklace he always wore.

"I'm going to show you something. Don't touch it, though." Cautiously, Valdir opened the bag and allowed a small blue stone to spill into his cupped hand. Pointedly keeping his hands behind his back,

Kennard craned his neck to see the stone better. It glowed.

"This is a matrix," said Valdir. "It is keyed to me, and it responds to my thoughts. But it is not very powerful. It can only do little things, such as making something look as if it is something else for a moment. The *leroni* have much larger ones in the towers where they work. By concentrating their *laran* on a big matrix, they can do wonderful things, like move clouds or rocks."

As Valdir rewrapped the matrix and put it back, Kennard asked, "Where do you get one of these?"

"Matrix mechanics, specially trained, keep matrixes. The *leroni* have more. When your *laran* awakens, we will find a *leronis* or a matrix mechanic, and see that you get one."

"How can I tell when that happens?"

Valdir smiled. "You can tell. When it seems to you that you can tell what people are thinking before they say it, you will know."

"When will that be?"

"Oh, maybe when you're ten or twelve. But don't worry about it . . . it will come."

"So I would have to go to a *leronis* to get a blue stone?"

"Yes." Valdir paused. "Matrices used to be found in the ground, but those places have long since been mined out. I suppose it's possible to find a loose one now and again, if a matrix mechanic spills a box of them, for instance. There could also be some lying around ancient burial sites, or near ruins from the Ages of Chaos. But I wouldn't go hunting for them. You could look long and hard for a lifetime before finding one."

''Can people with *laran* tell fortunes?''

''Some can see the future, yes. There's a little of that gift in our family. I saw you and Lewis before you were born.''

Kennard flinched. Maybe the woman had seen his future, after all.

Valdir grinned. ''It's nothing to be afraid of. Many people have it. You'll get so used to it, you won't remember when you didn't have it.''

The next day, Kennard saddled his pony to go riding again. The sky was only cloudy when he had walked into the barn, but when he rode out, a hard wind pelted his face with snow.

''No going riding today, young Kennard,'' said Edric. ''There's a blizzard coming.''

''I'm not going far.''

Edric shook his head. ''No, I've seen snows come so thick you could get lost between the house and the barn. Better take your pony back and ride some other time.''

''But what if someone's out there?''

''There are travel shelters all around, and several villages nearby. Anyone out in the open will find a thick stand of trees and huddle under the branches. I've done it once or twice myself.''

When Kennard came out of the barn again, he could barely see the house through the snow. Edric took him by the arm. ''Let me walk you to the door.''

A human-sounding howl cut through the storm. Kennard froze.

''It's just the wind,'' said Edric.

* * *

The wind outside rattled the windows in the Great Hall, but Kennard paid no attention as he sat looking out, face close to the panes.

Lewis and Dorilys played a child's version of castles next to the hearthfire. "Come on, Ken," Lewis called. "You'd think you had never seen a blizzard before."

Kennard shook his head.

After a time, Kennard sensed his father walk up behind him. Valdir sat on a sill, facing the boy. "What's troubling you, son? Did you leave something out there?"

Kennard did not know what his father would say if he told him about the woman. On the other hand, it was nearly impossible for him to keep things from his father. He brought out the doll from his indoor jacket and gave it to Valdir.

Elorie saw the motion, put down her embroidery, and walked over. "That's beautiful. Did one of the servants' daughters sew it for you?"

"But it's not done yet," said Dorilys, who had hurried over with Lewis.

"What are you doing with a doll anyway?" said Lewis.

"It's not mine, she dropped it!" said Kennard. "I took it to give it back to her."

Valdir touched Kennard's shoulder. "Who gave it to you?"

Kennard shrugged. "There was an old woman. I think the same one that chased me the other time. She had a blue stone like yours and she told me my future."

"Why didn't you tell us about this?" asked Elorie, concerned.

"I don't know. The kitchen folk said they heard

about a peddler woman with dolls. I thought it was her."

"I haven't heard of a peddler with a matrix," said Valdir, looking over Kennard's shoulder to Elorie.

Elorie shook her head.

"Let me keep the doll for now," said Valdir. "I'll get in touch with Dorilys' father and see if there's something we can do."

When the blizzard had ended, Kennard rode out of Armida with his father, Edric, and a few other guardsmen. Dorilys' father, Kennard's Uncle Damon, met them on the road, with his and Lewis' Aunt Ellemir. Valdir had used his matrix to talk with them during the blizzard—Kennard was not quite sure how that worked.

Damon led them to a spot on the road and signaled for a halt. Kennard dismounted along with the others. Valdir and Damon crouched down beside him at the side of the road.

Damon put a gloved hand on Kennard's shoulder. "Do you understand what you need to do?"

Kennard nodded and took out the doll. "I try to get her to come here with me."

Ellemir bent over him. "I'd think she'd like it if you called her by her name—Margali. She's been lost for a very long time and this is the first chance we've had to find her."

Kennard felt himself blush. Valdir had told him all that, of course, about how Margali had been fathered by a man with *laran* who had died before marrying her mother. Margali's mother married another man, and because neither had *laran*, there was no one to teach her about *laran* when it had awakened in her. Her father had been a matrix mechanic and had left a matrix with her mother to give to any offspring of their union. But with no one to teach or guide Margali, she had gone mad. Turned out by her parents, she wandered from place to place, avoiding the monitors sent from the *leroni* who had seen an unaccounted-for matrix in use from their Tower screens. All of it was so very complicated that Kennard had not understood everything, and had even forgotten the name.

"I'm sure you'll do just fine," said Damon. He pointed into the forest. "She's over there, just beyond the hill."

Kennard took the half-finished doll and waded through the powdery snow. Looking down from the hilltop, he saw nothing. Could his Uncle Damon be wrong? A pile of branches rustled. He caught a glimpse of a red plaid skirt. Slowly, he walked toward the rude shelter.

The branches parted. Margali ducked out, hair in front of her face as before. Kennard held out the doll out stiffly, as if it were a shield. The doll shivered in his hand.

Margali did not notice. "Oh, you brought my baby back." She took the doll and cuddled it.

"Would . . . would you like to see my pony? She's very nice."

"Not now. Saw before." She sat. Bringing out a needle and thread from a pocket, she began to finish the face.

"My mother said that was very good sewing."

"I sew good babies. Treat my babies nice, as a mother should, and give my babies to mothers who love them, as babies should be given."

Kennard shifted his weight. "Yes," was all he could think of to say.

She looked him straight in the eye. He fought the urge to run. Valdir said they would be watching Kennard, even over the hill, but old Mirella had told him stories about mad people and what they did. He put his hand back so his wrist touched the hilt of his short sword.

Slowly, Margali rose, looming over him. He took a small step backward and slipped. He fell against a snow bank.

Margali sat and made a strange noise. At first, he did not know what it was. She let out a wail and he realized she was crying.

"Afraid of me. Why are they always afraid of me, always push me out. I didn't hurt nobody. Not ever. Not nobody."

Kennard rolled over and crawled to her. "I'm sorry. I'm sorry. I didn't mean to."

Head down, she waved at him. "Go away."

He looked up, remembering his mission. "Why don't you come with me? We have some nice sweets in our kitchen."

"No," she sobbed. "They only pretend to be nice. Then they hurt me, or chase me, or make me go away. Have to stay all by myself . . . only me and my babies."

Kennard remembered what the kitchen folk had said. "We have rags for your babies. A whole pile. My mother keeps a big pile." He held his hand out even with his waist to show the height.

She wiped her nose on her sleeve. "Rags for babies?"

"A whole pile." He raised his hand a little higher.

"Oh." She stood. "All right. Some thread, too?"

"A whole lot. My mother has lots to spare."

She nodded. Holding her doll close, she followed Kennard up the hill. He took Margali's free hand and held it firmly in his, afraid she would run when they got to the top of the hill and she saw the horses.

But no one was there. Kennard dropped her hand in astonishment. Margali took a step forward and turned. "This not the right way?"

He looked up, down, side to side, and swung around to scan the woods behind him. "I . . . I don't know."

"Margali," said a voice from below. Kennard turned and saw a woman he did not recognize, kneeling, holding out her arms. "*Chiyu.* I'm sorry for what I did. I was wrong to turn you away. I love you, Margali. Please come back with me. I'll show you how to sew again, just like we used to."

"Mother. Mother, you come back, I knew you'd come for me. I knew it." She ran into the woman's arms.

Puzzled, Kennard walked down the hill toward them. As he came closer to the road, he saw Valdir and Damon and the guardsmen emerge from the trees. And on his right was his Aunt Ellemir, holding Margali in her arms.

"Yes, you're home, Margali. I'll be your mother now. I'll be there whenever you need me."

The next time Kennard saw Margali was in the Great Hall of Armida. Her hair had been washed and brushed and gathered in the back. Her clothes were clean. But she was not an old woman, as he had thought all along, but a girl not more than a few years older than Lewis. She sat on a large chair, legs tucked under her, sewing her doll. Ellemir sat next to her with her arm around the girl. Valdir read a book nearby.

Ellemir smiled at Kennard as he walked in. The older woman turned to Margali and stroked the girl's arm. "Being important is not being the first-born, or having lots of playmates, or even of having *laran*. It is to love and to be loved."

"Come and play, Ken," called Dorilys from the hallway. She stood next to Lewis, bouncing a ball.

Kennard found that he would much rather watch Margali work on her stitching.

Valdir looked from Kennard to Dorilys. "He'll join you later, Dorilys."

Lewis and Dorilys shrugged and ran off.

Valdir held out an arm. "There's always room for you here, son. I'll read you and Margali and Ellemir a story. There's one here of a boy who won fame and honor because of his brave deeds."

Kennard climbed up on the chair and looked at the pages over his father's arm as the story unfolded.

I'm A Big Cat Now

by David Heydt

David is a "generic young author" and the son of Dorothy J. Heydt, whose work has appeared in many Darkover anthologies, including this one. David is a first-year student at the San Francisco Academy of Art, and this is his first professional publication. He is following his mother's example in finding topics I think I don't want and writing salable stories about them. But it's really unfair to say I didn't want *a story on this theme, because never in my wildest dreams did I conceive of a story on this topic—a catman child in a Free Amazon Guild House.*

I don't think there are many writers, seasoned or not, who could have pulled this one off. Read and be amazed.

From the Annals of the Kadarin Guild House:

"In this year we built the palisade and dug privies and a well. Hunting was good, and we planted gardens. Joining us this year: Fiona n'ha Camilla and [here several words are scratched out] Rakhal."

"Well, I think you're all right, Fiona," said one of the two short-haired women in the room. Fiona slowly pulled her tunic over her head as the other Renunciate continued. "There are no complications of any kind, and your breasts should stop producing milk in a week, maybe two." Rafaella paused. "I am sorry, Fiona. I know it's hard for you." Rafaella had never had a child, much less lost one, but her heart was in the right place.

"Thank you, Sister." Fiona sighed. She was a tall woman with muscular arms and dark hair. A thin, white scar curved partway across her throat, a souvenir from her last encounter with her father's friends before joining the Comhi-Letzii. "Maybe a walk in the woods would do me some good."

"Of course. Go to it." Rafaella smiled broadly as Fiona left the medicine-smelling room.

The wind in the high branches wailed like a lonely and afraid baby while Fiona sat on a fallen tree in the forest in the Heller foothills. *I wonder how long it takes to get over?* she thought. A breeze ruffled her hair, and the cry echoed through the forest again. Fiona sat bolt upright. I *didn't* imagine that! As she got to her feet, she winced; her breasts were heavy with milk and they hurt. She should have brought her breast pump into the woods with her. Then she walked toward the sound as fast as she could.

It sounds almost like a drowning kitten, she thought, nearing the sound, and then she hurried all the more, the sounds of rushing water reminding her of the recent spring floods. She pushed aside a leafy branch and found the source of the cries. It sent a shot of cold into her heart.

Some kind of gray-furred animal had drowned in the river—a female with young. The infant lay on its mother's cold dead chest and nuzzled against her stiff body for the warmth and food that were no longer there. It was small and gray, a gray the color of fog in the early morning. It looked up at her with impossibly huge emerald green eyes. Pity rose in her, drowning out the voice of common sense that told her to kill it or at least leave it to die, and she reached to pluck it from its mother's breast. Even as it latched on and began, wearily, to suck, she remembered all that catmen had done to humans, the raiding, the slavery, the wars. Even as she turned to walk slowly back to the house, one more malicious thought reared its practical head: *This is a boy-cub. What will you do in five years when it must leave and no one will take it in?*

"Are you completely out of your mind?!?" yelled Siobhan. "Why didn't you just leave it—"

"Him."

"—*him* to Zandru and forget about it?"

"I—I couldn't. I just . . ." Fiona had no words to describe the horrible emptiness the cub's cry had found in her soul, and the joy that it gave her to have it against her breast. It snuggled closer, oblivious to the debate that raged around it. In front of her stood Siobhan n'ha Mhari, the Guildmistress of the new House. She was a large woman who might almost be mistaken for overweight, but even though she would make two of Fiona, every ounce was well-trained muscle. And she had grown up in the hills; she had seen what was left after catmen attacked a human settlement.

Behind Fiona stood the healer Rafaella. She came from Thendara and had seen many things, Terrans even, but no catmen until today. Her hand was on Fiona's shoulder, as if in support—or to keep her from running away.

Siobhan sighed. "Rafaella, is it possible that the loss of her child has . . . unhinged her somehow?"

"You make her sound like an addict deprived of his drug," Rafaella said. "A mother who's lost her child has a right to grieve. Grieving takes different forms. Sometimes a woman will adopt someone else's baby, or a pet, to soothe her grief—though I've *never* heard of anything like this. Still, you and I may feel that she is a few stones short of a house; but she was miserable this morning and she's happy now."

"I'm starting to get just a little tired of being talked about as if I weren't there," Fiona said. The other two continued to argue over her head.

"Is there any way she might be made to get better? What should we do about that—that thing?"

"Baby," Fiona said.

"Well, you're not going to like this, Mother, but I think it's better that she keep the cub, and try to rear it," said Rafaella quietly. "It sounds awful, but it's for the best."

Siobhan looked up to the high ceiling of the guild hall. "Merciful Avarra," she breathed. "So be it. But remember: five years. You have five years." Fiona left quickly, and, despite her fears for the future, she smiled at the bundle in her arms.

From the Annals of the Kadarin Guild House:

"Two. In this year we reinforced the palisade, and began work on the Great Hall. Hunting was not as good as last year, but our gardens flourished. The young cat-beast Rakhal grew very fast, and made many of the sisters uneasy. . . ."

"Kiya! Kiya!" The call startled Fiona and she turned quickly to see her fosterling come in with a

limping mockery of a child's run. Blood flowed profusely from his gray nose and mouth, and red flecked his furred hands.

"Rakhal! What in the Goddess' name happened to you? Slowly! so I can understand you," she interrupted a great quick drawing of breath, signatory to the rambling sentenceless rush of words that she had come to know well from Rakhal and the other children at the Guild House.

"Well, I was playing outside when Gwennis—you know, the one with the dark hair, Melitta's daughter, who never shares her knife, and did you know she knocked Aran out of a tree once when all he did was try to—"

"Rakhal," admonished Fiona. Yes, she did remember Gwennis, a forceful seven-year-old who had bossed her way into charge of most of the few other children at the Guild House, including one five years older than herself. As she reached for a small box of astringent *karalla* powder for Rakhal's bloody face, she realized with surprise that her one-year-old was nearly as big as the older Gwennis; she had not noticed since Rakhal was rarely seen with the other children. Come to think of it, she thought, I don't see much of my sisters. Since I've had Rakhal, I've been a kind of exile.

Rakhal continued, "Sorry. Anyway her and some of her friends just jumped on me and they held me mrphmmph grmmphrsss," his words become indistinct as Fiona cleaned his face and applied the medicine. "—I mean, held me while Gwennis started punching me hard (gasp), but I got my hand free and I scratched her—I know I promised not to but I couldn't help it (gasp) and she wasn't hurt bad I know because when I ran off she wasn't rolling around on the ground like in the stories (gasp) or anything like that—but then she was really mad and she called me a *'gre'zu'*—what does that mean *kiya?*—and she spat on me and kicked me . . ." Rakhal's breathless report died away.

"Kicked you where?" Fiona said worriedly. She'd already found a bad bruise above the knee and a multitude of scrapes and tiny cuts, but if there was anything else she didn't want to have to go looking for it.

"Where—where it hurts."

"Where?" Fiona knew that her puzzled expression was exasperating to Rakhal, but he wasn't being terribly clear.

"Where it hurts *bad, kiya.*"

Fiona almost laughed. "Did she kick very hard?" Rakhal shook his head, no.

"She slipped on a rock and fell on her back. Then the others let go and laughed and I ran away." Rakhal unleashed that awful grimace she had come to accept as a smile.

"Go lie down, and after a while you'll feel less nauseous." *While I go and clear your name,* Fiona thought. *Melitta has probably accused him of everything from rape to murder. Not that she can be blamed. I guess we all can be thickheaded about someone we love.* Fiona only hoped that this would not bring Rakhal's expulsion suddenly three years closer. She hurried off to the main hall.

Fiona walked into the hall, head up, back straight, trying to hide the rabbit jumping nervously around somewhere between her heart and her throat. The dry, dusty air didn't help any; she didn't need to start sneezing now.

Melitta stood at the head of the hall on Siobhan's

right, a dark storm cloud hovering between her eyes. Next to her stood Gwennis, who grinned maliciously and triumphantly as Fiona entered. Siobhan looked up as Fiona came closer. She clearly did not want to have to deal with this. "Fiona, what in Zandru's ninth hell happened?"

"I already told you!" said Gwennis. "That catthing attacked me and cut me real bad. See?" she said, proudly displaying the stained bandaging on her thigh. "So what do you need to talk to her for?"

"Shush! I've heard your side of the story, child. Now, where's Rakhal, Fiona? I want him here to answer for what he has," she glared at Gwennis, "or maybe has not done."

"Rakhal—" it came out as a squeak. "Rakhal is in bed, I thought it best until he recovers from being kicked in the balls."

"No *kiya,* I'm here," Rakhal's voice came echoing from behind them. Fiona turned, startled. "Where are the others?"

"Others?" asked Siobhan confusedly.

"Aran, and Jaelle, and Hillary, and Melora. I want to know if Hillary is all right. I think I knocked her down running away."

"Yeah, he did! I know 'cause she was holding his left leg, and he kicked to get awa—" Gwennis stopped suddenly.

"What?" said Melitta and Siobhan in unison.

Gwennis said nothing, and stared at her feet.

"Well!" continued Siobhan. "Rakhal, you are going to spend an extra hour every day with the fighting instructor learning to control your claws better." (Gwennis smirked.) "And you, Gwennis," (the smirk vanished) "are going to spend tomorrow helping Aran, Jaelle, Melora, and Hillary clean the kitchen after dinner. Also, excepting classes you will be confined in your room for the next week. Next time think twice about accusing someone of something like this."

Siobhan looked pleased, Melitta looked satisfied, Gwennis seemed about to cry, Rakhal was confused, and Fiona sighed in relief.

As Fiona and Rakhal left the hall, she joked, "So since when have you been taking a fighting class?"

From the Annals of the Kadarin Guild House.

"Three: In this year we completed the Great Hall, and began work on the main dormitory. Hunting continues to fail, but the gardens flourished in this rich soil. Entered this year, Camilla n'ha Rafaella and Clea n'ha Gwennis."

The traveler's a decent enough person, Fiona thought. He had eaten her meat stew with more delight than anyone else at dinner, so she was inclined to be fairly tolerant. *He's obviously frightened out of his wits in having to take shelter from the storm in an Amazon Guild House.* His eyes darted around nervously as if he expected to be impaled any moment.

The traveler was a wandering bard, and that was the other laughable thing about him; he was currently thinking furiously for songs that didn't have the male bias he was sure would get him killed. Then he began a hackneyed version of "Brave Raul the Hunter" with the protagonist's name and sex changed. The women had to bite their tongues to keep from laughing, but the children had never heard "Brave Raul," and wouldn't know scansion if it nipped them on the nose.

That could also explain his unrest, thought Fiona

with a start. Rakhal was sitting cross-legged in front of him with the other children; rapt with a happy grimace on his face. The bard kept glancing at him with obvious unease, and after the song he begged leave to go to bed, on account of a headache.

"Kiya!" shouted Rakhal, running toward his mother. "Wasn't that the bestest song?"

"Best," corrected Fiona with a smile. "And yes, it was fairly competent." *Poor man,* she thought.

"Kiya," said Rakhal. Fiona looked back at him quickly; his tone had changed and she knew he was about to ask some sort of difficult question. "*Kiya,* why don't we live in a village, like in the song? What's a city? Why aren't there more men here? Why—"

Fiona stopped him with a nervous chuckle. "One at a time, Rakhal. We don't live in a village because *kiya* . . . doesn't want to. A city is a very big village with a lot more people. And—" This was hard; she didn't know how to explain it in ways a child would understand. "Men don't live here because—because men can sometimes be—mean, and hurt us. One man—" How do you explain rape to a two-year-old, even if he is big and bright for his age? "One man—hurt *kiya,* and her father threw her out because of it."

"Why, *kiya?*"

From the Annals of the Kadarin Guild House:

"Four: In this year we completed the dormitory. For the most part, the construction of the Guild House is finished. The game began to come back, and, although weather has not been the best for it, the garden continued to be plentiful, thanks in part to the extra help gained with the completion of the dormitory.''

Rakhal ran into the room. ''*Kiya!* They moved me up again. Hillary came over with me, can she have a cookie or something?'' Fiona turned to see the two children standing next to each other, their heads almost level.

''Evanda! You'd be in Hillary's classes now, hmmm?'' She reached up and pulled down a clay pot and handed Hillary a honeycake. The sweet smell of the small gooey cakes wafted through the room, and she put the pot back. At least she never had to worry about Rakhal eating too many sweets; he didn't like them much, but she kept some around for Hillary who had been Rakhal's friend after that altercation two years ago. Hillary was fourteen now, and only a few finger breadths taller than Rakhal. Fiona still seemed not to notice just how tall Rakhal was.

''Oh, *kiya!* Aran's father came today. He talked with Siobhan and took Aran away with him.''

''I know, Rakhal. He's five today, remember.'' *And little more than a year to go for you,* she thought. She felt cold, and shivered. ''Hillary, how did classes go today?''

''Fairly well. We got to go hunting, and mush-head here brought down a wild pig, and left it for me to tell you about it.'' Rakhal grimaced sheep-ishly. ''Anyway, that was sort of the last song that broke the harp. He got lectured at about 'the re-sponsibility of his new status' and got sent off with me. I came back to keep him from getting am-bushed in the halls. As if any one would try.''

''Ah, well. Have another honeycake, Hillary?'' She pulled the pot down again; it was a motion she was used to as children in the Guild House showed up often to beg cookies and cakes from her.

"I suppose I could stand the responsibility," Hillary laughed.

From the Annals of the Kadarin Guild House:

"Five: Hunting was good, and the weather much better from last year. For the first time since the house was founded, we had a large food surplus, which sister Fiona n'ha Camilla prepares with excellent skill."

"No, no, no! Blast it, *use* your goddessforsaken right hand! Since you're born ambidextrous, you better believe I want you to use both your goddamn hands!" Darilyn, the fighting instructor, then proceeded to use a few more interesting metaphors while dodging thrusts from Rakhal's two wooden knives.

He laughed. "I don't know, Darilyn. Am I actually *capable* of that last one?"

"If you don't stop fighting one hand at a time, I can *make* you capable!" growled Darilyn in reply. The smell of sweat and sawdust twitched Rakhal's nose, and he bared his teeth happily. "You fight like a donkey-faced three-year-old!" she said.

"Nope!" Rakhal breathed as he rolled and thrust twice in succession, almost getting past Darilyn's guard. "I fight like a donkey-faced *five*-year-old, remember? Besides, I've beaten you before," he said between lunges, slashes, and gasps for breath. "Especially—when I pull tricks—like this." He rolled backward, barely avoiding a rapid combination of blows, leapt up, ran forward, and flipped over Darilyn's head, landing behind her with his practice knife across her throat. She slapped her hand against her thigh in admission of loss, and they separated.

"Fairly good," she admitted. Rakhal made a noise. "Your breathing was off. If you had had more opponents or had failed to dispatch me, you wouldn't have had the stamina for more than a couple minutes more. Even you." Darilyn grinned.

"You speak truer than you know," laughed Rakhal. "My legs and back are killing me." He stretched in an exaggerated fashion, making cricking noises with his tongue.

Darilyn took on a tone of mock admonishment. "Don't grow so fast next time. You're only a handspan shorter than me, and I'm as tall as any man you're likely to see. You have reach, and an extraordinary speed." Her voice became more serious. "But don't let yourself get cocky. That way you'll get yourself dead. Also you should try to keep your tail out of the way. The only thing that stopped me from grabbing it as you went for an aerial assault was knowing that if I had, you would have impacted the floor at high velocity, probably breaking several bones. Which wouldn't be good only a week away from—sorry. Pretend I never said it."

" 'S all right," he said, smiling sadly. "I really ought to be getting used to the idea. I just think I'll miss *kiya* the most. At least she hasn't been alone as much this past year." He grimaced. "I wonder how she's taking this."

Fiona fluttered anxiously around the small room avoiding furniture and other obstacles. *Goddess!* she thought. *He's only five! How can they do this to me? He's only five* . . . "Never mind that he's taller than me by three fingers," she laughed aloud. "I only wonder how he feels about this."

Then the alarm sounded and they had much more to worry about.

In the orange glow of the blazing fire figures scurried back and forth along the fire-lines. "How the hell did this get started?" yelled Rakhal to Darilyn through the din. "It's the middle of the spring floods!"

"You expect *me* to know?" she bellowed back as she shoveled. "Just keep working!"

"Rakhal!" called Fiona through the smoke. His dark shape loomed up in front of her suddenly, and she grasped at him. "Rakhal! Give me your shovel! Get back to the water-line with the other children. Go!" She pulled ineffectually at his shovel, and tried to push him away from the fireline.

"No, *kiya.*" She looked at him as he spoke, and it seemed as if the noise of the fire and the confusion raging all around her had died down to a quiet background murmur. "No," he said, again. "I'm not a child anymore, no matter how old I am. I belong here." He pulled away and ran to another place on the line where they needed more people.

Fiona stood watching him, paralyzed in shock. His voice came to her vaguely through the din and flame, and she saw his form hazily in the smoke. *When did he get so big?* she thought. Her strength failed her, and she collapsed in a faint.

". . . She's waking up. Fiona? How're you doing?"

"My—my head hurts," she said slowly as Rafaella's face swam into view. "And my—koff—lungs feel like they've been hung in the smokehouse to dry." She coughed again, and drank the water Rafaella's assistant gave to her. "Where's Rakhal?"

She grew wary at the sudden nervousness Rafaella showed. "Where is he? Has anything happened? Is he hurt?"

Rafaella was hesitant. "He's missing. No one's seen him since the fire, but search parties are out looking for him and others. . . ."

"Since the fire? How long has it been?"

Again Rafaella paused. "You hit your head pretty good on that rock, and the smoke you inhaled didn't help. It's been about a day. We're sure he—"

"Kiya?" came a harsh voice from the door, a form dark and backlit with sunlight. There was a cough. "Are you all right?"

"Am *I* all right?" Fiona almost laughed as the tears rolled down her cheeks. Rakhal stumbled into the tent, and she gasped. Half his fur was burnt off, and the exposed skin was a bright, inflamed red where it wasn't blistered. He coughed again, and then spoke again, before he collapsed.

"Rafaella, if you have burn salve, I'll kiss you."

From the Annals of the Kadarin Guild House:

"Six: In this year we had plagues, scarcity of game, blights, unseasonal rains and droughts, floods, culminating in a horrendous forest fire."

"Goodbye, *kiya,*" said Rakhal finally, after giving his farewells to everyone else. "I love you. I'll remember you, *kiya.*" Fiona sobbed. "Don't cry, *kiya,*" he said. "You have a great big family now. You'll be all right." But Fiona was crying, softly, and would not stop for hours.

Rakhal pulled his gray leather hood over his head against the rain, and walked down away into the valley.